J. EVAN JOHNSON

SNAPSHOT
OF THE
INEVITABLE

A NOVEL

Published by 20 Theory Books
ISBN-13 978-0-9967390-3-0

1.

Seth – Now

"Yeah, man . . . I know . . . The pictures were high quality . . . No . . . Nope . . . Listen, I'll talk to him and we'll see what happens."

Seth Brommels sits on the bus eying his stop coming up on the right. Holding the phone to his ear, he gets up and grabs the top pole to keep his balance.

"I gotta go, Cam . . . yeah . . . yeah . . . I'll let you know."

Seth snaps his phone shut and puts it in his camera bag. As he steps off the bus, he smiles and nods at the driver, a large man too big for the seat he is in. Once on the sidewalk, he walks down the street at a pace faster than usual. It's about one thirty in the morning in the city. The only people in the streets are those few homeless guys who sit in the same spot, day in, day out. Some cars drive by, but other than that, it's just him and the orange glow of the street lights. Normally, Seth takes the main streets home after a late photo shoot, but tonight, he just wants to get home. The photo shoot wasn't bad at all, but the location was absolutely terrible. The location he was asked to go to was a good two hours outside city limits, and without a car, that trip turned to four hours. Four hours on the bus going up, four hours going back, just for a measly fifty-dollar photo shoot.

He cuts down the back alley of a block of row homes, picking up his pace. The only thing he hears is the scuffing of his worn shoes on concrete in this completely dark alley. If it weren't for the moon, it would be pitch black. He focuses on the scuffing sound to calm his nerves, but nothing could help once he felt that strong poke in his back.

"Stop where you are."

Seth freezes.

"I don't know where you think you are going, but you aren't wise to come down these alleys."

A woman?

"So this can be easy, or hard, but please believe me, this is a gun in my hand . . . and I will use it." She starts feeling around Seth's pockets.

"You're not going to find much," Seth says.

The woman continues her search, not saying anything. Seth chuckles.

"Something funny?"

"Not really, I suppose. It's just . . . the poor robbing the poor."

"Who says I'm poor? I just want more money."

"I meant the poor in spirit . . . robbing the poor in money."

The woman stops. A few seconds later, she yanks off the camera bag from his back and rummages through that to find the two twenties and a ten. She starts to eye the camera. Seth peeks behind him with his hands still up to try to see this woman's face.

"Turn back around, Camera Boy."

Seth looks straight again. "Keep the fifty. Just don't take my camera. I —I need it."

"Looks expensive. I could get good money for it."

Seth hears her play with the buttons. "Please."

"You know . . . I could kill you right here . . . and you're worried about some camera?"

"I just need it, that's all. Please." Tension rises into Seth's chest, moving its way to his throat.

Seth hears another click, but this time he knows it is of the gun. Maybe he shouldn't have said anything. He feels the gun again, this time on the back of his head. A slight tremble scales up and down his body. He does the only thing he knows to do in a situation like this. Pray.

The woman hears his whispering. "What are you saying?"

Seth doesn't answer and continues whispering.

She nudges the barrel of the gun into the back of his head. "Hey. I asked you a question."

"I'm praying."

"Praying? Here? Now?"

"Now is as good a time as any. Plus, what else do I have left?"

"On the ground, face down, now." The woman pushes Seth to the ground.

Seth lies face first in a bunch of loose concrete. The smell of the earth rises into his nostrils from beneath it. He lies there for a few moments. A cold chill blows over his back. A few more minutes pass. Gathering a bit more courage, Seth looks behind him.

No one there.

He scrambles to his feet and flies to his camera bag. Everything is there but the fifty dollars. His camera sits in the middle of the bag. He hurries and stuffs it back into the bag, picks it up, and runs the rest of the way home.

Seth gets into his apartment, a rickety one bedroom on the second floor of a five-floor building, and runs back to the dining area table. He sets his camera bag gently on the table and flips on the lights directly above him. Drained, he sits down at the table, his heart still racing, and stares at the camera bag. He taps his finger on the table a few times before unzipping the bag with caution. He breathes a sigh of relief when he finds that there aren't any broken pieces lying around in the bag.

Seth holds the camera in his hand, a professional digital camera given to him by his church. This is Seth's prized possession . . . and he almost got it stolen. He sets the camera back down on the table and takes out the two lenses he carries with it. One is for closeups and the other medium range. He then pulls out a soft cloth and begins to clean the lenses. Meticulously, he wipes down every part of the lens, making sure it is ready for his next photo shoot. Now is when Seth gets his thinking time. At three o'clock in the morning, when everyone is asleep, Seth gets a moment to reflect.

"I almost lost ya there, dear friend," Seth says, talking to the inanimate equipment.

He thinks even more. *This woman—* Seth chuckles. Though his pride doesn't take a hit, he laughs because he was almost wiped clean by a female. He begins to wonder what she looks like. He didn't really have a chance to see her face . . . or anything other than her feet, for that matter. But he heard her voice. Her muffled voice (likely from a mask) had a Hispanic twinge to it, but it was rough around the edges. He might be imagining her voice, though. For all he knows, it could have been a guy with a higher voice.

He changes his mode of thinking, now focusing on the fact that he lost the fifty dollars from the photo shoot. He's already behind on rent by a month or two . . . or maybe three. The landlord is working with him and has been for the past year, but sooner or later, the help is going to stop. He needs to make some money, and fast.

Seth packs up his camera and slides the lenses safely into the bag. He zips it up and places it in the coat closet, top shelf. He then saunters over to his bedroom and flops onto the bed. After rolling and clawing his way into a comfortable spot and position, Seth stares at his ceiling.

"Thank you Jesus, for getting me through another day," he whispers. "I ask that you protect me as I sleep . . . protect my parents and friends . . . and help this woman who stole from me. Help her to see your everlasting light. In your name . . ."

Tally – Now

Tally Morales sits in an old, beat-up Impala, thinking about her latest victim. Parked in an alley very few would even dare look at, Tally reclines in her seat. Here is where she feels at home. In the dark of the city, a city where anything could happen, a city nicknamed the city of brotherly love, though she has found no "brothers" here. Indeed, she has found the place where she fits, but that is only because here is the only place she can be someone else, where she can blot out those things she deems unworthy of her time, of her memory. Here, in this city, she has control, and that's the way she will keep it.

But something strange happened tonight. Tonight, as she looked at the back of that guy's head, for the first time in a long time, she felt . . . sad. For what reason, she doesn't know. She gets mad at herself for feeling anything at all. She is supposed to be hard. Ice. This is all a business; a business that she is great at. But again, something strange happened tonight. There was this guy who probably knows he shouldn't have walked down that alley at night, hands in the air, facing away from her, but ready to die . . . for a camera? Or for Jesus? She pulls out the fifty dollars she took from him and throws it up on the dashboard. *He was saying his prayers.* Tally isn't much bothered by this man who was saying his prayers. She hears people all the time with their "Praise the Lord"s and "Hallelujahs," but there was something else there. Most of the people she robs get angry, cuss her out, make threats, but this man. He sounded vulnerable. He sounded like life was already doing a good job of beating him up, and she just made it worse.

Tally shakes her head. *No emotions, Girl. No emotions.* She looks at the dashboard to see a shiny card lying in with the money. She grabs it and finds it to be an ID card of sorts. It seems like her latest victim is a photographer for a church.

"Seth Brommels," she whispers.

She throws the ID back on the dashboard and reaches for the glove compartment. She snaps it open, grabbing at the stack of cash. She counts it under the dim fluorescent light beaming from the house next to her. Three hundred fifty-six dollars. A pretty good night. She then puts a rubber band around the wad of cash. Looking around, she gathers the fifty dollars and the ID she threw onto the dashboard and puts them in the glove compartment. Placing her hands on the wheel, she thinks a bit more. *Maybe it's guilt.* She shakes her head, flinging the thoughts away. She has a lesson with Ms. Xing tomorrow. As for the rest of this night, she must get Paul his money, a ritual she hates with a passion. Tally puts the car into gear and drives off, all the while wondering why she didn't take the camera.

Tally parks the Impala in front of an apartment building on the other side of town. She quickly steps to the main door, rushes in, and trots her way to the elevator so she can get to the tenth floor. While on the elevator, she lets the humming of the moving metal box soothe her. By the time she gets to the tenth floor, she is almost asleep. She reorients herself when the doors shake open, and picks up the pace again, galloping her way to the end of the hallway.

After a few seconds, she gets to the last apartment and knocks on the door gently, three times. A few moments later, the door unlocks. Tally opens the door just enough to slide in and shuts it behind her. Only the dim glow from a TV lights the area. In the shadows, she sees movement.

"Hey, Paul," Tally says.

Silence. Tally sees the flame of a lighter, illuminating the man's face. Tally hears the man take a long drag of a cigarette.

"How much?" he asks in a deep and gravelly voice.

"Three fifty-six."

Silence. For a moment, Tally thinks he knows that she is taking some of the money for herself. Out of guilt, she feels she must smooth things over.

"You did good," Paul says.

A small lamp flickers on, illuminating more of Paul's features. A hard face, unshaven. Muscular neck . . . muscular arms . . . muscular body. He taps his finger on the table. Tally pulls the money from her jacket pocket and walks over to the table. She looks into his eyes and sets the money down. Paul stamps out the cigarette in an ashtray and counts the money. Tally turns around to walk away, but Paul grabs her arm. Tally just looks. He pulls her over closer to him such that she sits in his lap. He then continues to count the money. Tally leans onto him, resting her arms around his neck, her face nuzzled close to his. Contrary to what she shows, this act absolutely repulses her. Unfortunately, this is a silent clause in her agreement with him. She gets a place to stay, protection, and anything else she asks for within certain boundaries, and he gets the money she lifts or cons from others . . . and sex. Though it seems he doesn't need the money, Paul still takes it just based on principle. He couldn't have Tally living with him for free. To him, she needs to earn her way. This repulses Tally even more, because it was her money from other ventures that got him started. Still, Paul isn't exactly the chivalrous type.

Behind him, the sun starts to rise as the skyline changes from purple to orange. She looks at the clock on the wall. Tally didn't realize it was so late . . . or early. Not giving Paul much time to think about anything else, she swings her leg over him until she straddles him. He smirks as Tally looks into his eyes. With both hands on her lower back, he pulls her lower half closer to his. Tally, still staring at the rising sun, begins to unbutton her shirt. Paul looks at her hand moving down her shirt, plucking each button, opening more and more of her chest to him. He looks at her face, noticing she looks outside. He stops her hands and holds both of them in one of his. He then turns his neck around to see what she is staring at. He snarls and nods.

"This city will be mine someday," he says.

Tally nods. "I know."

Paul stands up, with Tally clutching to him. He grabs her behind to prop her up and carries her into the back room.

2.

SETH – NOW

The morning is bright and full of life. In the streets, people walk all around, into buildings, out of buildings, many in suits and dresses. Seth sits on the bus and watches them all, but feels his attention waning. He wants to sleep, but the last time he fell asleep on the bus, he missed his stop, which in turn made him late to a photo shoot, which in turn made him lose money. He vowed to never make that mistake again. But a quick nap sounds enticing. . .

The bus comes to a halt and allows a few people off, while a new set comes on. The last person into the bus is a large woman with a tiny purse. Seth averts his eyes and looks outside again trying not to laugh. *Please don't sit next to me. Please don't sit next to me,* Seth thinks. Lo and behold, the woman stops right next to him and plops into the two seats next to him. The seats whine as her full weight compresses them. Seth inches over, pressing against the window. He looks behind him to see the whole row completely empty and gets agitated. For another twenty minutes, Seth sits next to the large woman, pressed against the window, hoping the next stop is her stop. When her stop is finally here, the woman takes a whole five minutes to get up, and when she does get up and leave, she leaves an old fried-chicken scent in her wake. Seth shudders and goes back to staring out the window.

About another five minutes of riding, Seth is the only one on the bus. Very few people seem to travel to the suburbs around this time. He stands up after seeing his stop from a block away and walks to the front of the bus. The bus comes to a screeching halt again, almost sending him through the front windshield of the bus. Sometimes he thinks the bus drivers do that on purpose . . . but he forgets the thought just as quickly as it comes up. He gets off the bus and walks up the street a bit before walking into a large parking lot. The sun beams on the façade of his destination, The Brigade School of Photography and Graphic Design. This is where he obtained his degree. This is where all his friends obtained their degrees. This is where they still work.

Seth walks into the massive building and down a hall filled with different pictures of landscapes and flowers. Eventually he gets to an open conference room. Two people sit in the room already. One is a stylish man wearing a Mohawk, thick framed glasses, and a polka-dot bowtie. Tony Jones he met in his first year in the school. He's energetic, but is mostly known for his brutal honesty. It's that exact brutal honesty that made him and Seth friends.

"Hey, Seth."

Seth smiles. "What's going on, Tony?"

"Nothing much. You good? You look like someone put you in a bag and beat you."

"Thanks. I'm good, I guess. Long night last night."

"Well, what happened?" A woman asks.

Seth looks out of his peripheral vision to see Brianna Connelly (Bree for short), a woman of astounding beauty, staring at him with ice-blue eyes. She pushes her curly blonde locks from her face. Seth grew up with Bree. They grew up on the same street, went to the same schools; their parents are still very good friends. Some have even said that they were destined to be together at one point, but Seth feels there's too much of a past there. He'd rather keep it at friends, for very specific reasons.

"I was robbed," Seth says while plopping into a chair.

"At your apartment?" Tony asks.

"No. In an alley. Just off Broad."

"Are you okay?" Bree asks. She hops from the corner and into the seat next to Seth, pressing herself closer to him.

Seth leans back in his seat. "I'm fine. My camera is fine. I'm out fifty dollars, though."

"Man, why were you in an alley?" Tony asks.

Seth looks at Tony. "Trying to get home."

"I always told you to move to the 'burbs."

"With what money? I'm barely keeping up with rent in the city. Rent, I remind you, that is already at a discounted rate because my landlord cut me a break."

"I don't know, Man. Maybe—" Tony props his glasses higher on his face. "Maybe you should get another job, like, supplemental income. You know, until the shoots start rolling in again."

"I can't do that. I don't have the time. If I'm not out on photo shoots, I'm in the church on photo shoots."

"You ever think the church is the problem?"

Seth glares at Tony.

"Just throwing that out there." Tony gets up. "Where is the rest of the United Nations? Always late. I'm going to look for Ranjit (pronounced Ran-jeet) and Cam."

As soon as Tony leaves the room, Bree leans her head into her hand and rests her elbow on the table. She stares at Seth.

"Do you need help?" she asks.

"Naw, Bree, I'm good."

She places her free hand on his. Seth doesn't budge. "What happened?"

"I was in the alley, already about to run, but like, out of nowhere, like she phases into existence—"

"She?"

"Yeah. It was a female . . . with a Hispanic accent . . . I think."

Bree says nothing but looks like she is thinking. Seth continues.

"She stuck a gun in my back and went through my stuff."

"You didn't see her face?"

"Nope. She had me stay facing away from her."

"So she just took the money and ran? And left your camera?"

"Well, kinda. I prayed and said some things. Begged for my camera. Then she left. But, if I were thinking correctly, I wouldn't have said anything."

"Seth, you could always move in with me."

Seth is thrown off by the change in conversation. "That's not a good idea."

"It seems that it is. At least until you get on your feet . . . or a little more established. Think about it. Tony, Ranjit, and Cam are roommates. Deb lives with her parents. We are the only ones striking it out on our own, and I have to work at a department store to do so." She smiles. "And you wouldn't have to be in the city."

"Thanks, Bree. I'll think about it."

"Please, really consider it." She rubs his hand.

The door swings open, and Bree snaps her hand away from his. Deborah walks in.

"Hey, guys," she says. "What did I miss?"

"Nothing yet, Deb," Bree says. "We didn't even start yet."

"Oh." Deb walks to the conference table and grabs a seat. She organizes the area in front of her. Deborah Chambers is a rather tall and slender woman, and good friend of Bree's. Some would be off put by Deb's almost near OCD organization, but Bree finds it interesting.

"Hey, hey." The rest of the crew comes through the door, with Tony leading the way.

Tony sits down in his chair. Ranjit and Cam sit across from him.

"Sorry we're late," Ranjit says. Ranjit Alomar, the stand-alone graphic designer of the group, is the most laid back. Nothing seems to bother him about anything . . . ever.

"Yeah. We were in the building but got caught up," Cam says.

"Yeah, let me tell you what they were caught up in," Tony says. "I saw both of them trying to run game on the freshmen girls."

"Hold on a minute," Cam says. "They asked us for advice and a quick critique of some of their photos. It's not our fault that they were hot chicks."

Everyone looks at Cam with skepticism. Cameron Rodriguez, a born "ladies' man" (so he thinks), rubs his chin, not feeling any shame for his actions.

"Everyone ready to get started?" Tony asks. He waits for any objections and when none come up, he begins. "Okay, first order of business: Seth got jacked."

Seth puts his head down. "Do we really have to talk about this?"

Tony continues. "He was paid fifty dollars for his photo shoot and some dude—"

"It was a female," Seth interjects.

The whole room goes silent. Cam and Ranjit exchange glances. Deb smirks. Tony looks shocked while Bree simply stares at him.

"Well," Tony continues, "That isn't the first time some woman cleaned a dude out . . . won't be the last. Just watch one of those divorce court TV shows. The guys always get cleaned out." Tony smirks.

"Can we move on?" Bree asks.

"Of course. I apologize. Anyway, we are off to a good month this month. In the pot is about two grand and jobs are aplenty. I have a list of about ten for the next coming weeks."

Everyone's mood changes, including Seth's. More jobs mean more money, which means they are closer to going full-time with their business. The six of them decided very quickly after graduation that they should go into business together, starting a photography company. They drew out plans to rent out a building and turn it into a studio, and to do destination weddings and runway shoots. Many of those goals remain, but each look at those goals with a different set of eyes. Eventually, reality had to hit and when it did, it hit each of them hard.

Unfortunately, it hit Seth the hardest. This wasn't going to be some overnight success story they've been accustomed to seeing on TV. They have resources and they have confidence, but it's taking a lot to get this ball rolling. Tony hands everyone a few papers.

"With Deb's help, of course, I worked out the schedules. Let me know if there are any concerns."

Seth grabs his paper and scans it, finding three jobs for next week, one of them . . . He looks to his side at Bree. She stares at the paper, trying to conceal her smile.

"Yeah, Seth and Bree," Tony says. "You guys have our first wedding. I've been in talks with the bride for months now. Very nice woman."

Deb smiles, but Ranjit and Cam frown.

"Why do they get the wedding?" Ranjit asks.

"It was the obvious choice," Tony says in his matter-of-fact way. "Seth and Bree are our best photographers. Period."

Ranjit shrugs his shoulders. No one had any objections to that.

"Plus," Tony says. "I can't have you and Cam hitting on all the bridesmaids. That's bad for business."

"No, no, no, my friend," Cam says. "*They* would be hitting on *me*."

"Anyway, you guys have your jobs. Oh, and more good news: The school is allowing us to use their facilities and waiving any of the fees for the rest of this year. Seems like more people believe in us than we thought. That's all I've got for right now. This meeting was short and sweet."

The room goes silent. Seth looks around to see everyone looking at their list of jobs to complete. He locks eyes with Bree. Her blue eyes are captivating, what's behind them even more so. Seth finds himself staring into them a few seconds too long.

"Looks like we have a big project coming up," he says while snapping his gaze away from her.

"We do. We need a game plan."

"I can ask the church group to see how they do their weddings."

"Yeah, and I'll do some research online tonight. Actually, you should come by so we can hammer out the details."

Deb is the only one who looks up.

"Ummm. I'm not sure what time I'm getting home from the church. I'm sure it will be late . . . too late to come by."

"Nonsense," Bree says. "We need to get on this. If you need me to, I'll pick you up . . . And I'll order a couple pizzas."

"Sounds like a good deal to me," Cam chimes in.

Seth looks at Bree again. He observes her heart-shaped face, and her high cheeks, small chin. She looks at him, drilling him with her eyes. Then, a light flash of playfulness crosses her face. She smirks. "Or we could meet up during the day tomorrow. How's lunch sound?"

"Lunch is good. That gives me enough time to do a bit more research tonight."

"Great," Bree says with a bit too much gusto. "Tomorrow it is."

"You should have taken the free pizza, Man," Cam says. "You should have taken the free pizza."

3.

TALLY – NOW

Tally steps off the train, excited for her upcoming lesson with Ms. Xing. She gets flashbacks of her early morning with Paul and shudders. Soon, so soon, will those memories be strummed away. She begins her trek through the city streets. With her hair covered by a silk scarf and her eyes covered with sunglasses, Tally hopes to remain anonymous. No one must see her, especially anyone who may work for or with Paul. She hurries into a building that has no signs on its front, but an open top floor that looks like a dance studio. She climbs the skinny stairwell to the top floor and knocks on the glass door, and then she enters the room.

Inside, the room is filled with the bright morning sun and various musical instruments. In the far corner is a piano, in another, a drum set. Every wall is covered with mirrors. In the middle of the floor stands a pedal harp. Tally smiles.

"This not place for hoods and eye coverings."

Tally turns around to see a short and skinny Asian woman.

Ms. Xing.

Tally removes her scarf and sunglasses. "Sorry."

The short woman places her hand gently on Tally's face. "You see? Beautiful woman. No need hood and eye coverings." She walks toward the harp and pulls up a stool. "Sit."

Tally sets the scarf and glasses on a table at the entryway and walks up to the harp, taking a seat where directed.

"Play."

Tally looks at the music stand but doesn't find a sheet of music. "Play what?"

"What's in your heart."

Tally places her foot on one pedal and her hands on the strings. "I can't think of a song."

"Play." The woman looks at Tally with a stern face.

Tally begins to glide her fingers along the strings of the instrument, still unknowing of what to play, so she starts the melody of "Mary had a Little Lamb."

"No. Stop. That not your song. I want to hear your song. Song from heart."

"I don't have one."

Ms. Xing shakes her head. "You play well. I taught well. This lesson is hardest."

Tally lets her hands fall down at her sides. "What do you mean?"

"Can't teach lesson. Only guide. Be there when fall. Hands up."

Tally places her hands back onto the strings. She closes her eyes and begins to play a tune, but the more she plays, the more frustrated she gets. The sounds coming from the instrument sound beautiful, but they are disjointed and inconsistent. Tally lets her hands fall to her sides again.

"Your song, jumbled. Your heart, jumbled. Move over."

Tally gets up to let Ms. Xing sit on the stool. Ms. Xing places her fingers on the harp and plays. The tune that resonates throughout the entire floor is a soft and beautiful one. Almost heavenly. She keeps playing on as Tally stares at her in awe. Never, for the ten plus years that she has known her, has she heard Ms. Xing play something so beautifully, something so original. The song is vibrant, full of life, yet sad and painful. Overcome with emotion, Tally's eyes well up with water. Ms. Xing looks over and stops playing.

"You see." Ms. Xing says, "My song. From heart. Connects you to me."

"You want me to play that? You know I can't play just from hearing. Where are the notes?"

"No notes. Song from heart continues. Song from heart, no begin, no end. Goes on forever. May change, but never stop. Can't put on paper. Take too many trees." Ms. Xing smiles.

Tally smiles. "Why the change in lesson? There are plenty more songs for me to learn. Why have me play something I can't learn?"

"You learn. Just different. Music opens door. Lets out pain." She motions Tally to sit back on the stool. "You hold lot pain. Need song."

Tally looks at Ms. Xing. For more than ten years, not only has she been an excellent teacher, she has been more of a mother than any woman she has ever known. Thus, Tally knows that every word Ms. Xing has said to her is right. She needs a song.

"For now, go back to Beethoven." She places a sheet of music in the music stand.

TALLY – THEN

"Tally, get down here. Ms. Xing will be here in a few minutes."

"I'll be down in a second."

"Talindra Alexandra Morales. Get down here now."

Tally trudges downstairs, being thoroughly annoyed at her mother. "She's not even here yet."

"That's not why I called you down."

"Then what is it?"

"Watch your tone, young lady." Debbie Morales stares Tally down until she relents.

"Yes, ma'am."

"I wanted to talk to you for a second before your lesson."

"Okay."

"Well, your brother is coming home for a few weeks this summer."

Tally rolls her eyes. "Great. I thought he was already out of school. Didn't he move to New Hampshire or something like that?"

"Where did all of this attitude come from?" Debbie sighs. "He did move to New Hampshire, but he is working on getting a new job down here."

"Why?"

Debbie looks at Tally like she just asked her what two plus two is. "To be closer to his family, of course."

Tally was always weirded out by her older brother for one reason or another. At one point, it was because he had this smarmy vibe to him, as if he were trying to get over on everyone. Unfortunately, he never really had to try too hard to "get over" on their parents. She also never liked the way he looked at her. He's never done anything to her, but she has caught him on several occasions staring at her with a look that can only be described as restrained, and hungry. Why a twenty–three-year-old man would look at a fourteen-year-old girl like that is beyond Tally's comprehension. Why a brother would look at his sister like that is even further past the grasps of her understanding.

"So, when is he going to get here?"

"He's coming today."

"And you are just telling me now?"

Debbie smiles. "We don't have to tell you all of the goings-on of our house. You don't pay not one single dollar of rent."

"But neither do you. Daddy paid for all of this."

"Excuse me?" Her face turns more serious.

"Nothing, Mom."

"It would be wise of you to mind your manners, Tally."

"Yes m—"

The doorbell rings, and Debbie is off for the door, leaving a trail of bergamot and neroli behind her.

Tally walks to the lavishly decorated music room and grabs a stool in front of one of the large pedal harps to await Ms. Xing's arrival. She begins to warm up and stretch her hands for today's lesson.

"Ahhh, Mi Vida!"

Tally looks behind her to see her father Roberto Morales, strolling up to her. He places a gentle hand on the top of her head and kisses her on the forehead.

"And how are you today, Lovely?"

Tally frowns. "You didn't tell me Fredo was coming home."

Roberto frowns. "You sure I didn't tell you? I remember letting you know."

"You didn't, Papa."

"I'm pretty sure I did. Maybe your memory is a little foggy?" His accent becomes thicker and his words speed up.

"Papa," she turns to look him in the eyes, knowing he is lying. His accent has always been a dead giveaway. "Why didn't you tell me?"

After staring at her for a few moments, he admits, "Your mother didn't want to tell you." He sighs. "She thought it would bring unnecessary drama into our home."

"Unnecessary drama? What does that mean?"

"I don't know. Her words. Not mine." He pauses and looks down. "It could be because the meltdown you had the last time he was here."

"Meltdown? That's not what that was. I—"

Debbie walks into the room with Ms. Xing. Tally immediately stops talking and stands to her feet.

"Enjoy your lesson, Sweetheart," Roberto says before he makes his swift escape. He greets Ms. Xing on his way out of the music room.

Ms. Xing is a petite woman, one whom Tally always found to be beautiful. She has her hair pulled back and into a bun. She knows Ms. Xing's hair is long because of that one time she'd seen her in a relaxed setting. Debbie threw one of her lavish dinner parties and invited Ms. Xing. This was around the time when Tally first started her lessons. Ms. Xing showed up and she wore a dress that was so stunning, Tally thought of her as some majestic deity from that point onward. Debbie, though, wasn't so fond of being showed up by the harp teacher. Ms. Xing never did get another invite.

"Did you warm up?" Ms. Xing asks Tally.

"Not yet."

She moves toward the larger pedal harp and grabs a stool along the way, dragging it to the front of the harp.

"On three," she says after taking a seat, "One . . . two . . ."

Ms. Xing begins plucking the strings of the harp. Tally follows suit and begins their fast-paced warm-up exercises. After a few moments, she stops and stares at Ms. Xing, who continues playing. She stares at her teacher and the rapid way her fingers move along the strings. She watches her until she finishes her warm-up.

"Ready to go?" she asks.

Tally nods.

"Where's your book?"

"Oh, I left it in my room. I'll run and get it." She pops up and dashes out the room, her shoes making a slight clicking along the marble floor. She dashes around the corner just to come to a complete stop at the foyer. Her parents turn back to her and smile brightly. She looks in between them to see her older brother and immediately, a chill goes up and down her spine. Alfredo Morales stands a bit taller than both parents, but is the perfect mix between the two. He has Debbie's almost pale skin, but Roberto's hazel-sometimes-green-colored eyes. Every time Tally has seen him, he was always impeccably dressed from the shirt down to the shoes. To Tally, he reeks of privilege.

"Hey, Tally. Been a little bit." He smiles at her.

"Fredo."

"Well, that's no way to greet your older brother," Debbie says.

"I'm in a hurry. Forgot my book in my room." And like that, Tally is off running upstairs for her room to grab her music book.

"Still snooty as ever," she hears him say as she gets to the top of the stairs. Her parents say something in response that was apparently funny, their laughs echoing throughout the foyer.

4.

SETH – NOW

Seth gets to his father's church, the Mighty Worship Tabernacle, and walks in. The building is big, but not mega sized, and is considerably new. They have only been in the building for a few months now, so people are still trying to get used to the space afforded them. Seth walks around like he knows the place well, waving and greeting the few people he sees in the halls. He takes the elevator to the upper level, where the offices are, and walks to the end of the hall to a set of double doors. He knocks once and opens the door to walk in. At a lobby type of area, he greets what seems to be a receptionist with a nod, though he has never seen this person before. He walks past the man and in the direction of the back rooms.

"May I help you?"

Seth looks back. "I'm sorry?"

"Do you have an appointment?" The man smiles, showing off a perfect set of white teeth. He's bald, and his goatee shows a few specks of gray. Yet still the guy has broad shoulders and a thick neck. He reminds Seth of a retired cop from the movies.

"I don't—"

"Well, I'm sorry. I cannot allow you to go back there."

"I was saying that I don't need an appointment. My name is Seth Brommels . . . Pastor's son."

The man squints to take a closer look at Seth. A few moments later, he smiles. "I apologize, Seth. Not having met you, I don't know that for sure. I'll call security."

"Security?"

A few moments later, the man is on the phone with someone from "security." Seth stands there gawking at the man. *When did all this happen?*

The man gets off the phone and stands up, towering over Seth. "Please, follow me."

Seth wonders what was said.

"Please keep in mind, Seth, that whenever you stop by, you must be escorted back to the Pastor's office."

Seth rolls his eyes. "Why?"

"Everyone must be escorted back, so don't feel singled out."

"I'm his son."

"Just policy."

"What policy? There wasn't such a thing as 'policy' before."

"Things change, Seth." He says his name with a type of nastiness. "Before the new building, there wasn't much need for 'policy' as you say it. But now . . . now is a different story."

"How so?"

The man says nothing at first, allowing Seth to examine the long hall filled with paintings and skylights above.

"Someone tried to stab your father."

Seth stops in his tracks. "What?"

"A man, obviously lit, walks to the front of the church as your father is giving the benediction. Right there in the open, he pulls out a knife and lunges for him . . . while he was praying. Thank God he opened his eyes in time to dodge."

Seth stands there quiet.

"There's no way that should have happened . . . and with 'policy' it won't again."

"But you're just a receptionist."

The man smirks and continues walking. "Not quite." They get to a door, and the man knocks. He opens the door, using his body to block Seth from seeing inside.

"Your son is here," the man says.

Seth doesn't hear his father say anything, but a second later, the "receptionist" lets him in.

Seth walks in and the man closes the door behind him. Sitting at a fancy-looking polished wooden desk, his father, Dr. Reverend Burt Brommels, stacks up a few papers and places them in a folder.

"What can I do for you?" he asks.

Seth is shocked at the impersonal tone. He takes a seat in front of the desk. "Hi, Dad, how are you? Oh, me? I'm well. Thanks for asking."

"Don't start this now, Seth."

"Start what? I came here to see how you're doing; going through more security than you would see at an airport . . . just to say hi."

"The security is a necessary change. I'm assuming you heard what happened to me a couple weeks ago?"

"Not from you. The secret spy slash receptionist told me just a few moments ago."

"Retired cop."

"What?"

"Dell is a retired cop."

I knew it, Seth thinks. "This was all Gretchen's idea, wasn't it?"

"No, this wasn't Gretchen's idea. The security is simply meeting a need . . . a need that is increasing in size in this ever-changing world. Look, is this visit more than to criticize what I do?"

Seth takes a few moments to calm his nerves. "I got a wedding."

"Oh, so you finally stop taking pictures of naked women?"

"Dad, they weren't naked. And it was a fashion thing."

"I know what I saw. It was close to pornography."

"Who's doing the criticizing now?"

Seth's father leans back in his seat. For a few awkward moments, he says nothing. "Congrats, on the wedding. Is there anything else you need?" Back to the impersonal tone.

"No, Dad. Thanks." Seth gets up from his seat. "I'll see you around."

Seth leaves without hearing another word from his father. He gently shuts the door behind him. As he walks down the hallway, he sees Dell the security guard/receptionist looking at him.

"All that trouble for a two-minute meeting?" he says in a soft voice.

Seth just looks at him and continues on his way, not saying another word.

Tally – Now

Late in the night, Tally sits in the beat-up Impala yet again after snatching only a hundred and two dollars over the course of the night. She figures it might be time to move into a new area, as people are starting to get the picture. She even considers stopping for a while so that cops don't get too suspicious. She throws the hundred dollars and change at the windshield. She deceives herself so easily at times and gets so angry over it. The real reason for the light night is that she let people go. The drunks from the nightclubs and the young twenty-year-olds who wear shades at night were abundant tonight. Tally let most of them go. She doesn't understand it. It seems that she doesn't have the heart for this anymore. That's not something she wants to tell Paul. He might laugh it off as a joke at first, but when he understands that Tally is serious, who knows what he would do. And Tally is serious. She can't do this anymore.

She shifts in her seat. Ever since she robbed that photographer . . .

She rummages through the glove compartment to see the fifty dollars and the ID still there. She scans the ID again and examines the man's face.

"Seth . . . Brommels." She lets his name slide from her mouth in a whisper. She looks at his perfectly trim goatee. His strong and firm looking chin. His deep brown eyes. She looks at the ID in confusion. *Why do I still have this?* She takes the money and ID and slides both into her boot, then gathers the rest of the money again to get to Paul.

5.

TALLY – THEN

"He's been here for weeks, and there doesn't seem to be an end in sight," Tally says into her cell phone. She sits in one of the guest-room closets, a room the size of a studio apartment. For as long as she can remember, she's gravitated toward the giant closet. Early on, it was her own play house. Later on, it became a museum of sorts, holding all of her mother's antique-looking clothing. Now, it's just a quiet and cozy spot that no one goes into. Her retreat.

"Didn't your Mom say he was staying that long?" her friend Tana asks.

"Yeah, but he doesn't look like he's getting ready to move anywhere. Plus, I thought I heard him ask Dad for a few more weeks."

"But you don't know for sure." Tana says as a statement as if she already knows the answer.

"I don't."

"So."

"So." Tally sighs. "You are no help. You know that?"

"C'mon, Tally. What's the big deal, really? It's not like you guys don't have space. I bet you don't even see him every day and you live in the same home."

"I don't see him every day, but when I do . . . something isn't right, okay? Something just isn't right with him."

"Okay." There's a pause before Tana says, "So, your parents out?"

"Yeah. Out at some dinner. With the governor or mayor . . . something like that."

"You know what we should have done?"

"Thrown a party?"

"Thrown a party. It could have been awesome. I mean, what are summer vacations for?"

"Well, we didn't, so . . ." Tally thinks about what would have actually happened had she thrown a party at her home while her parents were out. She isn't as aware of boys as Tana is, so she feels she wouldn't have much to do. She has had experience with alcohol and marijuana, but she doesn't need to throw a party to go back to that.

"Alright, Tana, I gotta go."

"Yeah, sure. Bye."

Tally hangs up and heads toward the front of the closet, where the light switch is. She cuts the switch off and places her hand on the door knob. Just as she opens the louvered door, the main door breaks wide open and Fredo's voice comes booming through. She slides back into the closet and presses against a few old dresses.

"It won't be too long. This will all be mine," Fredo says.

Tally moves and gets ready to come out when she hears another voice.

"Is that why you moved back? After ditching us?"

Tally looks in between the slats to see a slender woman with long brunette hair.

"I didn't ditch you all. I was making something of myself. And this will all be mine no matter where I am. My father already said so, so don't think I'm plotting something crazy here."

"So, why did you move back?"

Tally watches Fredo move closer to her and place a hand on her side. He moves in for a kiss but she turns away.

"I'm with Skip now. You know that."

Fredo looks plainly. "I know. But, to officially answer your question, I came back for you." He moves in again. This time she pushes him away.

"Stop it, Fredo. I'm with Skip now. You left. And we are done."

"Then why did you come here?"

"What? You invited me over."

"And why did you come?"

"Because you're my friend. And we are catching up."

"A friend?"

"Yes. You are still that, aren't you?"

Fredo's face is already red, but he seems to maintain his composure. "Yeah. I am. But does anyone know you're here?"

She looks down. "No. I couldn't tell anyone. I definitely couldn't tell Skip."

"Why?"

"You know why."

Fredo nods as his features begin to return to normal. "Want a drink?"

"I shouldn't."

"I'm not talking about anything super hard. Just a little cocktail or something. Catch up over drinks."

She looks at him for a few moments before nodding. "Let's."

Fredo nears the closet. The closer he gets, the more Tally's palms sweat. She moves to the side and crawls behind a few dresses to hide. She nervously anticipates the door opening, but it never happens. She skulks to the slats on the door to see Fredo rifling through the cabinet that is right next to the door. He pulls out a bottle.

"Sangria?"

"That's fine. Hey, where's the bathroom?"

He points at the door in the corner of the room. Tally doesn't see the woman anymore but stares at Fredo pouring the drinks. He carefully pours two cups of the deep red liquid, then with a casualness that makes her shiver, pulls a little bag from his pocket and removes a small white tablet. The tablet he crushes in between his thumb and index finger, and sprinkles what is now a powder into one of the cups. Then, he grabs another tablet and does it again.

She backs away from the door, almost in a panic. She's seen enough on TV to know that Fredo is trying to drug this mystery woman, but there isn't much she can do from within the closet. She must step out, but she fears her brother. She goes back to the door to look into the slits of light that shine across her face. She watches Fredo set the cups down and leave her vision. She faintly hears a click and knows he's locked the door. Her now clammy hands tremble against her wishes. A cold droplet of sweat slides down the nape of her neck as her insides turn to mush. She wants to jump out. She wants to scream. She wants to hurt Fredo. Instead, she swallows down the scream and makes herself as silent as she can.

The woman comes back, and Fredo hands her the glass with the powdered substance in it. Tally stares at the woman, hoping some long-dormant psychic ability would allow her to contact this woman who stands right in front of her.

But the woman takes a sip.

"So, what kind of trouble did you get into up there to rush back home?" she asks.

Fredo smiles. "No trouble. I just needed to be closer to family." He looks down into his cup. "And you. But . . . you are with Skip now. I respect that. I just wish there was still a chance for us."

She looks stymied and doesn't say a word.

"But I'm not trying to make this awkward." Fredo looks back up at her. "So, you? What's new with you?"

It takes her a moment to speak, but before she does, she takes another sip. "Me? Yeah, I'm back in school for my Master's."

"Yeah? In sociology?"

"Yeah."

"Your parents still weird about that?"

"Yeah and no. They still think I should have gone for a real degree." She smiles. "They just don't express their thoughts as much anymore."

Fredo nods and watches the woman take another sip that turns into a gulp. A few minutes of talking later, she goes to sit and stumbles to the edge of the bed.

"You okay?" Fredo asks.

"I don't know," the woman says, her speech becoming more slurred. "Fredo, help me." She falls back onto the bed, long strands of her hair covering her face.

Fredo walks up to her. "Sue."

The liquid still sitting in his cup gently rocks back and forth in his hand.

"Hey." He touches her face. "Sue."

She doesn't move, nor does she make a sound. Fredo paces back and forth in front of her for a few moments before gulping down the rest of the contents of his cup and setting it down on the carpeted floor. He moves closer to Sue, leans in, and kisses her.

Tally gasps and covers her mouth, hoping Fredo didn't hear the noise she just made, but Fredo stands upright and looks right at the closet. Tally leaps to the back of the closet quietly, and hides behind a row of large evening gowns. She holds her breath as the closet door opens. She remains completely still, for she knows Fredo is standing there, waiting. Eventually, she hears the door close again, but she doesn't dare risk moving at the moment. She doesn't move until she hears sounds and movements outside the closet. Still, her movement is limited.

"God," she says for the first time formally and alone, "please stop this."

She moves from behind the dresses, and back to the door, but she doesn't look through. She hears everything she needs to hear to know her quick prayer has gone unanswered. A tear traces down her cheek. She wipes it away with her forearm as she begins to hate herself for being too scared to step out of the closet. She hears Fredo's grunts and hates herself even more. She moves back to the corner of the closet behind the dresses and silently cries.

6.

Seth – Now

"So, I was online last night and found these amazing ideas for the posed shots."

Bree and Seth sit in a booth at an old diner down the street from Seth's church. Papers cover the table and empty plates sit on the side. Bree shuffles through a few of the papers and pulls out a printout.

"The bride says she wants mostly candid shots, but for the posed, she wants one with the groom, of course; her parents, siblings, cousins, aunts"—Bree flips the paper over—"uncles, friends, and a few coworkers."

"She said she wanted mostly candid shots?" Seth asks with a smirk on his face.

"I know, I know. This seems a bit outlandish . . . but that's what she wants. And we're getting paid to give her what she wants."

"Yeah." Seth takes a sip of his drink.

"And we have the chance to scout the place for lighting and all that fun stuff during rehearsal the night before."

"Cool."

Bree looks down at the table for a second. "And she has a few other couples who plan to get married in the guest list. We do well here, and we get more business."

Seth nods and stares at Bree.

"You don't seem so excited about this." Bree sets the paper down and frowns.

"Should I be? She sounds like one of those bridezillas."

"Where did you get that? We haven't even met her. And Tony says that she is nice."

"Of course she would be nice … on the phone … when she is trying to get a photographer for her wedding."

Bree leans back into her seat. "I don't get it, Seth. This is good money here."

Seth simply nods again, his expression stone cold.

"What is this about?"

"Nothing."

"Is this about Kylie? What she did to you?"

Seth flinches a bit. "Why w—" He rolls his eyes and looks out the window, nodding his head. When he turns back to Bree, he looks into her eyes, holding back the harsh words he so eagerly wants to spew. He smirks as he sees the change in Bree's eyes from playful and carefree to scared and guilty.

"Seth, I'm sorry. I don't know what I was thinking."

Seth puts up his hand. "Don't worry about it. Let's just move on."

"No, you don't understand. I didn't mean to say that. I know how hurtful that time was, and the last thing I would want to do is hurt you."

"Bree. Let's move on. Please?"

Seth and Bree have a stare off for a few moments before Bree looks away and nods.

"Okay. Fine. But again, I am sorry." She reaches for his face and places her hand on his cheek. Seth looks away.

"Seth, look at me." Bree's tone is softer, loving almost. She puts her hand on his face and rubs his cheek, forcing Seth to look at her. "I'm sorry."

Seth stares into her blue eyes as she puts her hand back down away from his face. She slowly blinks. At that moment Seth wants to kiss her, and he's sure she wants him to, but he refrains. He looks down.

"What are you doing tonight?" Bree asks.

"Dinner with Dad and Gretchen." Seth leans back. "I'm not really looking forward to it."

"Then why don't you reschedule. Hang out with me tonight."

"I can't. I blew them off too many times already. Well, I blew Dad off too many times already. I couldn't care less about Gretchen."

"I see. You know, we used to hang out a lot. What happened to that?"

"That was before things got . . . complicated. And aren't we hanging out now?"

"This doesn't count. This is business." She grabs a hair tie from her purse and pulls her hair back, putting it into a ponytail. "So what about after you have dinner with them?"

"I'm going home and I'm going to sleep. I'll likely need the rest."

Bree nods. "No back alleys this time. Okay?"

Seth smiles. "Okay. Now let's get the rest of this over with. Here's what I learned from the group at church."

****

Seth slumps in his seat on the bus as he heads to see his father and Gretchen. During moments like this one; moments in which he has a bit of quiet time, where he can become invisible in a group of people, Seth takes inventory on his life. He thinks about the upstart photography business with his friends and wonders if they will ever be successful. His thoughts then roam to Bree, gorgeous and petite, and absolutely enamored with him. He knows there are certain lines he doesn't want to cross in his friendship with her—at least, not again. He wishes she would find someone who could actually love her, because he knows that he isn't it. Nor will he ever be.

Love.

Seth cringes at the thought of the word. He sits up in his seat and looks out the window. *Not a bad night tonight.*

He gets up and pulls a cord that makes a beeping noise throughout the bus. As the bus slows down, Seth grips one of the straps hanging from the roof of the bus to steady himself. He walks to the front, greets the bus driver, and walks off. A few other people walk off with him. Seth is a good few blocks away from his father's home but figured a walk in Elkins Park while the sun sets wasn't a bad idea. Gives him more time to think.

He strolls down the sidewalks thinking about his near marriage to Kylie, what his mother would have thought, and how his entire relationship with her changed him forever. Jumping thought to thought, Seth finally determines that he isn't quite living the life he once believed he should have. He was supposed to be successful at something, anything, by now. He was supposed to have a well-paying job and married with a kid or two. Or he was supposed to be a preacher, following right in his dad's footsteps. He was supposed to be a great photographer, traveling the world, being admired by many for his creative talent.

But he is none of those . . . and that in many ways depresses him.

Seth looks at one of the houses and sees a boy and his father playing in the front yard. He smiles but picks up the pace to his dad's house. He doesn't need another reminder of how disappointed he is with himself . . . or even how disappointed his dad must be with him. But then, something else kicks in.

"Ah, Lord," Seth says. "I know I sound ungrateful . . . and I'm sorry for that. I have a roof over my head, food to eat, a job to somewhat pay for both, and good friends that I can trust. That's more than what most people can say."

He tries to change his disposition and thinks to himself, *The best things happen to the humble and the grateful.* A saying his father always said.

Seth gets to his father's home and rings the doorbell. The sun is no longer visible and the sky has turned from orange to purple, at some parts a dark blue. A few moments later, he hears high heels hitting wood floor and immediately braces himself for Gretchen, but when she answers the door, he is shocked by the huge smile she wears on her face.

"Hey, Seth," she says, "I'm so glad you came." Gretchen is a tall woman, taller than his father when she has heels on, and is all leg. In her heyday, she could have easily been a supermodel. She wears a modest skirt and blouse with the sleeves rolled up. Bangles on her wrist jingle at her every movement.

"Hey, Gretchen." Seth walks in.

"I'm almost finished with dinner, and your father is in the study."

Glad I came? Cooking dinner? What?

"O-oookay. Thanks," Seth says in confusion.

Seth walks by her, his face twisted, as she wears a perfect smile. He walks to the study to find his father flipping pages of a book. He looks up for a second to see Seth, then looks back down at the book.

"Son."

"Hey, Dad." Seth scans the room again. "What are you reading?"

Burt glances at Seth again. "A few commentaries."

"On what?"

Burt closes the book and leans back in his giant leather chair. "On the responses of Christ during his time on Earth before the death and resurrection."

"Responses of Christ?"

"Many people have studied the different situations Christ was presented with and how he responded. Sometimes he healed. Other times he waited. Other times he had something to say." He rubs his graying hair. "So if one could analyze those situations and Jesus Christ's responses—"

"It would shed a bit more light on how we can respond to things now."

Burt slowly nods. "I'm preaching a series on what it really means to ask, 'What would Jesus do?'"

"Sounds like good stuff," Seth says.

Burt nods again. "Have you been studying?"

"Not really. I still read . . . but not in the detail I once did."

"I see." Burt gets up from his seat and places the book on the bookcase. "Listen, Seth, I'm sorry about the other day. I should have told you about the security."

Seth says nothing. Burt sits on the edge of the desk and stares at the bookcase.

"You know what it's like to have someone charge for you with every intent on ending your life . . . and almost succeeding?"

"I can't say that I do." But Seth thinks in the back of his mind the fear he felt when he was robbed in the alley just a few days ago. He'd rather not get into that with his father, though.

"I mean, in my foolish days, I got into some trouble where my life was in danger. But it was never that close . . . or so it seemed."

Seth stares at his father, in part surprised by his candidness, and partly put off by it.

"Events like that . . . when you're praying, no less . . . they . . . they change you." He turns to look at Seth. "And before you know whether the change is good or bad, you just know . . . something is different."

For a while, no one says a thing. Seth looks at his father, who has turned to look at the bookcase again. A few quiet and awkward moments more, Burt leaves Seth in the study. Seth sits there, wanting to ask his father if that's how he felt when Mom died.

But the words never came.

"You ready to eat, Dear?"

Seth turns around to see Gretchen standing at the doorway, looking a bit more worn than earlier. Seth forces a smile and nods, getting up from his seat and walking by her. Seth notices that she wears a light and sweet-smelling perfume.

It makes him nauseated.

Tally – Now

Tally stands in the doorway of the bedroom, watching Paul stuff a bunch of clothes into a duffel bag. He says nothing to her, even as Tally stares at him, which she has been doing since he started.

"I gotta make a run," he finally says. "A big one. I'm gonna be gone for a while."

Tally keeps a straight face. "Where to?"

"Atlanta."

"How long are you staying?"

"A few weeks." Paul opens up the bottom dresser drawer and pulls out a few blocks of something that's covered with aluminum foil, plastic, and tape. He throws them into the duffel bag as well.

"Who are you staying with?" Tally wraps her arms around herself, unsure whether she should have asked that particular question. The last time she did, Paul beat her.

Paul stops packing. He stares into the duffel bag for a second. "I'm staying with one of my boys."

Tally leans to the side. "Can I come?"

"No."

"Why not?"

Paul glares at Tally. He says nothing, then continues to pack. Tally asked the question, but she already knows the answer. Paul isn't staying with one of his boys; he's staying with another woman. He's taken these trips several times over the years. At first, Tally was jealous and confronted him about it. Each time she did, bad things happened, so she learned not to ask too many questions, and not to seem fazed by anything he is doing. At this point, Tally just asks questions to see how much freedom she will have when he is gone.

"What am I going to do while you're gone?"

"Hold down the fort. I left some money on the kitchen table. Should be enough to get by." He zips up the duffel bag and hoists it around his shoulders. He stomps to the nightstand and pops open the drawer. He fumbles around but comes up with a shiny silver gun and stuffs it under his belt. A few moments later, he walks past Tally and out the door, without so much as a goodbye. Tally still stands in the doorway to the bedroom.

A sad-but-true fact about Tally is that she would rather have Paul here than be alone. When she is alone, her thoughts take over; her past starts to take stabs at her. She needs to keep moving, to keep busy. She walks into the kitchen and to the table to find only a few bills lying. Paul left her a hundred dollars . . . for three weeks or more. Tally stares at the money in disgust. She chuckles a bit before going back to the back corner of the bedroom. She picks at the air vent until the small grate lifts up from the floor, and she puts her hand in. She feels around and pulls out a small metal box. The black box is only unlocked by a numeric code, a code she handily flips the small dials to. Once she gets the box open, she empties the contents onto the floor. Rolls of cash and a card fall to the floor, and she unrolls each wad to count out the money. *Two thousand and some change*, she thinks. Tally considers the black metal box to be her bank, made up of the dollars she kept for herself after the many long nights of sticking people up. She picks up the card, the ID card that belongs to Seth Brommels, and stares at it again. It seems every time she sees the card—the picture of a smiling Seth Brommels—her emotions get jumbled. She feels guilty, yet excited for reasons she can't explain.

She flips the card over and finds the church phone number and grabs her cell phone. She dials the number. After a few short rings, she gets an automated message explaining the different events going on at the church and finally, the time of Sunday service. She hangs up and sits on the floor in the corner of the bedroom. She has this idea that is forming in her mind, but she knows in every way it is a bad idea. Yet still, a small part of her believes this is what she should do. It could be just a quick in-and-out thing. She pulls fifty dollars from her stash and places the rest back into her black box and puts the box back into the vent. She takes the ID and the money and sets it on her nightstand, making sure it is ready for her to take with her to Sunday service. Then she leaves the bedroom and turns on the TV with the hope of drowning out the voices of her past.

7.

TALLY – THEN

Three. Three times Tally counted Fredo did unspeakable things to Sue. When she knew it was clear, Tally stepped from the closet. She saw Sue, who was fully clothed, but the front of her pants was undone. She looked at her face and noticed her skin was pale, her lips turned a few shades darker. She moved two fingers to her neck to find a pulse but found none. At the moment, it took everything in her not to scream. Instead, she hurried out the room, and across the mansion, to her room, where she finished crying. She eventually cried herself to sleep.

The next day, Sue was gone, but the image of her on the bed in an unnatural position, her pale skin, and her blue lips, is one Tally can't forget.

Even a week later, Sue is on her mind.

"Tally, are you okay?"

Tally snaps out of her thoughts and looks up at her summer tutor. Debbie and Roberto insisted that Tally get a tutor for the summer instead of the break most other kids get, though during the school year, Tally gets straight A's. This always seemed like overkill to Tally, but she likes her tutor, Ms. Walker. That makes it bearable enough.

"Yes, ma'am, I'm fine."

"You sure?" Ms. Walker says.

"Yes, ma'am." Tally looks at her earnestly. "I am. Really. I'm good to go."

Ms. Walker eyes Tally for a few more seconds before continuing. "So, I understand the book at hand can be disturbing. Any time—"

"It's not disturbing. It's the truth . . . isn't it?"

"Many believe so. Many believe that man . . . is inherently evil. Many religious folk believe the same: that we are born into sin."

"And that's what Simon saw, right? He saw the pig's head for what it was . . . he saw it as the forces of evil . . . as Satan."

"This is true." She smiles. "So what other forms of symbolism are in The Lord of the Flies?"

"The glasses, the shell, Simon the character. All the characters, really." Tally shrugs. "There's a lot."

"Okay, Tally," Ms. Walker says. "Talk to me. What's on your mind?"

"Nothing. Why?"

"You don't seem to be engaged. Is it the story? Something else?"

"I'm fine. Really. Just tired."

Tally finishes out her lesson without issue and ends up in her room, on her phone, texting Tana.

Still can't believe you have summer school.
It's not that bad. Teacher is cool.
Did you see Fredo on TV this morning?

Tally freezes.

What are you talking about?

Fredo was on TV with a bunch of other people. Press conference. For that missing lady.

Missing lady? Calling now.

Tally punches in a few buttons on her cell phone and sticks the phone to her ear. Tana picks up immediately.

"What on Earth are you talking about?" Tally says.

"Do you watch TV? It's all over the news."

"What is?"

"The missing chick, Sue. Sue Goldstein."

Tally feels like she is going to be sick. "What was he on TV for?"

"It was a bunch of her friends standing behind her parents, offering support. They spoke to the press asking for help. Asking for anyone that knows anything to come forward. Her boyfriend talked, too. He was a wreck. I forgot his name."

"Skip."

"Yeah . . . Skip." Tana goes mum.

"They have a search out for her?"

"Yeah. Why do you sound like that?"

"I—" Tally turns toward the door to her bedroom to see Fredo standing there, watching her. "I'll call you back."

"Is everything okay?"

"I'll call you back." Tally rushes off the phone and clutches her phone at her side. She waits for Fredo to say something.

"Can we talk?" Fredo asks.

"About what?"

"Just a few things on my mind." He steps into her room. "Can I close this?" He points to her door.

"No."

He smiles and nods. "I figured as much." He shoves his hands into his pockets. "So, how are you doing?"

"Fine."

"Everything good?"

"Yeah."

"Good. Good." He nods and looks down. "You know, I talked to Mom and Dad, and we had the funniest conversation."

"It seems you three have nothing but funny conversations."

"Yeah. This one was really funny." He starts to laugh. "Somehow, though, we ended up talking about you. And you know what came up?"

"No idea, Fredo." She sounds annoyed, but grips her cell phone tightly to stop her hand from shaking.

"Mom talked about your little hiding spot you had when you were younger. She thought it was the cutest thing. You know what I'm talking about? The closet in the room across the house?" He looks up at her and pierces her with his hard stare.

She knows he's searching for something, and she is making sure she doesn't give anything away. "I know what you're talking about. Why are you here talking to me about it?"

He stares for a few more moments before answering. "No reason. I just thought it was a funny story."

Tally gives him a strange look. "Is that all you wanted?"

He blinks away his hard stare. "Yeah. I just thought it was a funny story, that's all."

"I don't see the humor."

"I guess not that funny, huh?" He smiles a bright smile.

"Nope."

"Hey, I'll leave you be. I just wanted to stop by and say hi . . . see if things are okay, you know, between us."

"Between us?"

"Well, yeah. We're brother and sister, right? We look out for each other, make sure the other is good and doing well. That's family." He starts on his way out. "I honestly don't know what I would do without you. My baby sis. You're almost all grown up. I remember when you were just this short little thing running around, following me wherever I went. Man . . . memories."

"Where are you going with this?"

"I'm just saying. We're family. A thought that just kinda popped into my head is that it would be heartbreaking if you weren't here."

Tally frowns. "Where would I go?"

Fredo shrugs. "I'm just speaking in general." He turns to walk away. "Man, you gotta let Mom tell you that story. Just the way she tells it is so animated." He waves. "Catch you later, Tally."

She waits until he is long gone before closing her door, curling up into a ball in front of the door, and crying.

SETH - NOW

After a long Saturday morning and afternoon, Seth and Bree sit at a table during the last parts of the wedding reception. Seth, Bree, and a few of the other vendors hired for the wedding enjoy a moment's rest.

"It's a beautiful night," Bree says.

"Yeah, it is." Seth looks around. A slight warm breeze blows through the courtyard-turned-reception area.

"When I get married, I could imagine my wedding being like this. On a warm summer night."

Seth smiles. "Yeah?"

"Well, sure. This is nice, isn't it? And look at those two." She points at the bride and groom. "Nothing else matters. Look at how into each other they are."

Seth looks at the newly bonded husband and wife as they dance in the middle of the dance floor. He stares at them, almost feeling the signals they send to each other. He grabs his camera and clicks a few buttons, then takes the picture.

"They're going to want this one." Seth smiles at Bree.

"Good call." Bree scans the room again. "You ready to get out of here?"

"Yeah." He finishes off his drink. "Off to your place?"

"My place?"

"Yeah." Seth starts to pack up his camera. "I know the game plan was for you to drop me off but . . ." Seth looks at his cell phone. "It's already eleven. By the time we get to my place, it would be around one, which means you wouldn't get back till . . . two, three, maybe."

"Yeah? So?"

"Nope. Can't have you do that. One, I don't want you driving through Philly at all times of the night. Two, I don't want you driving so late, period. People fall asleep on the road all the time."

"Thanks, Dad." Bree smiles.

"Ha ha. Look, I'll just take the bus from your place when we get there and—"

"So you can go through Philly at all times of the night, by yourself . . . with no car? No can do, friend. If I'm not taking you home, you're crashing at my place for the night."

Seth stares at Bree for a few long moments. Eventually he smiles. "Fine. I'll just get up early to get home and to church."

"Why don't you borrow my car . . . tomorrow."

"Then how are you getting to our meeting at the school?"

"Come pick me up."

Seth thinks for a bit more. "You're okay with that?"

"I suggested it, didn't I?"

"Well . . . let's get out of here." Seth grabs all of their heavy equipment.

****

"So what's all this commotion about your Dad beefing up security at the church?"

"You heard about that?"

Seth walks behind Bree through the hallways of her apartment complex, rolling a large suitcase of both his and Bree's cameras. They stop at her door, Seth breathing heavily from carrying the equipment.

"Make it to the gym much?" Bree chides.

"Funny. Real funny. Open the door."

"Okay. Opening . . . the door . . ." Bree's motions are slow and overly dramatic.

"Stop playing around. I'll wake all your neighbors."

"Okay, fine." Bree opens the door and Seth is immediately greeted by a strong scent of lavender. Bree turns on the lights. "Sorry for the mess. Didn't have much time today to clean; was rushing out the door to get to the spot."

Seth looks around. Bree's apartment is well kept. Everything seems to have its place. It is organized, clean, and smells good. He doesn't know what she had to clean . . . or what she's apologizing for.

"Still OCD with the cleaning, huh?"

Bree smiles and throws her keys on the kitchen counter. "Maybe."

"So where do I put this stuff?"

"Now that I think of it, we probably should have left that in the trunk. It has to go back to the school tomorrow."

Seth lets the equipment slide to the floor. "Thanks for telling me."

"You can just leave it there if you want."

"That's exactly what I was going to do."

Bree smiles again. For some reason, Seth scans her smile, searching for a hidden meaning that makes itself overtly obvious.

"I have to pee. Be right back." Bree disappears into the back room, giving Seth time to scan his surroundings.

Seth looks around the familiar apartment, being subtly reminded of the last time he was here. This is only his second time setting foot into Bree's apartment, so he takes his time in observing the area. She's always been neat. Seth was the one who was messy, even in growing up. Bree had the neat binder and folders. Seth had a bunch of loose papers. In high school, Bree had a locker organizer; Seth had a sandwich that was three months old and causing a rotting smell to come from his locker. Seth smiles and walks to the kitchen. It smells like bleach.

Eventually, Seth comes to a wall of pictures. Most of them are of her and her family, but one catches his eye. It's of him and her at their senior prom. Though they came with different dates, they spent most of their time with each other. Even when the night was over and they were back in their homes, Seth went over to Bree's house to hang out.

"Good times, huh?"

Bree's voice startles Seth, though he tries not to show it. "Yeah. Good times."

"Well, first let me show you around. You haven't seen the place since you helped me move, and that was, like, two years ago."

Bree goes around the apartment, showing Seth the area. The tour doesn't take long, as it is only a one-bedroom apartment. They linger in the bedroom for a few seconds too long, as Seth notices her jewelry box that used to be his mother's. She glances at him and back at the box before moving them along out the room in haste.

She sits down on the couch. Seth pulls up a chair and sits in front of her.

"So, tell me about this security stuff," Bree says.

"Well, someone tried to stab my Dad."

"What? Is he okay?"

"Yeah. He's fine, I guess. You know how my Dad is. If it did bother him too much, he wouldn't say anything anyway. How did you hear about the extra security? I didn't hear a thing until I went to see him."

"My Dad told me. Well, he kinda glazed over it a bit, sparing me the details. All he said was there's some extra security going on and that he was thinking of the same. Your Dad called him to talk. They talked for a while apparently."

"How is your Dad?"

"He's Dad. Same ol' Pastor Connelly."

"Yeah." Seth looks around, but his eyes are drawn to that picture yet again.

Bree turns around to look at the picture as well. Finally, she gets up and walks over to the wall. Seth notices that she took her shoes and socks off. Her toes are painted hot pink. Seth looks down at his shoes and tries to sneak them off, hoping he didn't make any stains on the carpet.

"Don't worry about it," Bree says, not looking at him but at the picture she now holds in her hands. "The carpet cleaners are coming on Monday." She turns around. "You remember this, night?"

"Like it was yesterday. It was one of the best nights from high school."

"Sure was." Bree yawns. "Senior prom. Such memories."

"Yeah, but not for our dates." Seth smiles.

"Well, Ron, wait, I think his name was Ron; all he was trying to do was get into my pants."

"That's what people do at prom."

"Did you?"

Seth pauses. "Well, no."

"Did you want to?"

Seth smirks. "If I wanted to, I would have."

Bree chuckles, then yawns again. "Ummm, you weren't Mr. popular in high school. You didn't have it like that."

"You're right. But I had a date that wanted it like that."

Bree sits on the couch next to Seth. "Really? And you ditched her?"

"Yeah. It was too much expectation. Too much built up. Too much pressure. I didn't like the situation. Plus, I just wanted to hang out with you."

"Yeah, I remember sitting there with … Ron … man, I gotta remember his name, and I was thinking how soon I could get this over with so we could chill."

Long pause. Bree sits on one end of the couch curled up under a blanket. Seth sits on the other side, trying not to press the bottoms of his shoes too hard into the carpet still.

"Listen, we both better get some sleep." Seth says. "Long day tomorrow."

"Sure will be." Bree gets up and saunters to a linen closet. "Here." She throws over another blanket. She goes back to her bedroom and comes back out with a pillow. She throws that over. "The couch folds out to a bed." For another moment, Seth and Bree stare at each other. Seth looks into her ice-blue eyes. She looks tired as her eyes are a bit glazed over, but he sees something else; something completely aware. He thinks he's just seeing things, but for a second, he thought he saw the look, the very same glint in her eye from some time ago.

Bree turns away. "Goodnight, Seth. See you tomorrow."

"Have a good sleep, Bree."

Bree dims the lights and goes into her bedroom, shutting the door behind her. A few moments later, Seth hears the water running from Bree's shower.

About an hour later, Seth is still unable to go to sleep. There aren't many noises he hears in Bree's apartment or the surrounding area, yet for some reason, he still can't sleep. He clutches the pillow, trying to get comfortable, and notices the pillow has a light scent of lavender. *Smells just like her,* he thinks. Seth turns over and begins thinking of Bree. Bree has been everything to Seth over the years, his best friend, his sister, the only one he could always count on to tell him the truth, but there is one thing he wishes he couldn't call her.

Lover.

Seth hears a slight movement.

Moments later, he hears a muffled creak of the floor, just by the kitchen. He stills. A sweet aroma fills the air. He can't see her, but he feels Bree walking by him. The blinds open, letting in what little light there is outside. That's when he sees her. She has her arms wrapped around herself as she stares out the window. Seth makes out her silhouetted figure. She's slender; always was. At times, he finds himself admiring her beauty. This time is no different. She turns to the side. Seth is unable to see it, but he knows she's looking at him. For what seems to be forever, Seth stares back, but says nothing. She eventually turns and starts to walk back to her bedroom.

"Can't sleep, huh?" Seth says.

"Oh." Bree sounds startled. "I'm sorry. Did I wake you?"

"Nope. Couldn't sleep, either. What's keeping you up?"

"Bad dream. You?"

"Don't know."

Seth feels the bed move and shift under Bree's weight.

"You don't know?"

"Not at all. I'm dead tired. Maybe it's just the different environment."

"I'm sorry."

"It's not your fault. And why do you say sorry so much?"

Bree stays silent. Seth rolls to the side to grab his cell phone and presses a button to illuminate the front and the area around them. He points the face of the phone at where he thinks Bree is to see her sitting on the edge of the bed, her back turned toward him. When she sees the light, she turns her head to the side toward Seth. He looks at her, noting the tight T-shirt and boy shorts.

"What was your dream about?"

Bree faces forward again. With a quick shake of her head, she dismisses the subject. "Do you need anything before I head back?"

Seth grabs Bree's hand. "Bree, what was the dream about?"

Bree lets her hand sit in Seth's but doesn't adjust her body to face him. She shakes her head again, this time faster than the first time.

"Fine." Seth says. "But it's just a dream. Everything will be alright." He lets go of her hand. "Here." He slides over a pillow. "Lie down."

"What?"

"Lie down. Get some sleep."

Bree now turns completely around to face Seth, eyeing him curiously. "I'm okay. I'll head to my own bed."

"Are those tears in your eyes?"

"No. I'm just . . . I'm just tired."

"Bree, lie down."

Bree thinks, then slowly lays her head down on the pillow, turning her back to Seth again. Seth lets his cell phone light go out and places the phone next to him. He thinks for a moment before placing his hand on her arm.

"Everything is going to be alright, Bree. You just gotta have faith."

Bree immediately recognizes what Seth says. "Faith isn't the same as when we were little, Seth." Her voice is strained. "Life isn't the same as when we were little."

"I know that. Trust me, I do. But there's a God—"

"Stop. Please, don't do this. Not now."

"What?"

"This. The God thing. I've heard it enough over my life. I know there is a God out there somewhere. I know He loves us and wants the best for us. I know He's forgiven us and all that other good stuff. I know."

The room goes silent again, Bree's words seemingly putting them in empty space. Seth thinks about what she said, keying in on her mentioning forgiveness. The way she stressed the word makes Seth curious.

"I'm sorry, Seth, I just . . ."

"There you go saying sorry again. Why do you say it so much again?"

Bree turns around to face Seth. "You get on my nerves."

"I know. Goodnight."

Bree sighs. "Goodnight."
Seth closes his eyes, but his mind still won't slow down.

8.

TALLY – NOW

Tally stands out in front of small brick building that looks like an old department store. On the front is a sign in plain letters that says "Mustard Seed Worship Center." She made sure she could get there right when service starts, and she made sure her attire wasn't overstated, but wasn't too "thuggish." Her goal is to blend without being seen. To not be remembered.

She makes her way into the church, smiling when someone greets her, and gets to a front desk that seems to be a security desk. A small man sits behind the desk and smiles at her.

"Hi. Do you happen to have an envelope?" she says to the man.

"I sure do." He hands her an envelope with the church imprint on it.

Tally quickly takes the money and the ID and slides them into the envelope. She looks at the smiling man. "Tape?"

The man picks up a tape dispenser and places it in front of Tally. She closes the envelope and seals it. She takes a pen that was next to the tape dispenser and writes Seth's name on it. She smiles. "Can you make sure Seth Brommels gets this?"

"Seth? He actually should be here now, in the sanctuary."

"That's okay. I'm kinda in a rush."

"So you're not staying? We have a wonderful service planned."

"I'm sorry, but no. I go to a different church already."

"Oh. I see. Well, if you are ever in the area again, please don't hesitate to stop by."

Tally is thrown off by the man's politeness. She takes a few steps back. "I will. Thank you. Have a good day."

"You, too, ma'am."

Tally turns on her heel and leaves the church. Initially, her steps were fast. She was in a hurry to get away from the building. After a block of walking, her steps become slower. She thinks to herself she has never attended a church service before. Another thought she has is of every person she has met that claimed to be Christian. They were all jerks. Some were snobby. Others used God's name to make a quick buck . . . or get a new car. She feels she has the whole Christianity thing already figured out without ever setting foot in a church. But her feet become heavy until she comes to a complete stop. She parked another block away, but she can't help but turn the opposite way and stare at the small brick building with the makeshift sign and its nice door person. Her eyes sting from holding back tears, as she tries to understand what is holding her in place. She thinks of Seth, a churchgoing man who she robbed, and finds herself hitting a new low point in her life. She finds herself to be a pitiful sight. Angry at herself for letting such emotion through, she hurries her way to her car, slamming the door when she finally gets in. She slams the wheel and furiously wipes at her face. Tally starts the car and sits there for a few more seconds before turning the car and driving *toward* the church. She slowly pulls into the church lot and parks the car. She realizes the further she gets from the church, the more it hurts. She doesn't quite know what "it" is that hurts, but she knows the pain. She knows pain, in general, all too well, and this pain is unbearable.

She gets out and saunters into the church, but finds only a single person in the lobby.

Seth Brommels.

Tally looks at Seth as he holds the envelope. She turns quickly to the front desk to see a different man than the one she had seen just a few minutes before. She smiles.

"Headed in?" Seth says.

Tally looks at Seth to see he was talking to her. For a split second, she just stares as he holds open a door for her. He's a little bit taller than she is. Chocolate complexion. The same goatee she saw in the ID. She nods and walks toward him.

"Thank you," she whispers and steps into the sanctuary.

TALLY – THEN

Tana sits in front of Tally, slack jawed, and completely flabbergasted by everything Tally just told her. She tries to form words, but nothing but a jumbled mess comes out. Tally watches her try to process what she said and the implications thereof.

"Is this a joke?" Tana asks.

Tally looks solemnly. "No. It's not." She continues to look at her friend. For some odd reason, she's taken back to when she first met

Tana. It was in the first grade. Tana and Tally were the only Hispanic girls in their class, and the teacher always got them mixed up. It was almost inevitable that they would end up best friends. Over the years, Tally has confided in her for almost everything, and there were no plans to stop now. Staying over Tana's house for the night provided the exact opportunity to tell her everything she witnessed in that back room of her own home.

"But he was on TV."

"I don't know how to explain that one. I just know what I saw." She fights every urge to cry.

"Did . . . did the police come to your home?"

"Not that I know of. And that scares me. He basically . . ."

"Got away with it."

"And she was dead." Tally pauses to try to squelch the trembling in her voice. "She was pale. Her lips were blue. And there was no pulse."

"Wait. You touched her?"

Tally nods.

"Girl, we gotta tell the cops." Tana jumps up.

"No." Tally grabs her arm. "I'm not telling the cops."

"What are you talking about? She was raped and left for dead. You saw the whole thing."

"Not the whole thing. Everything leading up to it. But I think he knows."

"Who? Fredo?"

Tally nods. Tana plops back down on the edge of the bed, hard.

"You mean he knows you know?"

"I think so. He's been watching me more than usual. And I can't see that look in his eyes anymore. Now it's like he's watching me but thinking as well." She curls up into a ball. "I'm scared."

"You don't think he would do anything crazy, do you?"

"You mean other than what he did to Sue?"

Tana looks like she's in deep thought. She eventually says, "Stay here with me. Come with us on our family vacation. It's coming up in like a week."

"What good is that going to do?"

"So when you tell the authorities—"

"I told you I'm not going to the police."

"You have to. Otherwise . . . he could do it again. Even worse . . . you could be his next victim. And I—"

Tally looks up to see Tana crying. This is a strange thing to her, because Tally has always been the crier. Tana rarely ever cries.

"Hey." Tally slides over to her and hugs her. She doesn't know what to say, being so shaken by her friend's sudden outpour of emotion, so she just holds her, and allows herself to be held.

After they both cry, they compose themselves. "I'll go. I'll go to the cops . . . tell them what I know." Tally looks at her. "But I can't go back there if I do."

"I know. We gotta talk to my parents first."

"No. We can't. They're going to go right to my Dad. He is going to flip his lid and go right for Fredo. That's if he believes them. If he doesn't, I gotta go back home, and Fredo will know for sure that I know . . . and . . ."

"Okay. I get it. So, let's go right now."

"How? Neither of us drives."

"I can ask Shep."

"He's not going to come all the way down here just to take us to the police."

"So we hoof it. It's not that far away. We've run longer distances in practice."

Tally considers what she said. "Fine. But we gotta go now while there's still some light out."

Tally sits in front of a desk across from a woman who called herself Detective Barringer. She's a taller woman with a hard face, but soft brown eyes. She offered Tally a drink, but she declined. She just wants to tell this woman what she knows and go on about her business.

"So, Tally," the woman says, "Did I say your name right?"

"Yes, ma'am."

"What is that short for?"

"Talindra."

"That's a very interesting name."

"Thank you, I think."

"For sure. Listen," she takes a quick sip of her drink that is steaming hot, "You came here to talk? Said you have information on the whereabouts of Sue Goldstein?"

"Yes, ma'am."

"Well, I'm all ears." She smiles a smile Tally could only describe as being genuine but hesitant.

"Sue." She stops. "Look, you can't tell anyone I told you this. And . . ." She starts to fidget.

"Tally. No worries. If this is a lead, I'm just going to follow it. There doesn't have to be any mention of who came up with info or anything like that."

"You don't understand." She looks with imploring eyes. "They'll know it was me."

"Who are they?"

"My family."

Detective Barringer smiles a little, but Tally knows her smile is completely from confusion.

"You have to help me out here," Detective Barringer leans in. "Start from the beginning."

"Detective Barringer—"

"Shelly. Call me Shelly."

"Okay. Shelly, I saw her. I saw her when she died."

"Sue?"

Tally nods.

"Okay. So, what's the story?"

Tally tells her the story and makes sure she doesn't leave out any details. She even tells her how she felt as things were going on. She gets to the point where she stepped out of the closet and felt for a pulse.

"Why didn't you call the police? Instead of running to your room, why didn't you call the police right away?"

"I was scared. And I didn't know what to do."

"Is she still there?"

"No. She was gone the next day."

Shelly leans back in her chair and stares at Tally for a few long, uncomfortable moments.

"Why should I believe you?"

"What do you mean? You don't believe me?"

"I didn't say that."

"Then what are you saying?"

"I'm simply asking. What is it that makes your story the one I should act upon?"

"It's the truth. And it's your duty to seek that truth, no matter what."

"Interesting answer." She gets up from her seat.

"Look, it's you all who asked for anyone with any information to come forward. I have information. I came forward. I—"

"Do you know what this information means? You can't. You're too young. You are a Morales. You are the daughter of Roberto Morales." She sighs. "The well-respected, intelligent, philanthropic, charismatic Roberto Morales." She starts pacing back and forth with an expression of disbelief. "And what you are telling me is Roberto's son, your brother, is responsible for the assault and death of Susan Goldstein."

"What I'm telling you is the truth."

Shelly exhales loudly. "Jeez, Kid. This is more than the truth."

"Is it?" She stands to her feet. "I have to go before it gets too dark."

Shelly nods. "Thank you for the tip. We'll look into it right away."

Tally stares at Shelly for an extended period of time. "Thank you for your time."

Tally is escorted out of the police station and meets up with Tana. They jog back to her house without saying so much as a word.

9.

Seth – Now

After service, Seth walks down the street to a small corner restaurant. As soon as he enters, he is greeted by an overpowering smell of potatoes and onions. His stomach growls. In the back corner, sitting at a booth, is a waving Cam. Seth spots him and sits at the booth.

"Ready for lunch?" Seth asks.

"You mean breakfast?" Cam says, still sounding groggy.

"Wild night last night?"

"Nope. It was pretty tame. Went to the salsa club . . . went home. Went to sleep."

"No company?"

"Wasn't feeling anyone there." Cam grabs a menu. "So, how was the wedding?" he asks with a smirk on his face.

"It was good. What's the smirk for?"

"No reason. Just . . . you and Bree . . . out all night long—"

"Working."

"If that's what you call it."

"That's what it was. I mean, we stopped and talked for a few, and I crashed at her place, but that was all."

That statement wakes Cam up. "You stayed the night?"

"Yeah."

"Hmmm." Cam's smirk turns to an all-out smile.

"What? C'mon, Man, you know nothing is going on between me and Bree."

"I don't know, bro. I kinda think you lead her on."

"How you figure that?"

"You don't see it, do you?"

"See what? I don't touch her with any intent. I don't look at her with any intent. I don't say anything that would imply that I want her. My intentions are loud and clear."

"True, but you let her do all that stuff to you. If you have no interest, you would tell her to stop. Otherwise, you show interest, and if you are not interested, you are leading her on."

Seth leans back in his chair, looking at Cam with an incredulous look. "You really think Bree is into me like that?"

Cam scans the restaurant, then leans in and motions Seth to come closer. He speaks in hushed tones. "I'm no expert on women, but I can tell a lot by how they move."

"What?"

"You think I'm just checking women out . . . well, I am, but I am also looking at how they move around, how they carry themselves. And Bree . . . Bree moves very gracefully, like a dancer. But she moves like this only when she's around you. Otherwise, she's Plain Jane."

Seth smiles. "You're crazy." He leans back again. "Bree doesn't see me like that, and I'm not leading her on." But Seth knows better. Deep in the recesses of his mind, in a place under a mental lock and key, lies a secret he never wants to get out, at least not to Cam. Not right now.

Cam shrugs. "Suit yourself. But tell me something. Do you not think she is hot?"

"I never said that. Bree is beautiful, and she is a great person. But she's also my best friend, one that I've known since I was little."

"So what you're saying is that you do want her, but you don't want to test the friendship boundaries."

"That's not what I'm saying at all. I don't want to be with her."

"There are only two options here. You either want her and are afraid to test the limits, or you don't want her and you are leading her on for some odd reason, maybe attention."

Seth frowns. "Why does it matter to you so much?"

"It doesn't. I just find it a strange thing for you to do. I mean, you and Bree never . . ." Cam balls his fists and starts thrusting.

"Nope."

"Never wanted to?"

"Nope."

"Hmmm." Cam rubs his chin. "I don't believe you."

Seth shrugs his shoulders, looking unfazed.

"But I know when I have pushed too hard. I'm dropping it. But as your friend, let me give you a bit of advice."

Seth looks Cam in the eyes.

"Clear the air. Make sure your intentions are clear. Otherwise, you may have a situation on your hands that you don't want. Now Bree doesn't strike me as the crazy type . . . but you never know."

Seth frowns.

"Next thing you know, she'll be looking through your trash trying to find where you are. She'll end up everywhere you are, then BAM."

Cam hits the table. "You're handcuffed to the bed and she's in black leather with a whip. Trust me, I've been there. Stuff like that . . . it changes you."

Another person talking about things changing them, Seth thinks.

"I'll be fine. Trust me."

For a few minutes, Seth and Cam sit in silence as they wait for their food.

"Well, I have some good news." Seth places fifty dollars and his church ID on the table. "You know what that is?"

Cam examines the money. "Fifty dollars. Real money."

"And my church ID."

Cam stares at Seth blankly.

"The money and ID that was stolen from me in that alley."

"Oh. You sure?"

"I'm pretty sure . . . well, not really."

"Maybe it was Bree."

"Naw. How would she get my ID back?"

"Stalker powers." Cam smirks.

"Shut up, Man. Seriously, no one could have gotten this."

"Unless your lady mugger dropped it somewhere."

"Along with the money? I doubt it."

"Did you tell any church folk about it?"

Seth shakes his head. "I only told you guys about it."

"Maybe she found out that she was going to hell for stealing from one of God's children . . . with gasoline draws on . . . no, gasoline lace panties on. Oooh, better yet, with a gasoline silk thong on."

"Cam . . . Really?"

"Sorry. Quiet night last night, remember?"

"Yeah. Anyway, it doesn't make any sense."

"Maybe it's a miracle."

"I doubt it."

"Wait. Hold on for a second. Maybe God knew you needed the money, so He worked it out."

"Not likely. If that were the case, he would have sent ten times this amount for my overdue rent."

"Well, that takes me back to . . ." Cam sits up in his seat. "Your lady mugger had a conscience."

"Yeah. Maybe."

"Man, when is the food going to get here? I'm starving."

"Hopefully it comes soon, 'cause we got to be out soon." Seth leans forward. "You know, every Sunday, you meet me here for lunch. You ever think of actually getting up early enough to go to church with me?"

"Not down this road, Friend."

"Huh?"

"You have your subjects. I have mine. New topic."

"Fair enough." Seth smiles. "So what happened with this chick handcuffing you to the bed?"

"Ah. Her name was Angelique."

As Cam talks about his wild adventure with the woman named Angelique, Seth scans the diner. A woman sitting by herself on the other side of the diner catches his eye. He blinks a few times.

". . . those marks didn't go away for a few weeks. Hey, you listening?"

"Huh?"

"You listening to the story?"

"Yeah. Whips, chains, all that. Listen, you see her over there?" Seth points.

Cam turns around. "The gorgeous mami in the corner?"

"Yeah. What do you get from her?"

Cam squints. "She doesn't look up much. Could be a self-esteem thing. She moves quickly . . . with precision. She doesn't seem to smile much."

Seth eyes the woman as she pays for her food and gets up from the table she was sitting at. "What do you see, Cam?"

"Pretty face, but she's cold on the inside. Maybe baggage . . . too many heartbreaks. I would stay away."

"I saw her at church today."

"And she ended up here?"

"Yeah." Seth gets up. "I'm going to say something."

"I wouldn't, Man. She looks like a rough one."

"I'll see you at the meeting."

Seth quickly weaves his way through the diner to get outside, but when he does, the woman he saw is gone.

Tally – Now

Tally stands, her back pressed against the cold concrete wall of an alley, attempting to hold her breath. The more she tries to hold her breath, the more and louder it forces itself out. She tries to even out her breathing, taking air in deeply and slowly to reduce the noise. She realizes that she played a risky hand today, following Seth after church into the café.

She peels herself from the wall, still trying to regain her composure. *What was I thinking?* She waits for another five minutes before stepping out the alley.

Just to run right into Seth.

He stands there looking at her with a smirk on his face. Tally gasps. For a few more moments, they remain still and silent. Seth speaks first.

"I'm Seth." He puts his hand out. "And you are?"

Tally doesn't move. She doesn't speak. Never in her life has she been so nervous in front of a man. She immediately thinks to the night she ran up behind him in the alley. If she had known . . . if she had known.

Seth slowly puts his hand down. "Okay. So, I see you in the church. We both are the last into service. Then after service, as I'm leaving, I see you again, and you know what I thought?" Seth stares at Tally.

"I thought that you have the absolute most beautiful eyes I have ever seen." Seth chuckles. "Now, I'm not hitting on you. I have no game whatsoever. I'm simply telling the truth." Seth furrows his brow. "But then I see you again in the diner. That makes me think even more." He begins to wag his finger. "I'm really seeing this woman a lot. A woman I know I have never seen before. In the church, in the diner, and running away from me down the street from the diner. I'm sorry, what did you say your name was again?"

"I didn't give you my name," Tally says.

"Ah." Seth smiles. "She speaks. And her voice. Her sweet, sweet, Hispanic voice." Seth wags his finger again. "You know . . . I find it funny that the very same day I get this back—" Seth pulls out a card.

Tally knows it's his church ID.

". . . and my fifty dollars from a crap photo shoot, I see you, a woman who I have never seen before, a woman with a Hispanic accent, not once, but four times . . . in a day." Seth smiles again. Tally feels nervous, guilty, and gushy on the inside all at the same time.

"So, tell me if I am wrong. Are you the one who gave this back to me?"

Tally slowly nods.

"Are you the one who took it from me in the first place?"

Tally nods even more slowly. She couldn't lie even if she wanted to. She feels trapped and lost at the same time, by this wonderful man named Seth.

Seth continues to smile. "Thank you for giving it back." He turns around to walk off.

"Wait. What? That's it? After what I did?"

Seth stops and turns to face her again. "What else do you want me to do?"

Tally stands there. She now starts to feel the burning of oncoming tears as she shakes her head. *Not here, not now.* "I don't know." Her voice comes out strained.

"Listen. You gave it back. Why? I don't know, but I know I've been praying for you. I hold no ill will toward you . . . Beautiful Eyes."

Tally's thoughts change for a quick moment. She's outside without her usual sunglasses and scarf. She quickly grabs them from her purse and puts them on. She sees that Seth looks at her strangely.

"I have to go," she says. "I'm sorry for . . . the alley." She turns around and walks away. Not for even a glance does she look back.

****

Tally rushes away from Seth and doesn't turn around until she is a good three blocks away. She realizes that she parked about five blocks away and continues to walk down the street. Her mind races from thought to thought, most of them about Seth. When she does get to the car, she plops in but doesn't drive anywhere. She doesn't want to go back to Paul's place, and it would be great to talk to someone about her day. She decides to drive to Ms. Xing's studio.

Once in front of the studio, Tally rushes out, not caring for who sees her. She once again climbs the skinny stairwell and knocks on the glass door. She enters and sees a boy and a girl, each playing the harp. They look up at her. Ms. Xing sits next to the girl, helping her get her notes correct. She turns around and looks at Tally.

"Maria, Andrew, this Tally, my best student."

"I'm sorry, Ms. Xing," Tally says. "I know I don't have another session until—"

"Sit." Ms. Xing points to the harp Tally always plays.

"I can come back at a different time."

Ms. Xing looks at Tally plainly. "Sit."

Tally walks over and sits in front of the harp. "I just need to talk."

"Play."

"Play what?"

"Your song."

"I still don't have one."

"Play."

Tally looks at Ms. Xing, then at the bright-eyed children who stare at her in anticipation. Tally puts her hands up to the harp when Ms. Xing stops her.

"What I tell you about hood and eye covering?"

Tally takes off her sunglasses and scarf.

"Now, play."

Tally starts playing. She is finally able to string a few good notes together. The melody she plays sounds good to her, but she is unsure of how it sounds to everyone else. Tally starts to get the feeling that she is doing well when Andrew's expression turns into one of awe. Ms. Xing smiles. Tally abruptly stops.

"Why stop?"

Tally looks at Ms. Xing confused. "I don't know. I had nothing left."

Ms. Xing smiles again. "You will." She turns around. "You two, play. Page three of books."

The children flip through to the beginning of their music books and play. Ms. Xing motions Tally to follow her as she saunters to the back room. Ms. Xing offers Tally a seat at a small wooden table. Tally looks around. The back area seems to mostly be a break room of sorts, with a small stove in the corner and a few cabinets hanging above. The area is lit by a single light bulb near the back corner of the room.

Ms. Xing grabs a couple of small teacups and sets them on the counter next to the stove. She grabs an oven mitt and gently pours tea into the small cups from a black cast-iron teapot. She sets the pot down on the stove and tosses the mitt aside, finally joining Tally at the small wooden table with two hot cups of tea. She slides one cup in front of Tally, then takes a sip of hers. Tally slowly puts her lips to the teacup and takes a sip.

"Mint."

Ms. Xing nods. "Good for body." She smiles. "And for breath. Man downstairs could use it."

Tally smiles. "Don't be mean."

"It's true."

Tally takes another sip of her tea. "I need to talk to you."

"Why you think I bring tea? Talk."

"Okay. For starters, there's a lot you don't know about me."

"There's lot I don't know about lot of people. I still love you."

"Thanks." Tally smiles. "But you know life hasn't been really easy for me."

"I know."

"Even when you were giving me lessons when I was younger . . . at my parents' house."

"I know. Why buffer statements?"

Tally looks at her and shrugs her shoulders. "I got into some things as of late and . . . I'm not sure what to make of it." Tally's chair creaks as she leans back into it. "I . . ."

"Do you need help?"

"No. Well, yes. But no." Tally sighs. She grabs her purse and digs in it for a few seconds. She takes out a small pistol and sets it on the table in between her and Ms. Xing. Ms. Xing looks unfazed.

"What do you need with that?"

"I stick people up."

"You're a thief?"

Tally nods.

"Why?"

"It's complicated."

"Make it simple."

"I don't know . . . I just made one bad choice after another . . . and I ended up with this guy. He . . . won't let me go. I want to leave, but he'll just track me down . . . and I have nowhere to go. He's a bad man." Tally looks down at her cup of tea. "A very bad man."

"You go to police?"

"I can't. That's too close for comfort. They'll get suspicious, and I'll go to jail."

Ms. Xing nods. "I have place for you. You stay. No money needed. Free lessons for now, too."

"I can't."

"You can."

"No. Really, I can't. I don't want to be in hiding for the rest of my life, either."

"So what to do?"

Tally looks down at the gun and back up at Ms. Xing. "I have to kill him."

"No." Ms. Xing grabs the gun and puts it in a drawer, locking the drawer with a key and putting the key in her pocket. "We find another way."

Tally has tears in her eyes. "I've done it before. I can do it again."

"Different situation then."

"Was it really? It feels the same."

"You good person on dark path. I help bring you out."

Tally sits there, staring off into space. "I went to church this morning."

Ms. Xing sits back down in her seat. "Not bad place to go."

"I didn't want to go. There were things I had to do."

"Stealing?"

"No. Giving."

Ms. Xing looks confused; a rarity for the woman.

"I robbed this one guy . . . and before I could get away, he prayed. Right there in the alley. I had a gun to his face and he prayed. It's a crazy thing to do, given the circumstances."

"Did you shoot him?"

"No."

"Then he not so crazy."

Tally pauses to reflect. "I suppose not. But, I robbed him anyway . . . and felt terrible for it." Tally sips her tea again but still stares off into space. "So I gave him his stuff back."

"Was he cute?" Ms. Xing asks with a bit of laughter in her voice.

Tally looks up. She smiles and internally thanks her for some levity in the conversation. Tally nods. "He's cute."

"So what happened?"

"I went to the church and gave his stuff back, then I went into service, then I went to get something to eat. Saw him everywhere I went."

Ms. Xing nods.

"I . . . I had to follow him. I wanted . . ." Tally looks Ms. Xing in the eyes. "I wanted to see more of him. But I got caught."

"By him?"

Tally nods. "I lingered around just a tad too much. He put a few things together and figured that I was the one who robbed him. But . . ."

"Yes."

"But, all he did was thank me for returning his things." Tally smiles. "He said I have beautiful eyes. Who does that?"

"No man I know."

"I know. Exactly. I keep asking myself who this Seth Brommels person really is."

"Why don't you ask him?"

"Because I can never see him again. He could call the cops at any point. Too risky."

"Why didn't he call the cops then?"

"Maybe he did. I don't know."

"I say you leave bad man and find Seth."

"Again, not that easy."

"Well, when you think straight, here key." Ms. Xing places a key in Tally's hand. "Opens room in back. You help teach. Lessons free."

Tally grips the key as if a piece of gold. "Thank you." She stops talking to focus her energy on keeping her eyes tear-free. "I'll get this all figured out."

10.

TALLY – THEN

It's been a little over a week since Tally went to the police station and spoke with Detective Barringer. Nothing has happened yet. Fredo is still around, though he isn't in the house as often. Where he goes during the day, she doesn't know, but she knows for sure it isn't to work a job. She's watched every time when the Goldsteins were on TV, pleading, begging for new information; for her captor to let her go. Every time, it made her gut wrench.

She hears the doorbell ring in all its obnoxious glory and gets up to see who it is. She hears a couple voices as she gets to the top of the steps at the foyer, but can't recognize but one; the voice of the maid. She trots downstairs to get a look at who is at the door. Her mother always says she's "too nosy for her own good," and Tally is staying true to that word. When she gets to the door, the maid is ushering the person in and rushing to get someone. Who she sees stops her in her tracks.

"Hello, young lady," Detective Barringer says.

Before Tally can say anything else, she asks her name.

"T-Tally."

"Mi Vida. Go to your room for a second, please."

Tally turns around to see her father galloping down the stairs.

"Yes, Daddy." She gives one last look at the detective before turning and heading upstairs.

Once she gets to her room, she gently shuts the door, her mind reeling. She wonders if the detective is here to arrest Fredo. She desperately wants to know what the detective is talking to her father about. Tally grabs her portable CD player and jams the headphones over her ears to drown out her thoughts with music.

Later in the night, Tally goes on a search for her father, eventually finding him in the music room, sitting in front of the baby grand piano. He simply stares at the keys, but doesn't play a tune. A shiny glass sits on the top of the piano within reaching distance for him. It's filled with a brown liquid.

"Daddy?"

He doesn't act startled. Rather, he slides his view up to Tally and gives a weak smile. "Mi Vida. You should be sleeping."

"Are you okay?"

He returns his gaze to the keys of the piano. "I'm not sure."

"What's wrong?" She sits on the piano bench with him and huddles up close.

"Nothing I can say." He places his arm around her. "Could you do me a favor?"

"Anything."

"Could you play me a song on your harp?"

A nervous energy runs through her. "Of course." She frowns. "I don't know any good songs, though."

"That's fine. Play what you can."

"Let me go get my music book." She jumps up and dashes out the music room.

She gets to her room and snatches up her music book, just to turn around to see Fredo at her door. She hesitates for a moment before squeezing by him and dashing back downstairs. She shakes off the strange feeling she has when he looks at her.

"I have my notes," she says.

"Play me your favorite. Your favorite song."

"Okay."

She gets set up in front of her harp and plays her favorite song, a somber tune by Bach. She concentrates on not messing up any notes, so much so that when she finishes, she has a little sweat on her brow. She lets her hands fall to her sides and smiles at her father with love and admiration. He holds his cup and smiles that same weak smile.

"I want you to keep up with your lessons. Okay?"

"Yes, Daddy."

"I'll make sure Ms. Xing is compensated adequately and . . . and . . . You are a great harp player. You are a great person. And I am proud of you. I'm so very proud of you."

She becomes shy. "Thank you, Daddy."

"Now, go back to bed. Get some rest."

"Daddy, who was that woman earlier?"

Roberto's face slightly hangs. "No one. No one important."

"She seemed pretty important to me. She had a badge clipped to her belt." She looks on expectantly.

He takes a sip from his cup. "I'm afraid I cannot say too much about that. Just . . ." His eyes start to glimmer, but she is unable to tell if his eyes are glassy from the drinking or if he is crying.

"Just know that I love you. I always will. And I want you to make good decisions, ya know? Good decisions in life. I've done everything I could to make sure you and your brother have the space and opportunity to become someone."

"Why are you talking like that?"

He opens his mouth to speak but doesn't say a word.

"Talindra, it is well past time for you to go to sleep. Up to your room."

Tally looks at the entryway to the music room to see her mother in her nightgown, arms crossed.

"Now," she says.

Tally gets up from her seat and leaves, giving one final look to her father. She passes by her mother without so much as a single glance her way.

The next day, the police, led by Detective Barringer, enter the Morales residence and arrest Roberto Morales. Tally realizes it looked nothing like how it is on TV. There was no screaming. There wasn't a fight. There was just quiet, and sadness; a deep and profound sadness.

Tally walks the entire home aimlessly while her mother fake cleans. She doesn't understand. She went to the detective because of what she'd witnessed. She knows for sure she hasn't said a word of her father, so why he was arrested, she doesn't know. She paces the music room floor, enraged.

Fredo shows up at the house in the middle of the day. He calls for their mother but finds Tally first.

"I just heard."

Tally keeps pacing.

"Did they say what they arrested him for?" He waits for an answer, but Tally offers none. "Look, Tally, I know—" He starts pacing back and forth with her. "I know you aren't a fan of mine, but—"

"Aren't a fan?" She stops in her tracks. "Aren't a fan. Fredo, I despise you. You know what that means? I hate you. I hate you more than anyone, more than anything on the face of this planet."

"Now come on, Tally."

"I mean what kind of punk are you? What kind of lowlife individual are you?"

Fredo doesn't say anything. He stares at Tally with a gaze so intense, she can feel the burning in her own eyes. She feels her control of her anger slipping.

"And you come here talking about you heard. You heard what? That Daddy was arrested for something you did? That—" She stops because she knows she has said too much. "Leave, Fredo. Don't come back. Ever."

Fredo's eye twitches. He looks down and away from Tally as if he is trying to find the words to say. Instead, he backs up, slowly. Before long, he is turning around and striding toward the large front doors to exit their home. Soon after, Debbie trounces in.

"Was that Fredo, Dear?"

"No, Mom," Tally answers and gives a hard stare at the maid, daring her to say something. "Where are you off to?"

"The police station. I will be back."

"Okay, Mom."

Later in the night, Tally lies in her bed, her back facing the door. With her headphones on, she silently mourns the fate of her father while seething in anger toward her brother.

She doesn't feel it in time: the presence of someone else in her room.

She feels a hard yank on her arm, pulling her to be flat on her bed, then a sharp force to her stomach. She struggles to get air, and musters a low-level scream. Towering above her, with his knee jammed into her abdomen, is Fredo.

"Breathe, Tally," he says.

She tries to get air, but as soon as she takes in a deep breath, he jams a cloth over her face. She smells something sharp that burns in her nostrils. A few seconds later, everything goes dark.

11.

SETH – NOW

Seth sits in a meeting with his friends as Tony speaks to the group.

"Okay, guys. Good week last week. Actually, great week last week. This coming week, we have a bunch of stuff happening, so check your folders often. Oh, and Seth and Bree: great job on the wedding. I saw some of the pics. Good stuff. Good stuff."

"Thanks." Seth says. He digs into his pocket and pulls out some cash. "Here's more to the pot."

Everyone but Cam eyes the money curiously.

"What's this?" Tony asks.

"It's the fifty dollars I owe from that photo shoot. The one I got robbed after."

Tony frowns. "Seth, Man, don't worry about it. Keep your money. Things are hard enough as it is, you don't owe us anything."

"But I do. This is the money from the shoot."

Everyone stares in silence.

"How did you get it back?" Deb asks as she wipes her hands with antibacterial gel.

"She gave it back."

More silence.

"Look, I don't know why. Me and Cam were trying to figure it out."

Everyone looks at Cam. He shrugs his shoulders. "I thought she was feeling a bit guilty."

"Over fifty bucks?" Ranjit asks.

Cam shrugs his shoulders again.

"Did you see her?" Bree asks.

Seth nods.

"She was easy on the eyes," Cam breaks in, "but I could tell she was carrying a lot of weight."

"Seth?" Bree seems to want Seth's opinion.

"Well, she was beautiful. I mean in that rare-quality way. It's hard to explain, I guess."

"You didn't go to the police?" Deb asks.

"Nope. What for?"

"She robbed you. She's a criminal ... with a gun. She threatened your life. I could go on," Tony says.

"I know, I know."

"I think our friend here has a little crush on his assailant," Ranjit says.

"No. I don't. It's more so that I have another opportunity to see prayer work."

"Hmmm. Alright. Let's move on." Tony glances at Deb. Deb in turn takes the money from Seth and places it in her bag.

Tony continues to talk, but Seth doesn't hear much of what he's saying. Bree nudges him and leans in close to his ear.

"Can I talk to you after the meeting?"

Seth nods. He glances over at Cam and notices that Cam is staring right at him. Cam smirks and turns his attention back to Tony.

****

After the meeting, Seth and Bree walk around on the school grounds. They eventually come to a bench and sit down.

"It's beautiful out."

"It is." Seth says. He looks at her as she scans the field around them, likely looking for some good pictures to take.

She looks back at him, catching his glance yet again. And again, he doesn't stop looking at her, hypnotized by her eyes. She smiles, feeling shy under his gaze. Bree sighs and shifts in her seat.

"So, what's up?" Seth asks.

"I'm concerned."

"About what?"

"This whole robbery thing."

"There's nothing to be concerned about."

"Maybe. You said she was beautiful . . . in a rare way. I'm just curious . . . do you have some sort of a crush on her?"

"What? You're kidding, right? C'mon, Bree, you know me better than anyone else. Think about it."

"I know, but . . . you looked different when you talked about her."

"I don't know her. She's pretty. That's all."

Bree looks away. "Do you think I'm pretty? Do you think I am beautiful?"

Seth pauses. "Where are you going with this?"

"Just answer the question. Please."

Seth looks at Bree, noticing she doesn't look him in the eyes. "I do."

"Then why?"

"Why what?"

"Why aren't we together?" She looks him in the eyes now.

Seth flexes his jaw a few times. He looks at Bree but doesn't say anything.

Bree holds his gaze for a few moments before turning away. Her face turns red and she shakes her head. The wind picks up again. Now, Seth smells her sweet scent. Like flowers.

"Remember our first year here?" she asks.

Seth knows where this is going. He doesn't answer.

"I had just got the apartment and you came by to help get my things in. You were the only one who helped. Everyone else was busy."

"Look, Bree, I—"

"Hold on, hold on. I know we said we wouldn't bring this up again, but . . ." She places her hand on his. "You were the only one who came. Not my boyfriend, not even my parents . . . You helped lug all this stuff into my apartment, because you were my friend. We didn't get finished until nighttime and by then, you were too tired to go back to your parent's place, so you stayed with me." Bree looks Seth in the eyes. "You remember that?"

Seth looks down. He looks at her leg, which seems to be shaking vigorously. "I remember."

"Do you remember it all?"

Seth nods. "We both did some things we shouldn't have."

Bree frowns. For some time, she doesn't say anything. "We made love that night. You held me close to you . . . like you loved me."

"What we did was wrong."

"It was all wrong, Seth." Bree smiles to conceal pain. "You're the son of a pastor. I'm the daughter of a pastor. We grew up in the church, went to Catholic school, and there we were rolling around naked, biting on each other like some animals. We both were in committed relationships. You with the woman you were supposed to marry. Yes, it was all wrong."

Seth finds this conversation more and more uncomfortable.

"But you know what? That night changed me. We gave in to each other and . . . it felt good. Those things that we did, I never did with anyone before . . . or after. I only wanted to do those things with you. Even while I was dating other guys, I could only think about you and that night."

Long pause.

"Seth, I love you. I knew this even before the night we made love. I never could say it, but now that we are here, there it is. I love you, and I want to be with you. We're both single now . . . I mean, I know we've made our mistakes and done some weird things, but . . ."

Seth looks up at the sky. He says nothing. Bree stops and stares at him.

"I take it you don't feel the same?" she whispers.

"I just really don't know what to say."

"Tell me you love me, too. That you will always be there for me. That someday you are going to marry me. And that it could be us dancing in the middle of the floor completely into each other, like nothing else matters, at our wedding."

"I *will* always be there for you. But . . ."

Bree wipes at her face. "Just not in that way, right?"

"I just don't see all of that for us."

Bree nods. "So what was that night to you? Other than it being wrong."

"It changed everything . . . not just you . . . and I didn't want anything to change."

"So why did you do it?"

"Why did you?"

Silence.

"Look, we both were vulnerable in some way that night. I don't know. There was something there, but . . ."

"Go on."

Seth shakes his head. "That's it. There was something there, at the time."

"Please stop beating around the bush and tell me what you feel." Bree's voice comes out soft, yet agitated.

"I cheated on my fiancée with you, Bree. I didn't get married, because of what happened that night. I went through the public embarrassment of calling the whole thing off solely because of that night."

"So you blame me for what happened between you and Kylie?"

"No. I blame myself."

"Yet, in reality, neither one of us is to blame. Kylie herself is to blame. She treated you badly the whole relationship."

"But I loved her."

"Why? How? How could you love someone who treated you like trash, yet look completely past me? I'm the one whose shoulder you cried on whenever she did something dumb. I'm the one who was there consoling you. I'm the one who went through it with you. Everyone else didn't want to be bothered. I dove right in because you needed it. And now . . . this woman . . . this woman who freaking *robs* you gets more attention than I do?"

"It's not like that."

"What is it like, Seth?"

"You're my friend. One of the best I have, and I never wanted to nor do I want to hurt you. But please hear me clearly, you are my friend. I want to keep it that way."

"So we aren't together because you want to stay friends. I get it. Fine. So why couldn't you tell me this before?"

Seth slowly shakes his head. "I don't know."

"Really? So, what was virtually every interaction we've had since that night? I fawned all over you for years. Every interaction we had was laced with *that* tension. You mean to tell me that you were just playing a part? It was fake? A lie?"

"No, it wasn't."

"But you had no intentions of being with me. You just kept me stringing along."

"That's not true. I had feelings for you. I just didn't know how to deal with them then. I still have something for you now, but the friendship has always been more important to me. C'mon, Bree. You know I wouldn't lead you on. That's not me. You know that."

Bree slowly nods. She gets up and grabs her bags. Seth notices a sparkle of a tear in her eye. He still doesn't say anything. He can't. Even as she turns around and walks away, he doesn't chase her down. Even as she gets in her car and drives away, he doesn't flinch a bit. All he can do is watch her.

For a while, Seth sits by himself. No one steps onto school grounds on Sundays, so he took some time to pray. Eventually, he feels a rough pat on his shoulder.

"What are you still doing here, Man?" Cam says.

"Same to you."

"I had a shoot. Needed the school studio."

"Well, I'm just relaxing."

"Liar." Cam sits on the other side of the bench.

Both sit in silence for a few moments.

"She had a thing for me," Seth says.

"I know."

"But I wasn't leading her on."

"I know. You were feeling her, too."

"But I couldn't pull the trigger."

"That's because she isn't the one for you, Friend."

"It's something in my gut, Cam. Something in my gut telling me to keep that option off the table with her."

"And you listened to your gut. There's nothing wrong with that."

"Then why do I feel like trash?"

"Because life would have been easier for you if you had pulled the trigger. Now, many things are uncertain. And you hurt her feelings, I assume."

Seth nods.

"Give her time. Give yourself time."

"Yeah."

****

Seth steps up to the door of his father's house. He finds it strange that he was invited to another dinner so soon after the last, but he makes nothing of it. As he steps up the porch, he hears the pat of a few raindrops on the street. He lifts his hand to ring the doorbell, but before he could, Gretchen opens the door wide.

"You made it," she says. "Please come in." She ushers Seth in.

"Thanks." Seth eyes Gretchen curiously. "Where's Dad?"

"He went out to grab a few more things for dinner. Make yourself at home."

Seth sits down on the leather couch in front of the TV.

"I'm making lasagna. Is that still your favorite?"

"Yeah." Seth gives her a strange look.

"Good. I spent most of the day making it." She walks back to the kitchen. "You don't drink, do you?"

"Not really."

"Oh. Well, I have a bottle of Malbec, if you would like some."

"Thanks." Seth gets up from his seat, even more confused than he was before, and goes to the bathroom.

Coming from the bathroom, he sees the door to his father's study is open; only a desk light illuminating the area. Seth goes in and looks at the giant bookcases filled with various books. He grabs one off the bookcase and thumbs through it. *I used to be so into this stuff*, he thinks. He puts the book back and grabs another. After thumbing through it, he slides that one back. He moves down the bookcase and grabs a book that's just out of reach. When he pulls the book off the shelf, something thin and flimsy falls to the floor. Holding the book, Seth looks at what fell to the floor.

A picture.

He picks it up and looks at it. The picture is old. Some of the color is faded. He sees his father and he holds Gretchen in his arms. Seth right away notices that his hand is rested on Gretchen's butt.

Seth flips the picture over to see a note:

I just caught on to where your hand was . . .

—Always yours to touch
Gretchen

Seth flips the picture back to the front to see the date in small yellow print. July 18th, 1993. He was only eight years old then. Seth squints.

It was three years before his mother died.

Seth quickly slides the book back into the case and stuffs the picture in his pocket. He distinctly remembers Gretchen coming into the picture a couple years *after* his mother's death. He remembers the conversation he had with his father about how and when he met Gretchen. Seth remembers exactly, because he asked his father those questions the first day Gretchen showed up into his life. Next to the day of his mother's death, it was the worst day of his life. *It was in '97, Seth* thinks. *He said he first met her in '97 . . . at a church conference in Texas.* He feels a pulse deep in the pit of his stomach. He tries to gather himself, but too many thoughts run through his mind. *Why did he lie? Is that really him in the picture? Is it really her?* Seth pulls the picture back out from his pocket and stares at it for a few more seconds. *It's them.* He hears Gretchen's laugh coming from the kitchen. *Dad must be home.*

Seth stuffs the picture in his pocket and leaves the study. He gets to the doorway of the kitchen to see his father and Gretchen making out. They seem to be into it as Gretchen sits on top of the counter, Burt grabbing her hips. Seth turns away and clears his throat.

"Oh," Burt says. "Hey, Son." He walks over and pats Seth on the shoulder. "How are you?"

Seth is again thrown off, this time by Burt's excitement.

"I'm good. How are you?"

"Blessed."

Seth avoids rolling his eyes.

"Help me set the dinner table, will ya?"

Burt walks back into the kitchen to grab some plates. Seth follows and grabs the forks, knives, and cups.

"Seth, were you staying the night?"

"I didn't plan to. Gotta get back and get some sleep for a shoot tomorrow."

"I'd rethink that plan of action. It's raining pretty hard out there." Burt looks at Seth.

"I should be fine."

"Suit yourself."

Seth hears the low rumble of thunder.

****

Most of the dinner was considerably civil, as was the last one, and that makes two good dinners in a row. Two good dinners in a row makes Seth cautious.

"So," Burt says, "As you can see, Gretchen and I are pretty . . . jovial tonight."

"I noticed."

"Well, we have a lot to be excited about."

"The church is doing well?"

"Of course it is, but that's not why we're so excited."

Seth leans back in his chair. "Okay."

Gretchen grabs Burt's hand. Seth focuses on their hands together.

"You're going to be an older brother," Burt says.

"What?"

Gretchen smiles wider than Seth has ever seen before. "I'm pregnant."

Seth stiffens and doesn't say anything. A minute or two passes before the smiles that were plastered on Burt and Gretchen's face turn to frowns.

"Well, aren't you going to say anything, Son?"

Seth clears his throat. "Aren't you two a bit old to have a baby?"

Burt looks shocked by the comment. Gretchen remains still.

"I guess I should have thought better, thinking you would actually be happy for anything Gretchen and I have going on."

Seth doesn't say anything. The only noise hears is the heavy rain outside.

"You've always been so focused on yourself. Everything is about you. Nothing can be about anyone else, and God forbid if something happens without you knowing about it or being a part of it."

Seth and Burt have a sort of stare off.

"I wonder, Dad, if you really thought about this. I'm pretty sure you didn't, but I know who did." Seth eyes Gretchen. "I'm not too sure how you thought I was going to react, but any sane person would think this was a bunch of mess."

"We have put up with a lot from you, an—"

"From me? You've put up with a lot from me?" Seth chuckles. "You're kidding, right?"

"Now, Seth—" Gretchen tries to speak.

"I don't want to hear anything from you. You've already said enough."

"You better watch your tone with her." Burt grips the edges of the table.

"Just like you. It's just like you to defend her when she needs it not. Kinda a funny thing. I don't ever remember you defending Mom this way."

"That's it." Burt hops up from his seat, flinging it to the ground. He stomps over to Seth and grabs for him. He grabs him by his collar and lifts him out the seat until he stands to his feet.

Seth stares into his father's eyes, not flinching, not squirming, but instead, digging in his back pocket and pulling out the picture he found earlier. He grabs it and puts it in front of his face.

Gradually, Seth feels Burt's grip loosening.

"Where did you get that?" Burt asks.

"Does it matter? Just the simple fact that it exists brings up some more important questions; questions like why did you lie to me? Or even better, were all those arguments you and Mom had about *her*?" Seth points at Gretchen without looking her way.

"I didn't lie to you."

Seth glances at Gretchen, who seems to be stuck in place.

"You did lie to me. You told me you met her *after* Mom died. A couple years after, as a matter of fact . . . at a church convention." Seth wags the picture in Burt's face. "From the looks of it, you two were quite cozy well before then . . . at the freaking Jersey shore."

Burt looks away from Seth and at Gretchen. Gretchen remains still, with her head cocked to the side slightly.

"Get out of my house."

"What?"

"Get the hell out of my house." Burt puffs his chest out.

Seth smiles. "Gladly, you slimy bastard." He lets the picture fall to the floor and walks to the front door, with Burt and Gretchen following him.

Seth swings open the front door so hard it makes a dent in the wall. He stomps out into the storm, not looking back. He can't tell, but it sounded like Burt slammed the door shut. It was either that or a low rumbling of thunder.

12.

TALLY – NOW

Tally gets back to Paul's place and throws her bag on the floor. She flops onto the couch, exhausted. For a moment, she allows the silence to calm her, to perform its ritual of healing on her, but that moment is short lived. She gets up and goes to the window. The storm outside rages and shows no signs of letting up. She thinks about the offer Ms. Xing laid on the table for her. Tally again considers it, but is afraid of what Paul would do. She then thinks about Seth. She's not too proud to admit that she is "crushing" on him, but she knows there is no way they could ever be together. He's a church boy. Her first time in church was earlier in the day. Even though Ms. Xing thinks the opposite, Tally believes a guy like him is too good to be true. Yet still, there's a part of her that holds on to hope. She turns away from the window and scans the apartment. Paul is going to be back soon, and things will have to go back to normal. Back to sticking people up, or, worse, be forced to run drugs for Paul. Tally shakes her head. Normal isn't working anymore, and after the events of the day, she doesn't think normal is an option.

Things have to change.

She sits at the kitchen table, her knees pressed together and her feet shoulder width apart, contemplating her next move. But within a few moments of thinking, Tally hears the whispers. She suddenly feels cold and jumps up from her seat to grab a blanket. She tries to drown them out by turning on the radio, but the whispers are too loud. They tell her that she's worthless. They tell her that she's powerless.

They tell her that things can never change.

Tally shakes her head. She is reminded of her parents and how terribly they treated her. She is reminded of her brother. She is reminded of jail and talking to that wacko psychiatrist. She is reminded of so many things she keeps buried deep inside her. She can't take it, so she grabs her jacket and umbrella. A drive in a storm is better than mental torture in an empty apartment.

****

It doesn't take long for Tally to calm down once she's out the apartment, but with nowhere to go, and no desire or gun to make some quick money, she just drives. The rain gives way to powerful wind gusts that shift the car to the left and right while she's driving. No one is on the streets, so even if she wanted to, she couldn't make any money. As she comes to a stop at a light, she sees one person, almost stomping down the street. She squints to see who it is, but the person cuts down an alley behind a few houses before she can see. *It can't be.* She follows the person down the alley.

Eventually, she drives up behind the person and stops. The man with a blazer keeps walking, despite her headlights shining behind him. The man stops at the edge of a fence, seemingly to allow Tally to pass. Instead, she gets out the car. She knows who the man is.

"It's three o'clock in the morning. What are you doing down this alley again?"

The man squints. "You're kidding me, right? What are you, a stalker or something?"

"No, Seth." Tally looks at him. He is completely soaked. "Get in."

"Why? So, you can rob me again?"

Tally notices his voice isn't as soft as it was earlier. He sounds outright mad at something. She hopes it isn't her.

"You're soaking wet and it's a little cold. You're gonna get sick."

"Look, thanks, but no thanks. I don't even know you."

"Why are you down this alley again?"

"It's a shortcut." Seth starts walking on his way again. "And I have no umbrella."

Tally watches him as he walks down the alley. The rain starts to pick up again. She hops back into the car and drives up right behind Seth. She honks her horn and waits. Seth keeps walking, but this time, closer to the side. Tally stops the car and gets out. She pops open her umbrella and jogs up to Seth. Seth sees her and shakes his head.

"What do you want?"

The raindrops are coming down harder. Tally hands Seth her umbrella, and instead of turning around to leave, she stands in front of Seth. In a matter of seconds, Tally is soaking wet, but she doesn't move. She stands looking at Seth. She can't move. She doesn't want to move. She doesn't want to leave him. But eventually, she turns on her heel and gets back to her car.

That was weird. He must think you're weird now.

Tally starts to drive by Seth, when he moves directly in front of her. She pumps the brakes. Seth walks to the passenger side and knocks on the window. Tally leans over and pops open the door. Seth gets in.

"Thanks."

Tally nods. "Where to?"

Seth doesn't answer. Tally looks his way to see him looking straight forward, as if thinking. She thinks she sees tears streaming down his face, but she can't tell. Could be rainwater.

"I don't know," Seth chokes out.

"I could take you home."

Seth doesn't look at her. "Go straight. Right at the end of the drive. Left at the light."

Tally starts driving.

"So this is your spot? Your territory?"

"Huh?"

"The alley. This is where you always go to get people?"

Tally is stunned by the question. "I . . . It doesn't work that way."

"So how does it work?"

She is reluctant to answer. "I drive around certain spots, looking for a certain type. Well, that's what I used to do."

"Used to?"

"I can't do it anymore."

Seth opens his mouth to say something but shuts it and remains silent.

"So why are you here?" he eventually asks.

"I don't know. I went out for a drive an—"

"At three in the morning?"

She glances over at Seth. "Yes. At two in the morning. I couldn't stay at the place I was."

Seth gives her an incredulous look. "And you just happened to run into me in the same alley you robbed me."

"I was following you to see if it was you. You're the one who went down the alley. Plus, you were the only nutcase out in a storm at three in the morning without an umbrella. I had to see who that was."

She glances at Seth to see him smirk.

"So, what's your name?"

Tally pauses. "After the light, then what?"

"Straight for a few minutes. I'll let you know."

Silence.

"Tally. My name is Tally."

"Tally. That's an interesting name."

"Now it's my turn."

"For what?"

"To ask questions. First one: Why were you outside in the middle of a storm at three in the morning?"

"Because I didn't have an umbrella."

"Fine." She slightly purses her lips. "You don't have to tell me."

"Tell you what?"

"Church Boy had a booty call and got caught in the rain."

"Is that what you think happened?"

"I'm just guessing."

"Well, you guessed wrong. Pull over. My complex is over there." Seth points.

Tally pulls over and puts the car in park.

"Thanks for the ride." Seth places his hand on the door handle.

"It was a joke."

"Huh?"

"It was a joke . . . the booty call thing."

"I know. Anyway, I guess I'll see you around."

"Will you?"

Seth thinks for a moment. "I don't know. Maybe."

"Well . . ." Tally starts to fidget. She doesn't look at Seth and seems to be lacking the confidence she once exuded. "Is there a way that turns to a yes?"

"What do you mean?"

"Do you . . . want to go out . . . sometime?"

Seth lets go of the door handle and looks at his hands. He starts to say something a few times, but ends up saying nothing.

"It sounds crazy, I know. But I had to ask. I . . . just . . ."

"I have to decline." Seth shakes his head. "You held me at gunpoint. You . . . you freaking stalked me all day. I mean . . ." He grabs the handle again and cracks the door open. "I appreciate the ride and all, but I don't think it's a good idea . . . for us to . . ." Seth gets out the car and into the rain. He walks to the front of his building and disappears without looking back.

Tally sits in the car, feeling bad for being rejected, but feeling worse for asking in the first place. She thinks it was too soon to ask something like that, but she was afraid that she would never see him again. She had to ask. She puts the car in drive, thinking to herself what a stupid move she just made.

TALLY – THEN

Her neck hurts, and she has no feeling in her arm. She opens her eyes to see that her arm hangs above her, cuffed to a pipe. She tries to wiggle her fingers but can't. She looks around to get a feel for her surroundings. She's in a basement, this she knows for sure. The unmistakable smell of mold fills the air. There's one light, a single light bulb in the corner of the room, but her view of the light it produces is mostly blocked by a pillar.

Her head throbs whenever she makes too sudden a movement, so she takes it slowly in trying to stand to her feet. With her free hand, she feels her nose, realizing it must have been bleeding. The dried blood sticks to her skin and stings when she scratches it off. She freezes at hearing footsteps on the wooden floor above her. The steps are heavy and slow. Her heart races as those footsteps reach steps she cannot see. Moments later, the echo of the footsteps reaches the basement. She sees a shadow back toward where the light is. Before long, Fredo stands in front of her with a pained expression. She won't say his name. She refuses to even acknowledge the pig, that disgusting vermin. She looks away and screams.

He looks at her after her screams turn to wounded purrs. "I bought this place a couple years ago," he says. "A rundown little shack a man of my stature wouldn't be caught dead in." He shrugs. "No neighbors. And no one knows we're here . . . so scream if you must . . . but no one is going to hear you."

"Why are you doing this?"

"Because I'm a lowlife. I'm some punk. Remember?"

She says nothing.

"But seriously, your words mean nothing to me. But your words may mean something to someone else . . . and I can't have you going around telling everyone what you saw. It's as simple as that."

"Let me out of here."

"I'm afraid I can't." He turns around and heads toward the light. "I'll see you soon, Sis."

"No, please."

He cuts the light off.

In the darkness, she hears his footsteps again, this time moving up the steps and back onto the wooden floor above her. She tries her hardest to listen until there are no footsteps to be heard. A loud boom reverberates throughout the shack, which Tally presumes to be a door. Then silence. Complete and utter silence. She slides back down to sit and cries.

There's a dirty window on the side wall, close to the underside of the upper floor. If she gets at the right angle, she can see light outside, but just barely. She marks into the concrete wall behind her with her nail, leaving a chalky looking "I" to mark a day. She figures to perform the ritual every day, so she doesn't lose track of time. She closes her eyes and pretends she's sitting in front of her harp, holding her free arm up and moving her fingers in a way that she would as if she were playing. She does that so she doesn't lose track of herself.

She believes someone will come for her. Someone will know she is missing and they will come rescue her soon. She just has to hold on.

She hears the footsteps again moving across the top floor and toward the steps that lead to where she is. Before long, she sees Fredo as he walks in casually.

"Good morning. How did you sleep?"

"I didn't."

"That's a shame." He looks like he doesn't care much. "I got you breakfast."

"My hand hurts."

He ignores her. "I figured maybe we could sit and eat and talk."

"I said my hand hurts. Can you take these things off?"

Fredo considers what she asked. "I don't think I can. You gonna try anything funny?"

"No. I just want to have some feeling back in my hand again. Look, it's turning colors."

He squints to look at her hand that is still cuffed to the pipe. "Fine. But if you try anything, I will hurt you. I will hurt you bad."

She says nothing and waits for him to walk over to her and uncuff her from the pipe. He takes off the cuffs and she immediately grabs for her wrist. He sets the cuffs aside and pulls out of a plastic bag a styrofoam container. He hands it to her and takes a few steps back. He sits down next to the bag, legs crossed on the concrete floor, and pulls out another container. She sits as well. Her stomach growls as the aroma of something sweet and baked hits her nostrils. She opens her container to see a Belgian waffle topped with fresh blueberries and strawberries. Stacked in the corner of the container are packets of maple syrup and a plastic fork and knife.

"I know waffles are your favorite."

She hates it, but knows he's right. She's always loved waffles.

"I'm not the bad person you think I am."

"You think a waffle will change what I think of you?" She scowls at him.

"Maybe not." He chuckles. "It was an accident, though. Sue. What happened to her was an accident."

Tally doesn't say anything. Unable to hold off any longer, she tears into her food. She would much rather eat in silence than continue any conversation with Fredo, so she does just that. Toward the end of her meal, she notices that he stares at her. She slowly stops eating, her stomach starting to turn.

"What do you want from me?" she asks. "You want me to say that what you did wasn't bad? That you aren't at fault? That you aren't letting your own father take the fall for your actions? Terrible, disgusting, inhumane actions."

He seems startled by her words. "I just wanted a moment to explain."

"Why explain anything to me? Why not explain everything to the police?"

He looks down at his hands in his lap. "It really matters what you think of me. It always did."

"You know what I think of you."

"And that pains me. But if you'd just listen to my story, maybe you would have a change of heart. At the very least, you would have some perspective."

Tally looks to the floor, being confused by this talk Fredo wants to have. She thinks hard and quickly about why he has anything to say to her at all; about why she is being held captive in a dirty and musty basement. The realization hits her hard.

She isn't being held here just because of what she saw.

"I have to go to the bathroom," she says.

He stares at her for a long and uncomfortable time. She stands to her feet. "Really bad."

He nods and pulls out from his waistband a small gun. "Nothing tricky."

She tenses but can nod vigorously. He leads her upstairs. Tally takes in as much as she can without being too obvious.

Woods outside.

Sunny day.

Dirty place.

One floor.

No phone.

No doors on any of the rooms.

They get to the bathroom, another room with no door, and he stares at her. She doesn't move. After a few seconds, he motions for her to go ahead. She timidly steps into the bathroom and stares at the toilet, turned brown from Lord knows what. She turns back to look at him.

"Would you rather go on yourself?"

She shakes her head. He steps away from the doorway and she hurriedly uses the toilet.

Once finished, she walks to the sink to wash her hands. There's a mirror above the sink, but it's as grimy as the rest of the bathroom. She stares for a few seconds at her distorted image, trying to make out how much of a mess she looks. It doesn't take too long for Fredo to ease into her periphery.

"Let's go."

She looks at him and considers making a stand, but thinks better of it. The bathroom is too confined, and he is too strong. She steps out the bathroom and starts to follow him back down to the basement when she sees an opportunity:

His gun sitting on an end table.

She acts like she doesn't see it at first, not understanding why he would leave it there and not have it on him. She believes he just figures that he is stronger and he could simply overpower her if need be. She flits her attention toward the gun again. She's almost to the basement and decides to take the opportunity.

She dashes for the end table and grabs the gun before Fredo could react. She holds it up, aiming it at him, her hands shaking. With a casualness that makes Tally shake even more, Fredo simply hangs his head. He takes a step in her direction.

"Don't," she screams, tears threatening her vision.

Fredo sighs, but stops. "What are you going to do, Sis?"

Without thinking, she pulls the trigger. She keeps pulling the trigger.

But no shot fires off.

Fredo moves smoothly without haste to her as she still pulls the trigger. He gently pulls the gun from Tally's grip. "You didn't load it," he says and shoves the gun back to his waistband.

She stands there, shaking harder by the moment.

"So you would kill me?" Fredo says.

She looks up at him, enraged. He shakes his head. And with a quickness she can't keep up with, he punches her, just under her right cheekbone. She flies backward, hitting the ground hard, her head bouncing off the wooden floor.

She sees little specks of light crawling around her vision as she stares up at the ceiling. Her body won't move. Then, she sees Fredo again. His mouth is moving, but she doesn't hear what he says. The edges of her vision turn black and she fights the darkness with everything she has left. Eventually, she succumbs to the growing inkiness.

Anything seems to be better than the fear.

13.

SETH – NOW

Seth gets into his apartment and throws his keys onto a nearby table. Still shivering from his soaking-wet clothes, he plops on the seat in the kitchen area. After everything that has gone on, the only thing he can think of is about the picture he found of his father and Gretchen. Millions of questions run through his mind, but no answers.

Seth shakes his head and reaches for his phone. He calls the only person who could help him sort through what's going on in his head.

But Bree doesn't answer.

Seth sighs. He sneezes and then decides to take a warm shower. More questions pop into his head. He asks himself why he couldn't just be with Bree. She's beautiful. She's was into him. They have a good history with each other. They rarely argued. But to Seth, something is off. Everything seemed good on paper, but his gut always told him to keep his distance. Maybe it's because of fear. His mind drifts back to his Dad and Gretchen. He sits at the edge of the bed and digs in his nightstand drawer. He pulls out a laminated piece of newspaper. He looks at the headline and accompanying picture. He first saw it on page three, though to him, it was front-page news. Even though he already heard the bad news, the moment he saw it in the paper, he knew it was real.

He flipped. He cried until he couldn't cry anymore. He prayed until he couldn't speak anymore, until his knees started to hurt from kneeling on hard, wooden floors. But nothing could bring her back. Nothing could bring back the joy he felt in his heart when his mother was around. Nothing.

He rereads the article, looking at the picture of her next to the text. The black-and-white printout is the only picture he has of her. He never had the guts to ask his father for a real picture of her, and when he moved out of the house those years ago, he was in a hurry.

There was a tornado watch that night, Seth remembers. Winds picked up and rain came down in numerous, long, continuous streams, making visibility on the road near impossible. She went out just after she and his father were arguing. If he had known she wasn't going to come home, he would have spoken up and begged her to stay . . . at least until the storm passed. But he said nothing as he curled up in a corner in his room praying for his parents to stop going at each other's throats. He never knew what they argued about, but he knew they argued often. At one point, they stopped arguing, and there was an eerie silence that settled over the entire house. When she eventually left, he ran to his window and sat. He fell asleep waiting for her car to be parked in front of the house again.

Seth slides the laminated piece of paper back into his drawer and lies down to sleep. It takes a while, but eventually he closes his eyes and falls into a fitful sleep.

TALLY – NOW

"Focus, Tally."

Tally stares at the strings of her harp while sitting in the middle of Ms. Xing's music room. Ms. Xing hovers around her, organizing the room, intuitively listening to Tally play works by Beethoven. "I can't."

"Something on mind?"

"Something is always on my mind."

"Tea?"

"No, thank you. I would like to take another crack at that song thing you were teaching me."

"Your song?"

"Yes, ma'am."

Ms. Xing motions her hand to urge Tally to play. Tally starts trying to form "her song" as she places and plucks her slender yet strong fingers along the strings of the harp. It takes a few tries, but Tally eventually gets a nice stream of uninterrupted play going. She concentrates hard to keep the notes flowing, though she knows some parts were disjointed.

Exhausted, she drops her hands to her side. Ms. Xing stares at her.

"It sounded terrible," Tally says.

"Yet beautiful to me. Disjointed, yes. Sad, yes. But beautiful still."

"It sounded sad?"

The old woman nods.

"I don't know if I'm getting this whole 'my song' thing."

"You are. It takes a while. Takes everyone a while."

"But why? Why does it take so long? And why am I doing this?"

"Release pain. Discover self. Take long because you retrain mind."

"What do you mean?"

"You first played songs by others. When jump into your song, it nothing more than other songs put together. Somewhere, you get to most basic of craft. Notes. You put notes together, then you play your song. It's deepest form of expression. Enough for now. Make tea. Talk." She walks to the back room to put a black cast-iron teapot on the stove.

Tally sits there motionless at first but eventually takes a seat at the table in the back room. She watches Ms. Xing make a pot of tea.

"Hungry?" she asks. "I make ham-and-cheese sandwiches."

"With the crusts cut off?"

"Like when you were little?"

"Yes, please." She looks down, almost embarrassed at the request.

Ms. Xing smiles and prepares lunch for the two of them. When she sits down at the table holding the handle of the teapot with an oven mitt in one hand and a plate of sandwiches with the crusts cut off in the other, Tally feels surprisingly . . . bad.

"I don't get it."

"Get what?"

"I have nothing. I am about nothing. I'm a thief. I stole from people for my own means. I'm living off their money as we speak. I tell you this and show you the gun I did it with. You, in turn give me free lessons, food to eat, tea to drink, and . . . you're always here. I don't deserve any of it."

"I don't know who is more deserving."

"There are plenty more people who are more deserving of your time . . . of your love. Those kids I saw the other day. They deserve it more. Some of the other students I see pictures of on the wall . . . they deserve it more. I'm a grown woman. I made my bed. Now—"

"But I will not let you sleep. Not until you make better bed. I hope for best . . . for you." She pauses. "You deserve more. That's it. Nothing else to say. You deserve more. You realize that, you in much better shape."

Tally looks down at the sandwiches. She grabs one off the plate and starts eating.

Both women drink tea and eat in silence. Tally continues to look down at the table, taking notice of the wood grain. She looks up to see Ms. Xing staring at her.

"I saw him again," Tally says.

"Who?"

"The cute guy I told you about, Seth."

"The anti-bad man?"

"Yeah. He was walking in the same alley I robbed him in just last week."

"Cute guy not so smart?"

"I don't know. It was weird. I was driving around—"

"Stealing?"

"No. Not at all. I was driving around to clear my mind . . . and I couldn't be by myself. It was raining and I see him in the alley."

"You see man walking in alley at night in the rain?"

"The rain stopped for a few seconds, and he was on the main street when I first saw him. He was on the side where the street lights still work. He goes down the alley, and I follow behind him."

"How were you sure it was him?"

"I wasn't, really. I—" Tally pauses to think. "I guess it was more of a hope. I don't know. I wanted it to be him. That make sense?"

Ms. Xing nods.

"I wanted it to be him so bad."

"So what did you do when you found it was him?"

"I told him to get in the car. He was soaked and the wind was starting to blow. He was going to get sick."

Ms. Xing smiles.

"What?"

"You steal from anti-bad man, then tell him get in your car. He gets in?"

"No. Well, not at first. But I was legitimately concerned for his health. He's too pretty of a man to have a runny nose and sneezing all over the place. I bet you even when he sneezes, it looks like a work of art. But anyway, it starts raining again and I give him my umbrella. Right when I'm about to give up, he gets in."

"And?"

"I dunno. Something was off . . . with him. I was so nervous and excited, maybe a little turned on, but he was . . . I don't know. Something just didn't feel right. But I tried to make a few jokes. They didn't land too well. Then I really messed things up."

"You asked him out."

"Yeah. How did you know?"

"Know you well. Very well."

"Well, I shouldn't have done it. He probably thinks I'm some crazy chick. I rob him, give his stuff back, stalk him, then ask him out." She sips some tea, letting the mint aroma rise to her nostrils and fill her lungs. It gives her energy. "But I'm not crazy. I just know I will never see him again."

"What makes you so sure?"

"He doesn't want anything to do with me. And who could blame him?" Tally shakes her head. "Just my luck, right?" In a trance, she looks at the steam still rising from her cup.

Ms. Xing gets up. "Come." She motions Tally over as she walks out of the back room and to the large standing harp. "Play."

"Ms. Xing, I don't feel like playing."

Ms. Xing taps her on the shoulder. "Play."

Tally sets up a stool at the end of the large standing harp and plucks at the strings, looking at Ms. Xing with a puzzled expression.

"What am I playing?"

"Your song."

"Again?"

The old woman doesn't say anything but stares at Tally and then at the harp. Tally looks down, sighs, and plays. This time, the tune she plays starts off a bit shaky, but after a few moments, Tally plays with a continuous flow of notes. After a few more moments, Tally locks in a trance of sorts and she continues to play. Her fingers pluck the strings gracefully and the more she does, the more she realizes she isn't playing just notes anymore. Each note matches a reflection of her emotions. The sounds she makes hurt her as they resonate throughout her body. Her thoughts are no longer on trying to play notes, but on her life; on her past tribulations, on her current crappy situation . . .

On Seth.

She stops abruptly and stares at the harp. She slumps a bit as she lets her hands fall to her sides. The sounds of the notes fade in her mind, but the emotions remain.

"How was that?"

"Beautiful."

"It doesn't feel like it."

"It was perfect. Sad, but perfect." She places a hand on Tally's shoulder. "Now we need happier tune."

14.

Tally – Then

She wakes sensing her arm hanging above her head, feeling the worst she's ever felt in her life. Her face hurts. She cannot feel her arm anymore. Sluggish, she stands to her feet. It's pitch black, but she knows she's in the basement again, and cuffed to the pipe along the far back wall. She remains quiet, listening for anything, but only hears a low hissing of some sort, hoping it isn't a snake.

She moves around enough to get the blood flow back in her arm, the sharp and tingling pain only adding to the pain she feels from everything else. As she moves her arm, she realizes she has a little more freedom to move. She notices she can now move across the wall, still cuffed to the pipe. It doesn't take much longer for her to hear shuffling from the level upstairs, then the heavy footsteps headed toward her level. She freezes and doesn't move until Fredo stands in front of her as a looming figure of darkness. He stands there, she knows, observing her. She doesn't say a word.

"Dad's dead."

She doesn't move.

"Did you hear me? Dad is dead."

It takes great effort to understand what he is saying, and when she does, she feels nothing. Emptiness. All she can manage is a curt nod.

"That's it?"

"That's all I have left."

"He was our Dad, for goodness' sakes."

"Goodness? What do you know about goodness? He's dead because of you."

"No. He is dead because of his actions. His DNA at the scene."

"What scene?"

"Where he buried her body."

She feels like she is going to be sick.

"Just thought I'd tell you that."

"Why? So, you can torture me more?"

He doesn't respond.

"Like, what do you want from me?"

He stares at her with a gaze she instantly recognizes and she feels a rush of cold air.

"You haven't eaten all day."

"I'm not hungry."

"The lies you tell. You need to get some meat back on your bones."

"What are you, Mom, now?"

"No. I'm not." He states as a matter of fact. "I'm not a lazy, good-for-nothing twat that sits around in a lavish house all day, ordering maids and butlers around because it's what rich people do."

She looks at him for a quick second before returning her gaze to the floor.

"But you're her favorite," she says.

"Yeah, well, she was never mine. The stuff she put Dad through."

Tally has no idea what he is talking about, but she doesn't press any further.

"Anyway, I'm setting some things up for you upstairs. Making it a little bit more habitable."

"So?"

"Well, that is, unless you like being cuffed to a pipe."

She doesn't say anything simply for being confused. She knows he's kept her hostage because she's the only other one who has seen his crimes. He doesn't know she said anything to the police, but still. His main concern was keeping her out of the equation. Why does he keep her now, she wonders. Furthermore, why he is setting things up for her is a mystery.

"I'll get some grub," he says with a nonchalance that is both annoying and scary. He turns around to leave the basement but stops. "You know I forgive you."

"For what?"

"For trying to kill me. I mean if you think about it, I saved you."

"What?"

"From being a murderer. I saved your life . . . your conscience. I saved you."

"You set me up. You didn't leave that gun out in the open for no reason."

"It was a lesson learned. You're smarter and wiser for it now, aren't you?"

She looks back to the floor.

"I'll get us some food."

She looks on the basement wall as she carefully makes another mark with her nail. Six, she counts. For the past few days, Fredo has been working upstairs for the bulk of that time, crashing and banging sounds echoing throughout the basement. Lately, he's said nothing to her. He would either drop off some food and leave, or escort her to the bathroom, but neither of those times did he say much. She finds herself wanting to have a conversation, but she doesn't start one herself.

He comes downstairs and stares at her for a few moments.

"Upstairs is finished."

"What are you doing?"

"Come on." He moves to uncuff her from the pipe. She instinctually flinches. She lets her hand down to her side but doesn't move otherwise. He turns and heads upstairs, and without saying another word, she follows. He takes her through the main level again, but this time, points out the back room and the thick wooden door that hangs in the doorway.

"I don't get it."

"I figured its better than being cuffed in the basement."

"Going home would be even better."

"That's not an option. But here, at least, you will be a little more comfortable."

He grabs her arm and pulls her to the room. She scans the room. It's well-lit with incandescent lights. There are two large sets of curtains that she rushes to, only to find the windows have been boarded up. She shuffles her feet along the dusty wooden floor.

"No," she says.

"What?"

"I'm going home." She takes steps toward the doorway.

"Fine." Fredo moves aside.

She storms past him, but every nerve ending in her body is on fire. She stomps past the kitchen, by the living room, and out the front door. She looks all around to see nothing but thick, dense forest.

"Of course without food or drink, you wouldn't really survive. And you're not much of a camper . . . or a hunter." She hears his voice coming from behind her. Tears blur her vision. She looks all around the house, but still doesn't find anything but forest. Not even a vehicle. She concludes that he must hike his way to the little shack. She turns and looks at Fredo. He leans against the front of the shack. He waves her over, but she doesn't move.

"I'll get us some dinner together. You should check out your new digs. I got you some clothes, too."

As she stares at him, a feeling of dread settles over her. "I want to go home now," she says a little more earnestly.

"Tally, there's no way that's ever going to happen."

In a moment of boldness, she screams. Nothing of what she yells is intelligible, nor does any of it seem to faze Fredo. The final thing she says comes out clear, all while shocking and scaring her to her core.

"Just kill me already. Isn't that your end game here? You know I'm the only link to your . . . junk."

He stares at her as she breaks down into a sobbing heap. He walks over to her and gently grabs her arm, helping her back to the shack.

"I don't want to kill you. I couldn't. I love you."

In a blur of emotion, she doesn't hear much of what he says, save for that last part. She hears the emphasis he put on "love" and shivers. Still, she lets him lead her back into the broken-down shack.

15.

SETH – NOW

Seth gets off the bus and heads into the school studio to set up for a photo shoot. He lacks enough sleep to have any spring in his movements, and if he could find a comfortable-enough spot, he would easily steal a few moments of shut-eye. He constantly thinks about this past weekend, about his father and Gretchen, about his mother, about Bree, about the woman who robbed him but had a change of heart. He shakes his head. He heads into the studio to set up and sets his bag down. He moves lights around to get the proper placement and changes the background paper to plain white. His movements feel labored.

"You look tired."

Seth looks at the studio room entrance to see Bree.

"Well, I guess you can say this Monday morning really sucks. The weekend wasn't the best."

"Really?" She walks to one of the lights to help Seth set up. "Well, mine was great."

"Liar. You spent most of your weekend with me."

"Exactly."

Seth pauses, searching for something to say. "I tried calling you last night."

"I know. I didn't really feel like talking."

"You mean you really didn't feel like talking to me?"

"Maybe. Look, Seth, I'm sorry for how that talk went. I opened a can of worms that probably should have stayed closed. I'm not mad at you or anything." She takes a step closer to him. "In fact, I understand where you are coming from. And for putting so much pressure on you, I am sorry."

Seth considers what she said. "But your feelings are your feelings. And that's how you feel."

"I'd be lying if I said they weren't. I'd be lying if I said I don't want to be with you . . . that I don't love you." She folds her arms. "But the friendship is more important."

"I appreciate that. But you know I never ever at any point want to hurt you. It kinda hurts me when you are hurt. But I'm not saying that to make anyone feel better or anything. I'm just saying that I hold our friendship to such a high level that I don't want anyone messing it up . . . including us."

Bree nods and looks at the ground. "I understand. Because for a second . . ."

"What?"

"It's silly. Forget it."

"Naw, go ahead. What were you going to say?"

"I was thinking that . . . you know . . . you didn't want to be with me . . . for other reasons."

"What other reasons."

"I dunno. We're . . . different. You've never dated a white girl before, have you?"

"I haven't, but that wasn't a factor."

"Well, you would be silly to think there isn't a difference . . . you know . . . and a potential added pressure."

"Bree, it wasn't a factor. I mean, is the fact that I am a black man a factor for you?"

"No. Never was. Never will be. You're simply Seth to me."

Seth stares at her for a few moments before unpacking his camera. "So does that mean you still wanna be my friend?"

"I guess so. Somebody needs to make sure you keep it together."

He smirks. "Listen, I called you last night about something else, though."

"Yeah?"

"That dinner at my dad's . . . worst dinner ever."

"I don't remember those being entirely fun."

"No, but this one. This one was the straw that broke the camel's back."

"What happened?"

"Well, Gretchen is pregnant."

Bree's mouth opens wide. "Get out."

"Yup. So, that whole thing was—*is*—awkward. But I got into an argument with my Dad, which is nothing new, but . . . I found something that threw me off. A picture." He looks to see if he still has Bree's undivided attention. "A picture of him and Gretchen."

"What kind of picture?" Her face turns to a frown.

"A normal picture of two people having a good time with each other."

"So what's the big deal?"

"It was dated before Mom died."

He looks at her as she processes what he just said. Her looks range from confusion to realization to shock.

"You . . . you don't think Gretchen is one of the reasons why . . . you know . . . why your parents argued so much."

"I do. That's exactly what I was thinking. I don't know for sure, though, but when I confronted Dad about it, he seemed more pissed than usual. It simply doesn't add up."

"I don't know, Seth. Something doesn't feel right about this."

"I know. This whole situation doesn't add up."

"No, that's not what I'm saying." She walks in close to him. "I know you. I've known you all my life. I know when you get a hold of a slight thing, insignificant or not, you dig and dig until there's nowhere left to go."

"Yeah. Your point?"

"This may not be the topic to dig in on. Seriously, what do you hope to find?"

Seth stares at Bree for a moment, not shying away from direct eye contact as he would normally do. "I honestly don't know. I don't even know if there is anything to dig for." He moves away from her and starts playing with his camera. "But that's the thing. I don't know, and the only way I will know if there is something is if I search it out. If I get nothing, I'm comforted. But if I find something . . ."

She stops him from toying with his camera and grabs his hand. "Seth . . . what are you looking for?"

He holds her hand and gently rubs it with his thumb. "Nothing."

"So you put a wall up now?"

"It's not a wall. It's the truth. I hope I find nothing."

She looks down. "You can't do this to yourself. Not anymore. Nothing is going to bring her back."

"I know." He snatches his hand from hers and attends to his camera again. "I don't want to bring her back. I'm not that selfish . . . and it sucks down here." He looks through the lens for a second, then brings the camera down away from his face. "But I will honor her. She deserves more than that, but that's all I can give . . . and that's more than what Dad gives her."

He continues to change the settings on his camera and hears Bree start to walk away.

"Be careful, Seth."

Seth doesn't say anything in return, and Bree leaves the studio.

TALLY – NOW

The last few weeks have been quiet for Tally. Rarely did she go out, and when she did, it was to get to the school for her lessons. She's been helping Ms. Xing with lessons as well, and the old woman has become more persistent in her pleas to get Tally to stay at the school. She politely declines each time, but it's getting more difficult. To Tally, Ms. Xing doesn't understand the type of danger she is putting herself into by taking her in. Paul will find a way to track her down. He's done it before.

Every now and again, the man named Seth crosses her mind, but for only a brief moment. She usually brushes any thoughts of him away before she can get too deep into her own fantasies and delusions. She understands that anything with Seth is a foregone conclusion.

It just wasn't meant to be.

She looks out the large living room window after taking a disappointing lukewarm shower and putting on a tank top and underwear. She crosses her arms in front of her, holding herself, thinking of what her next move is going to be. She's running low on the money she kept from Paul and with no real way to pull in any more, she's getting nervous. She doesn't want to ask Ms. Xing for the gun back to start stealing again, but it's not looking like she has much of a choice.

Paul should be coming back soon. Thinking about it, Tally realizes he should have been back. It has been four weeks, almost five. A few times last week, she tried to call his cell phone, but immediately got his voicemail. Her mouth forms into a snarl as a stiff realization starts to set in. For years, it has been all about what Paul wanted, never about what she wants. She feels the sting of oncoming tears. Her whole life has been about what others wanted and what they wanted for her, or from her, never about what she wanted. She feels trapped.

Such a range of emotions she tries to keep in check, because she knows when she is emotional, she is sloppy. She makes bad decisions when hyper emotional. But with each attempt to quell the turmoil that churns within her, it becomes worse. She starts to cry. A few tears turn into a flood of tears and she finds herself on the floor sobbing in the worst way. She cries herself out of energy and lies on the cold linoleum floor curled up in a ball asking why she has had such a terrible life.

She learned quite a bit from her excursion to church, most importantly that there is a being who is with her at all times; during joy, sadness, and pain. This being is a shoulder to cry on, a strong leader, and smart, full of wisdom, all in one. It was the complete opposite of what she was led to believe over the course of her life, yet she knew what she was learning was true. She silently gave her life to him, as the church folk say. She didn't want to walk down a stupid aisle. It's way too showy. People weren't even supposed to know she was there. Yet, there she was, virtually crying her eyes out as some big lady was rubbing her back. She kept asking her if she wanted to walk and Tally each time shook her head no. Enough was already happening to her just sitting in the very back of that church. But at that moment, she was scared, and asked Jesus Christ what he wanted to do with her life . . . because the pain was becoming too much to bear.

She finds herself asking again: *What do you want from me? I don't have anything to give. Not anymore. They took it all from me.*

She sits up and paws at her face, taking deep breaths to calm the surges of sorrow threatening to overtake her again. Then, faintly she hears something . . . or maybe she saw it . . . or she felt it. Whatever it is, it was clear.

"It" told her to move.

She doesn't know what to make of it. She starts to think she made it up in her mind and somehow heard . . . or felt something that never happened. *But what if . . .* She gets to her feet and paces back and forth in front of the window. *What if this is that mysterious stuff I heard in church?* She comes to an abrupt stop. *Is Jesus speaking to me?* She shakes her head, thinking there's no way the Son of God would have anything to "say" to her. She doubts he says much. She has heard too many people say that God "told them" to do this or that, all things contradicting.

But there "it" is again.

She starts to get jittery, continuing to battle herself in her head. She ponders what "move" means. Surely it can't mean physically. There's no way she can leave this place now. She doesn't want to think of what Paul would do. *Maybe it's spiritually. Maybe I need movement within my spirit. That makes more sense.* She pulls her hair back and forms a pony tail, then lets it drop.

What if it's both?

She decides to stay put, but she doesn't feel great about it.

An hour later, she gets dressed, packs her things, and leaves.

16.

Tally – Then

It's been three more days in the shack. Three days locked inside her new room that has very little. Fredo has come by once in the last three days. He dropped off a cooler filled with food, another duffel bag with snacks, and a bucket with a top. When she first opened the bucket, a rush of cleaning chemicals burned her nose. She realized he isn't going to be around for a while, because that bucket was supposed to be her toilet.

At first, she just relaxed as much as she could on the dusty cot. But it took not even five minutes for her to become angry at everything and everyone.

She's all alone with her thoughts. She tries to pretend she's sitting at a harp, plucking the strings, but even that feels awkward now. She screams a few times before plopping back onto the cot. She wonders what is taking so long for someone to find her. Has Tana gone to the police like she said she would if she went missing? And what of this Detective Barringer? She can't be that stupid to believe that she simply walked out of her home voluntarily, not after all the things she'd told her.

She gets up and bangs on the thick wooden door, but hears nothing in return. She doesn't know how much longer she can take this. She walks in circles around the small room.

She doesn't know what pass she's on, as she's lost count after fifty-two, but she stops in the middle of the floor. She hears noise outside the thick door and dashes toward it to try to listen. She hears very little other than the slight tap of footsteps. She pulls away from the door and observes the entire wall. For such a beat-up shack, her little room of captivity surely seems to be sturdy. She presses to the door to try to hear something again. She hears voices, one of which she is sure is Fredo's. But who is the other voice coming from? She pounds on the door with a balled fist. For a while after, everything goes silent. The only thing she hears is the low humming of electricity feeding the light bulbs. She leans on the door and slides down to the floor. She positions herself to sit propped up by the wall and closes her eyes, rapidly losing hope that someone will find her.

Tally is awakened by the sound of the locks on the thick door moving. She hops up and stands in the middle of the room. When Fredo appears, she feels a strange surge of relief. She hates herself for that.

He hands her a bag full of toiletries, a cloth, and a towel.

"You need a shower."

She doesn't move at first, but when he cocks his head to the side, she takes a few steps toward the bathroom with no door. He doesn't immediately follow behind her but grabs the bucket that is halfway filled with cleaning chemicals and waste that was sitting in the corner of the room.

She takes a few steps toward the bathroom and picks up on a scent. When she looks into the bathroom, she sees that it has been cleaned. But the scent of cleaning chemicals isn't what forces her to move away from the bathroom.

"Where are you going?" Fredo asks.

"What's that smell?"

"The bathroom. It's clean now."

"No. Not that." She continues moving away from the bathroom, trying to figure out what that smell is.

"Tally, get to the bathroom. Don't make me do something that I'll regret."

She stops and turns to look at him. "Who were you talking to earlier?"

"What do you mean?"

"I heard through the door . . . something. I heard you and someone."

"I doubt that. The room is soundproof."

She looks down and heads back to the bathroom. She knows that scent, and doesn't believe herself to be crazy yet. Just before stepping into the bathroom, as he walks by her with the bucket, she asks, "When's the last time you talked to Mom?"

He stops dead in his tracks, but doesn't turn around to face her. "I went to see her yesterday."

"Is she good?"

He keeps going on his way out the door. "Yeah."

Later in the night, Tally and Fredo sit at a small table in what could be called the living room, eating dinner. Incandescent bulbs fill the area with light and a bit of warmth. She looks outside but sees nothing but darkness. Not even the moon is out to dimly illuminate the trees. It's as if she stares into a bottomless pit. She has a feeling something moves in that bottomless pit, she just has no idea on what. She picks at her food.

"Not hungry?" Fredo asks.

She shrugs. She doesn't feel much like talking. In fact, she's shy under his piercing stare. He made her put on a dress he bought her that's way too tight and short. He says he had no idea of her size, but she knows that's a lie.

"You look great tonight."

She remains silent.

"Aren't you going to say anything?"

She shrugs again. This time, she feels pressure behind her eyes. Against her will, tears force themselves out, and before long, she's sobbing.

"C'mon, Tally. Cut it out."

But she can't. No matter how hard she tries, she can't stop crying.

"I said cut it out." He slams the table with his fist. "Go to the bathroom and get yourself together."

Not unlike a trained animal, she gets up from the table and goes to the bathroom like he says. She looks in the mirror, noticing the bags under her bloodshot eyes. She continues to scan the spaghetti-strap dress that barely covers her top. She feels disgusting. She grabs a few pieces of toilet tissue and wipes her eyes. Then, she blows her nose. All the while, she's thinking she can't do this anymore. She has to get out. She would rather take her chances out in the pitch-black wilderness than stay and be ogled by the violent and repulsive creature she used to call Brother.

Plus, she knows, it's only a matter of time before he starts to escalate in his actions.

She comes out the bathroom and sits back down, catching Fredo staring at her legs.

"You okay?"

She nods. "Sorry."

"It's fine." He acts as if he has not a care in the world. "I was saying a few minutes ago that you look wonderful. Do you know how beautiful you are?"

She doesn't know how to respond to his weird statements. "I'm thirsty." She gets up, but so does Fredo, and that makes her pause. "What am I going to do, Fredo? Really. I'm going to hit you with a plastic bottle? Really?"

He looks frantic at first, but wipes it all away with a smile. "On the floor in the kitchen, there are a few sports drinks." He sits back down. "Could you grab me one, too?"

She walks a few feet to the kitchen, knowing he is watching her every move, and gets to an opened pack of sports drinks. She kneels down and grabs two when something catches her eye, sitting inside one of the broken cabinets.

A rusty metal pipe.

She stands quickly as to not linger and give up her newfound discovery. She walks back to the small table with two drinks in hand, calculating different ways to get to the hopeful weapon. She returns to her seat across from his and goes back to silently picking at her food. She doesn't make eye contact, but she knows he's staring at her again.

"Hey, Tally."

"Yes."

"You ever been with a man?"

All of her insides freeze at the question. "No. Why do you ask?"

"Well, I'm sure you had friends that have, right? That Tana. She's a wild one for sure. I'm sure she's done something of the sort."

"Maybe."

"Aren't you at all curious?"

"About what?"

"About what it's like . . . to be with a man."

"No."

"C'mon. Really?"

"Really." A strand of hair falls in front of her face. She quickly snaps it up and pulls it behind her ear.

"Do you know how beautiful you are, though? I mean, you would have made some man very happy."

Tally still doesn't peel her eyes from her plate for fear of the look Fredo is giving her. She knows where his line of questioning is leading to; she just needs the right opportunity to act and end this nightmare. Something about what he said bothers her, though. "What do you mean, 'would have'?"

He takes a deep breath and exhales through pursed lips. "Are you done eating?"

She quickly nods and decides not to push her question any further. "Back in the room?" She gets up from the table.

"Yup. I'll be back in a few days to check up on you."

"You're leaving now? It's pitch black outside."

"You sound like you care."

She shrugs. She doesn't care, but she's trying to keep him talking while she figures out what to do. A nervousness settles in the pit of her stomach, knowing that if she doesn't make a move soon, she's as good as dead. Even up to this point, death hasn't been a thing to her. She's never had to experience it so much as she has when around Fredo. And her own mortality never came into question until now. Now, she is as sure as ever that she is going to die if she doesn't do something. No one is coming for her. She bets no one is even looking for her.

She looks him in the eyes, knowing exactly what he's been hinting at all night. It all fits; the looks when he would visit, the earnest 'I love you,' and the comments he's made all night about being with a man. She knows he wants her, which is so disgusting it isn't human to her. But this is what she must use to her advantage. Somehow, tonight, she has to take her freedom back. And it is apparent, he isn't going to simply give it to her. Tonight, she must rid the world of Alfredo Morales.

17.

Seth – Now

Seth moves around his father's church with purpose, not paying much attention to the various looks he gets while walking directly to the pastor's wing. He gets to the double doors as a woman presumably on the church staff steps out. She gives Seth a smile and holds the door for him. He thanks the woman and returns her smile, but as he steps in, his smile fades to a frown. Dell, the retired-cop receptionist sits at the little desk in the lobby area. He looks at Seth blankly.

"I need to see my Dad."

"Do you have an appointment?"

"No. It will only be a few minutes . . . like last time."

"Well, his schedule is packed. I'm afraid he doesn't have a few minutes to spare."

Seth eyes Dell for a moment, trying to read him.

"Can you give him a call real quick?"

"I cannot."

"I don't see why you can't."

"Because I was told not to disturb him for the next hour or so."

"Tell him it's important. Or you can tell him who is requesting to see him. I don't care. I just know I need to talk to him, so I would appreciate it if you would call him and tell him his son is waiting to speak with him."

Seth continues to stare at Dell, watching Dell show signs of his patience wearing thin, and feels triumphant in a way. He isn't sure why, but he feels he said enough to get the retired cop to move.

"You know, Seth, the world does not, nor will it ever revolve around you."

Seth frowns. "I never said it did. Look, for all this time you are wasting, I could have had my little talk with Dad and been about my way. You know what?" He starts toward his father's office. Dell quickly jumps up and moves beside Seth. Seth strides to the office and gets to the double doors. He swings them wide open, ready to give his father a few words about his overly eager receptionist.

But no one is in the room.

Seth looks around. The desk is cleaned off, which tells Seth his father wasn't in all day. Usually, there would be some sign of work, of studying. He glares at Dell.

"Where is he?"

"I told you his schedule is packed. Now if you do not remove yourself, I will be forced to do it for you . . . and I have a feeling you won't like the way I do it."

Seth looks around again, feeling defeated. He leaves the office. At the end of the hall, he sees two men dressed in white shirts, black ties, black pants, and hats.

"These gentlemen will escort you out of the building."

"Who says I'm leaving?"

"I did."

"It's a church. Its doors are always open, remember?"

"This is true. But right now, you are trespassing . . . an arrestable offense. So, instead of taking you in, I'm kicking you out. But if you would like to get locked up, I can by all means oblige."

Seth looks at the guards, then back at Dell. "You're a jerk."

"And you think the sun doesn't set until you lay your head to sleep, and it doesn't rise until you get your lazy ass out of bed to eat your bowl of Fruit Loops."

"Funny on several levels. Especially given how you don't know a thing about me."

"Really?" Dell chuckles. "Seth Brommels, son of a Burt Brommels, born and raised in the church. Was supposed to someday lead this church, to follow in his father's footsteps, but decided to take pictures of trees, clouds, and naked women. Soon after making that life choice, he left the church for another that would condone his lasciviousness, thereby turning his back on his family and future."

Seth freezes. "From the sounds of it, you've been talking to my Dad."

Dell says nothing and stares at Seth. Without peeling his vision from Seth, he says to the guards, "Please escort this young man off the premises."

Seth puts up no more resistance and follows the one guard with the other close behind, through the church and out of the building, his mind set ablaze with thoughts of who this Dell guy is.

Tally – Now

Tally lies in the small and creaky bed in the back room of the school, thinking. She stares up at the plain-looking ceiling, contemplating whether she made a mistake. The longer she lies, the more she has to convince herself that Paul isn't coming back; that he isn't going to go after her. That some holy being was communicating with her, telling her to leave. A few hours before, she was sure she made a mistake and almost turned around. Ms. Xing stopped her. Since that moment, Tally has done nothing but lie in bed.

She rolls to her side despite the protesting groans of the bed, to look at the floor. A sliver of sunlight from the large front window makes its way to the back room floor. She stares at the bright, albeit small bit of light, waiting for it to disappear. It does disappear, but all too abruptly. Ms. Xing steps into the doorway.

"You okay?"

Tally doesn't say anything immediately. She takes her question into deep consideration. "I don't know."

Ms. Xing sits at the foot of the bed and stares at Tally, expecting her to speak on her troubles. Tally glances at her. "I'm all jumbled up on the inside."

Ms. Xing remains quiet, allowing Tally to process what she wants to say.

"I'm scared."

"Don't be."

"It's not that simple."

"Why not? Fear is illusion. Fear is not reality."

"It has become my reality. What if he comes back? What if he comes looking for me? What if he finds me?"

"You can't spend life worrying. If that happens, we will deal with it. But until then, we live . . . we breathe." She places her hand on Tally's leg. "Things will be okay. Come help clean up."

Tally helps clean the floor up, which doesn't take long, because there just isn't enough foot traffic for it to be a real nuisance. She gets through with that and heads toward the office, which is right next to the small area with a kitchen and a bed. She starts dusting file cabinets and cleaning off the desk when she sees it.

An envelope with big bright red letters on the front: OVERDUE.

She doesn't touch it but makes note, and continues with her cleaning.

****

Later in the night, as she lay in the bed unable to go to sleep, her mind drifts to that envelope. She's seen a bunch of them at Paul's place and knows they're overdue bills. *But why would the school have overdue bills?*

Ms. Xing usually locks up the office before she leaves, but she needs to get back into that room. She pops out of the bed and scrounges a couple things from the drawer in the kitchenette. She goes to the locked office door with a screwdriver and a couple paperclips in hand. *One of these must work.* She tries the screwdriver first with little success. Then, she tries the paperclips. Still, no dice. A thought pops into her head, and she bounds to her purse and pulls out an old card in the shape of a credit card. With a bit of finagling, she gets the office door open and sneaks in. She steps lightly to the desk and flips on a small lamp. Nothing was moved since she last saw it. She moves some papers aside and grabs the envelope. After grabbing that one, she finds a couple more.

She stares at the ever-increasing pile of overdue bills, wondering how the school hasn't been shut down yet. She takes in a deep breath and exhales slowly. *She can't lose the school.* Slamming the bills back onto the desk, she pushes herself away and leaves the room. On the verge of tears, she walks to the kitchenette and to the drawer where she knows the gun was placed, but finds the drawer empty. She sighs and slams the drawer shut, knowing that sticking people up wouldn't get her enough money anyway. She stands in the dark, thinking. The idea hits her hard, hard enough to physically take her breath away. There was a time in her past when she was on her own, and money wasn't an issue. What she did during those times gives her pause. Still, she finds no other option.

18.

Tally – Then

She places her hands, palms flat, on the table. She doesn't want to be too obvious. In this moment, subtlety is her friend.

"Are you seriously leaving right now?" she asks.

"Is that any of your business?"

"Well, I would like to stay out of that room for as long as possible. So, if you aren't leaving right away . . ."

He watches her as she smooths the dress out to cover more of her legs, but it's a useless struggle.

"And can I change into some jeans or something?"

"Why would you want to? You look great. Don't you want to look great?"

She doesn't answer, but watches him as he scans her body.

"What are you doing? Staying? Or going?"

He furrows his brow. "What are *you* doing?"

"What do you mean?"

"You are mighty inquisitive about what I'm doing."

"Like I said, I don't want to go back into that room." She swallows down the fear that's rising in her chest. "And you asked me something a few minutes ago . . . that made me think."

"And what might that be?"

"If I had ever been with a man. I haven't been." She sits and wraps her arms around herself. "Tana has, though, for sure. She told me it isn't much."

He bores a hole into her with his eyes. "Then I'm sure Tana hasn't been."

"I don't think she lied. She regretted doing it."

"It was with some high-school kid, right?"

She nods.

"Well, there's her problem there." He chuckles. "Boys don't know what they're doing. I'm sure she would think differently if she were with someone older."

"Older, like your age?"

"Sure."

She shivers. "So what is it like, then? Or, what is it supposed to be?"

"Well, it's definitely more than what Tana made it out to be. It's—" He leans forward in his seat. "You know what it's like to be thirsty. I mean really, really thirsty. And you first get that sip of water. That satisfaction right at that moment, the relief, but the urge to drink more. Take that second and stretch it out over many, many pleasurable seconds. That's what it's like when done right."

"I think I get it. It feels that good?" She squelches the desire to run and scream.

"Even better."

"You want another drink?" She stares at the empty sports drink container.

"Please."

She gets up to wobbly legs, knowing she is playing a dangerous game. But she's in this now. She has to see this idea through. "That kinda makes me sad."

"What do you mean?"

"Well, I would have made some man happy. That's what you said. And he would have made me happy. I know what the end is here. I'm not long for this world."

"That's not true."

"I'm not leaving here."

"Eventually. With me."

She nods and kneels down to get a drink. "But that doesn't mean I'll ever experience that . . . satisfaction . . . that pleasure."

When she stands again, he still sits in the seat, but his back is facing her. She sees his reflection off the large front window to see him seemingly in deep thought.

"I can show you," he says.

She keeps her face plain, knowing she's in a tug of war. She wants to get just close enough to the edge.

So she can push him over.

She forces a smile so it sounds like she is happy when she speaks. "You're my brother. That's gross."

"No one would ever know" is all he says, still keeping his back toward her.

For a long few minutes, the shack is filled with a dead silence. She takes those moments to steel herself. Forcing its way into her mind is a memory of her father. He told her no matter what she did in life, she would be successful. Because she's adaptable. Because she's a survivor.

Because there's a fire in her like none other. She misses him. If he were around, none of this would have happened to her. The fact that he no longer lives hasn't quite settled on her yet, but not lost upon her is the one responsible for his death sits in front of her now.

"Tana told me she went down on him to start. What does that mean?"

"She put her mouth around his . . ." He points to his lower area.

"Oh. Really?" Tally knows full and well what it means. She also needs a way to continue on her made-up story. She takes a silent deep breath. "I think I . . . I want you to show me."

He hesitates and begins rapidly tapping his hand on the table. When he stands, he has such a perplexed look on his face, she believes he's about to throw her back into the room and leave. Instead, he walks over to her and drops his pants and boxers to the floor.

"I can guide you, but you have to show me what you know first."

She stands there frozen, holding the sports drink in one hand. He leans back after grabbing the drink from her hand and placing it on the countertop.

"Okay. I don't know much."

"Have you seen one before?"

She shakes her head vigorously.

"Well, first thing to do is—" He gently takes her hand and places it on his crotch. "Kinda massage."

"I get it." She kneels in front of him and moves her hands along his thighs. "This is what Tana said she did."

"She teased him." He looks up for a moment then looks back down at her.

She looks up at him, his manhood in her vision. "Then what?"

"Then you pretend it's a banana you don't bite into. You suck."

"Okay."

He closes his eyes and leans his head back as she grabs his manhood again. She finally sees her opportunity, knowing she has to be fast, but also knowing he is completely and utterly vulnerable. With her left hand, she grabs his manhood, and with her right, she balls her fist. With every bit of might she has, she uppercuts him in his groin. He screams in a way that sounds more like a squeal and crumples to his side. He swings a hard fist at her as he tips, catching her on the chin and sending her falling. Her vision is blurred, but she forces herself to keep focused. He lies writhing on the floor, shouting obscenities into the air. She squints, looking for the metal pipe, finding it in the exact spot she remembered, and gets to her feet. He only catches a glimpse of her as she holds the pipe high above her head and sends it down to collide with his skull.

She lifts the pipe again and sends it down as it connects with the side of his head, this time making a crunching sound.

He doesn't scream any obscenities any more. In fact, Fredo Morales lies on the floor, his blood pooling under him and a panicked Tally standing above him.

Well water. Probably pretty dirty. And a generator out back with a stock of oil nearby. She never heard it while locked in the room, so maybe it *was* soundproof. That's how things worked in the shack.

Tally looks at herself in the broken but cleaned mirror after taking a shower. She has bloodshot eyes, likely because she's been crying all night. She cried as she dragged Fredo's weighty lifeless body to the room. She cried as she emptied the room of any useful items and when she closed and locked the door.

All she could do is cry.

She must keep telling herself she had to do it, that Fredo was going to kill her, so she had to kill him to be free. She puts some comfortable clothes on and still tries to coax herself into believing she did the right thing.

She thinks, *At least I didn't put his head on a stick as an offering to the beast.* Still, there's much to be said for the evil deeds she has done, even if they were for the sake of freedom.

Once dressed, she begins scavenging, looking through the entire cabin for useful items and food and drink. From there, she can somewhat guess as to how many days she can survive before she finds herself in dire straits. She finds Fredo's cell phone, but nothing is on it, not even a text. She searches for a signal but gets none. Here, she gets the idea to travel outside until she gets a signal. She packs a few snacks, and a couple sports drinks in a bag. With Fredo's cell phone in hand, she leaves the shack. Today, she decides to go straight.

Tally takes another inventory check, determining she has only a couple days left worth of food. She's tried four routes already in attempt to find a signal on the cell phone. Straight from the front door. The complete opposite end from the back of the shack twice, and from the side. She grabs the cell and jams it into her pocket. She doesn't keep it on, nor does she turn it on until she feels she's far enough from the shack, simply to preserve battery life. A phone charger is not one of the things she found in her scavenging. Last she checked, the charge was only at twenty-five percent. Each time she's gone out, she trudged through the thick forest, hoping to find an opening first, then when she didn't find that, she popped on the phone to see if there was any sort of signal.

She doesn't feel like she has the energy to go through all of that today. Clouds cover the sun, giving everything a dreary look. She doesn't want to stop, because the moment she does, all of the emotions will bubble over. She can't break down now. Her life depends on it. Still, she finds it difficult to shift her mind away from Fredo, who now is likely rotting in the back room he imprisoned her in.

She stares outside, wondering how Fredo made it to the shack and back. He didn't drive his way here, that's for sure. He had to hike, but how did he know where to go? She steps outside into a slight drizzle of rain. She looks for something—anything—that would tell her how he knew where to go; maybe a mark or something. She points out where the generator is and where the well is. She uses those marks to make sure she knows where she's going. She starts searching trees and within the brush, looking for markers, looking for anything that could help.

She decides to take a path in a circle around the shack. She does circles around the shack for the entire day, not finding anything, fearing that this was a waste of her time. She sees the shack from afar off, in between the thick trunks of trees and hanging vines. Dejected, she stomps back to the shack. As she steps to the door, fear settles in on her even more. She's running out of food, and running out of a charge. She's low on energy and low on hope. Her cheeks glisten with a sheen of sweat that mixes with her tears. She's done nothing to deserve this, any of this. She's done the right thing and she's going to die for it now. She finally wipes her eyes and gives a last glance out into the forest when something catches her attention.

Something moves in the brush.

She dashes in the shack to grab Fredo's gun that she placed on the counter on the broken-down island. She grips it and runs outside, thinking if it's an animal of some sort, she could kill it and add a day or two to her food stock. Slowly, she creeps up to the area, but when she realizes the movement doesn't stop as she gets closer, she gives up on the idea of it being an animal. *But if it isn't an animal, what is it?* She steps closer to where the shaking is to find a heavy rock on a wood plank. She struggles, but she moves the rock, and the shaking stops. She moves back and waits. Moments later, the shaking begins again and the wooden plank moves. It rises into the air and to the side. Tally pulls the gun and aims it at the moving plank. It's thrown to the side by a set of hands. For a moment, she thinks it's Fredo somehow, but when she sees a woman's face popping out of the ground, she gasps.

"Tally." The woman climbs out of the ground, much to Tally's chagrin.

She can't believe it. She lowers the gun and drops it to the ground. She doesn't move still.

"Tally. Are you okay? Are you hurt?"

She says nothing, but a fresh batch of tears force out of her eyes.

"Tally?"

"I killed him," she says. "Are you here to throw me in jail?"

"What?" Detective Barringer eases from a hole in the ground, eyeing Tally cautiously.

"Fredo. He's dead. I killed him." She falls to the ground and begins to sob. "Are you going to take me to jail?"

"Tally, no. I'm here to take you home." Barringer steps to her and kneels down, placing a gentle hand on Tally's arm.

Tally shakes uncontrollably as sobs storm through her smaller-than-it-was body. She tries to speak in between sobs, but she's unable to catch her breath. Barringer inches closer to her, close enough to wrap her arms around her and hold her. She embraces Tally, rocking back and forth, trying to calm and soothe her.

"Shhh, it's okay," Tally hears her say, though she is unable to stop the storm of her tears from terraforming her emotional landscape. She can't help but cry. Life as she knew it has been irrevocably changed, and what it is to be now scares her more than anything.

The past few days have been rough, but not as rough as being held against her will. She was rescued on a hunch by Detective Barringer. Things were terrible in the little shack of horrors, but nothing could have prepared her for the storm that was back at home.

After traversing the length of a two-mile underground tunnel with Detective Barringer, she was taken to the hospital. Welcoming her were the flashes of cameras and a gang of journalists, reporters, and just plain ol' nosey people. While in the hospital, she found out on TV that the Goldsteins were under investigation after her father's death. She wondered how much else she was going to find out from news reports and the like. So, when Detective Barringer came into her hospital room to check on her, she pinged her with a bunch of questions.

"Why were the Goldsteins under investigation?" she asked.

"You shouldn't worry about any of this. You should focus on recovering."

"I'm going to find out anyway. That's all the news is reporting. Why not tell me?"

"Maybe your mother should be the one to tell you. She is on her way now."

"But I asked you. I didn't ask her for a watered-down version of what happened. I went through hell. I deserve to know that much."

She sighed. "They were thought to be responsible for your father's death."

"I know that much. Saw that on TV. I'm asking why. Daddy didn't kill Sue."

"But he did hide . . . he hid the body."

"So, he knew what Fredo did."

"And he helped cover it up. And . . ." She looked at Tally as if debating if she should say more. "It's not the first time."

"Oh, my God."

"An unsolved case in New Hampshire and . . . look, I'll spare you the details. The Goldsteins were enraged, and understandably so. They were out for blood, though. We had to look into them."

"But you found nothing, I'm guessing."

"Not anything that we could take to court."

"So, it's like what the report said. Daddy killed himself."

"So it seems."

Tally nodded. "So, what took you so long? To find me. What took you so long?"

"There were quite a few things that slowed us down. Listen, why don't you rest. Your mother is coming to see you, and we can pick this all up tomorrow. Maybe we can start to discuss a little bit further what happened in that shack . . . only if you're up to it."

Tally nodded.

Eventually, her mother showed up and hugged her, but it wasn't a warm and firm embrace like Barringer gave her. Her mother's hug was too hard, as if it was for show. Her mind swirled with too many thoughts to delve into it, but she knew there was a burning question she was going to have to ask her soon.

19.

Mathias – Then

Mathias Reid stares at his reflection in the bathroom mirror. Day seven of his new life as a police officer, and he's already starting to show some wear. He splashes some water in his face and dabs it dry with a towel. None of his first week was what he expected. First, for the most part, all he does is drive around in a car while his partner handles every situation. Not that he has a problem with learning the ropes a bit, but he graduated top of the academy. He should have done something interesting by now. But that brings up his second gripe. His partner is, to say the least, weird. He's not in any way what you would call by the book, but the force swears up and down by him. According to many of the guys at the station, he is the best they have, so when they paired him up with Dell Crawford, Mathias instantly thought *power team*. Maybe he overstated his own value to the force a bit, but it was hard to ignore the possibilities. They would clean up the city streets just like in the crime novels, or in one of those procedural cop shows. It only took seven days for him to figure he had been living in a dream.

But it took less than that for it to crash.

"Ready for another exciting day on the force?"

Mathias looks to his left to see his fiancé, Wren, leaning in the doorway, with a tired but satisfied smile on her face. Her hair is tousled and she holds a sheet to her body.

He has never seen a more beautiful woman.

"If exciting is what you call it." He puts the towel down and gives her a kiss. "I'm not doing much."

"Good." She places her head in the crook of his neck. "You know I support you . . . I fear for you just as much, though."

"I know." He doesn't know what else to say. He simply doesn't feel like getting into the "discussion" about him being a cop, about how dangerous things are now as opposed to ten years ago, how he's smart enough to do something else—anything else that would give him more money. His dad was a cop. His grandfather? A cop. It's in his blood. He couldn't turn his back on what seems to be his heritage. He couldn't turn his back on justice.

Justice is in his blood.

"I left you something in your bag," she says. She drops the sheet and lazily walks to the shower.

He eyes her curves in the mirror. She isn't petite, but she isn't what some would call "thick." She doesn't belong in a music video, nor on the runway. She's average, but perfect, he thinks, because she has personality for days. A bright and big smile made him weak in the knees when he first saw it. He wondered if anyone else knew what he knew: that she was the most beautiful creature to ever walk the face of this planet. Her laugh is one of a kind, especially when she laughs at her own terrible jokes. He smirks and instantly digs through his bag to find a pair of lace panties, the ones she wore last night, to be exact. He strolls back to the bathroom, tangling his fingers in the lace of the underwear and stares at her for a moment, only getting a steamed-up silhouette of her body in the shower. He strips and enters the shower with her.

SETH – NOW

Seth sits at a large round table in one of the conference rooms at the school. He's more than a half hour early for the group meeting and toys with his camera, trying new functions, relearning old ones, and finding ways to combine the two. He's doing everything in his power to clear his mind, but something keeps gnawing at him. He must talk to his father. He sets his camera down on the table and leans back in his chair. He stares up at the ceiling, once again bringing to the forefront of his mind images of his mother.

"Dude, you are here early."

Seth looks toward the doorway to see Cam, carrying his camera and a bulky bag.

"So are you. And you're never early."

"I had a shoot. No point in going out now. So"—he sets his camera on the table and the bag on the floor under the table—"here I am. So, what about you?"

"I'm just here. Had nothing else to do today." He stares back up at the ceiling. "You ever think about your past and consider key moments that make you question everything?"

Cam twitches his nose and looks at him strangely. "Getting philosophical on me again?"

"You're the only one I can with. Everyone else, they don't understand the world like we do." He looks over at Cam and smiles. "You know, us being geniuses and all."

"Ahhh, Friend, there's nothing like inflating our egos," he chuckles, "but what's wrong?"

"I honestly don't know. But I think something is off, and it all started with a photo. One of my dad and that chick."

"Gretchen?"

Seth nods. "The date on the pic bothers me. It basically paints this picture: Dad and Gretchen were cozy well before my Mom died. If that date is correct, they were cozy when my Mom was still alive."

"Meaning your Dad had an affair?"

"That's what I'm thinking. And maybe that's what they always argued about. Maybe that's what they were arguing about—" He clenches his jaw muscles.

Cam leans in. "What?"

"What if . . . the night Mom got into that accident . . . what if that's what they were arguing about beforehand? What if my Dad drove her out that night? Why didn't he stop her? It was storming outside. Why didn't he stop her?"

Cam looks at Seth wide-eyed for a few moments before sitting back in his seat and whistling. "That's deep stuff, Man. But, I dunno, don't bite my head off, but I don't see how that matters to how things played out. Like, why does it matter what they were arguing about if the point is they were arguing? They could have been arguing about a paper plate. Don't you still have those same questions, then?"

"Maybe, but what if there would have been no arguments at all if it weren't for this?"

Cam raises his eyebrows and shrugs. "There's just no way of knowing. All you can do is speculate."

Seth starts rocking in his seat. "Yeah." He starts packing his camera. "I tried to talk to him."

"Your Dad?"

Seth nods. "He sent his bodyguard on me, and he banned me from the church."

"Banned from a church? That one is new."

"Yeah. But I have to talk to him. I need to see his face when I ask him who, what, when, where, and why. That at least ends some of the speculation."

"Seth," Cam sighs. "I am telling you this as your friend. You should let it go. You're going to go through all this just to find out what? I mean, this sounds more like a closure thing . . . and I think you still may be messed up over what happened to your mom. That's understandable, but I think you need to find another way to deal with it."

"Deal with what?"

Seth and Cam look to the doorway to see Bree finding a seat.

"Is it already time for us to get going?" Seth asks.

"Just about. What's going on?"

"I'll talk to you about it later."

Bree looks at him strangely but says nothing more.

****

After the meeting with the group, Seth moves forward with attempting to speak with his father again. He knows he's running a risk by setting foot on church grounds, but he remains a bit skeptical on the notion of a church "banning" someone from the property.

An hour later, he gets to the front doors of the building and steps in. He immediately looks for Dell and pushes toward his father's office. He gets to the lobby area again to find someone sitting at the receptionist desk, but that person isn't Dell. He walks to the desk as if nothing transpired a few days before in that very room.

"Hi," he smiles.

The woman is younger, and seemingly not interested in anything he has to say. Her hair is nice-looking enough, tied up in a bun. She clicks away at a keyboard, though even that seems to be a task, because her fingernails are quite long.

"I thought I told you not to come back here."

Seth looks to his side, from the direction of the long art-filled hallway, to see Dell casually strolling up to him.

"Look," Seth holds his hands up in a surrender type of fashion. "I didn't come here for trouble. I just want to speak with my father. I was coming to set up an appointment."

That stops Dell in his tracks. "An appointment?" He chuckles. "I bet."

"No, I'm serious. I just want to talk to my dad."

Dell bores a hole through Seth with his eyes. "How long do you need?"

"Five minutes. Tops."

Dell nods. "Stay here." He disappears down the long hallway and into Burt's office.

After a few minutes, Dell comes back out. "Five minutes." He nods toward the office doors.

Seth quickly makes it to his father's office, knocks, and enters. He sees his father sitting at his desk, reading his Bible. He takes his reading glasses off and stares at Seth. Seth knows he's wasting time, but he finds it difficult to ask anything.

"You wanted to talk?" Burt asks.

Seth snaps to. "I did. I . . . things ended weird with us last time I was around. I just wanted to clear the air, I guess."

"I'm sure you wanted more than that."

Seth thinks for a second, trying to understand the hidden meaning behind those words. "Look, I'm just going to ask you straight up. Did you lie to me about Gretchen?"

Burt adjusts in his seat. He stares at Seth even more, just like he used to do when he was younger. "Before I answer that, may I ask you a question?"

Seth shrugs his shoulders.

"What are you looking for?"

"What do you mean?"

"I mean, after I answer your question, I would like to not hear of it again."

Seth takes a few steps toward the desk. "I'm not looking for anything in particular, nor do I really want anything out of this."

"Then why ask?"

"Because it would clear a bunch of things up."

"Things like what?"

"Like if she's the reason you and mom were . . . not getting along."

"Ah. This is about your mother."

"Not just her. This is about you as well. Can you answer the question, so I can be on my merry way? I think I'm running out of my five minutes." He glares at his father, hoping the jab landed well.

"Yes." Burt says plainly, without emotion.

"Yes what?"

"Yes, I lied to you about Gretchen."

"Meaning you cheated on Mom."

"No. I never said that."

"So what did you lie about?"

Burt leans back in his chair and folds his hands in front of him. "I made it seem like I met Gretchen *after* your mother died. That isn't true. I met her years before, as you could tell from the picture. We went out a few times, but nothing came of it while I was still married to your mother. I never cheated on her. Gretchen was a good friend whom I could talk to about my issues. She was always there."

"And nothing inappropriate happened?"

"No. I mean, there was tension there. We never acted on it while I was married. She knew how important that was to me, and she didn't want to be *that* type of woman. So, what you saw in the picture was about as far as it ever went."

"Why lie?"

"Because I knew if anyone had any bit of this information, they would blow it out of proportion. With me being a pastor of a church, I would have been under extra scrutiny . . . all for something that was nothing."

"So then Mom dies, and you run right to her?"

Burt looks perplexed. "Not in the slightest. When your mother died . . . I closed myself off from everyone . . . even when I was up in the pulpit. I didn't talk to her for a while because . . . because I felt guilty. I would ask myself each day: what if I talked to Jolene the way I talked to Gretchen? What if the contents of my heart were opened more to your mother and less to Gretchen? We would have argued less, that was for sure." He looks off to the side. "But eventually, I got to a point where I couldn't feel sorry anymore. I couldn't be depressed anymore. I had to move forward. And throughout that process, Gretchen was there. She—"

A knock on the door. Dell pokes his head in. "It's been a few more than five minutes, sir, and we need to get you to LA."

"Just another minute, Dell." Burt stands. "I hope you can learn to understand, Son. My life, my marriage with your mother . . . nothing about what I told you was easy." He walks to a coat closet and pulls out a coat and briefcase. "Please let Tina know when you are leaving, so she can lock up." He slides his coat on and stands in front of Seth. Slowly, Burt offers his hand to Seth. Seth cautiously shakes his hand and Burt pulls him in for a hug. "Maybe we can have those dinners again?"

Seth shrugs.

"I know, I know. The last one didn't go so well. Just . . . let me know when you're ready. We'll be here."

Seth nods, and Burt hurries out the door, leaving it wide open.

20.

BURT – NOW

Burt walks out the front doors of the church with Dell close behind. He slides into a limo quickly and scoots down a seat as Dell sits and the driver shuts the door behind them.

"So?" Dell says.

"So?" Burt retorts. He smiles smugly.

"We don't have to worry about him anymore?"

"I would say not."

"What did you say?"

"Some of what he wanted to hear. Enough to back him off."

"You sure?"

"I know my son." He looks at his watch. "ETA?"

"One thirty."

Silence.

"You know, Dell, sometimes the best way to defend is to misdirect."

"Is that what you did?"

"It's what I'm best at doing."

"Fair enough." Dell keeps his arms crossed and looks out the window.

"Any update on the files?"

"Still, nothing, sir. We are"—he adjusts in his seat—"quickly approaching the point in which we've exhausted every resource."

"They're out there, Dell. They're out there. Keep looking."

"Yes, sir."

Burt and Dell never make it to the airport to get to LA. In fact, they drive right past the airport and into an empty warehouse, where Burt takes his briefcase and sets it in the middle of the dark space, on concrete floor. He promptly leaves the warehouse and hops back into the limo so that it can take him home.

Burt – Then

"Isn't it the charity dinner that only rich people go to?"

"I don't think so. Why?"

"Usually, when charities hold this stuff, they invite rich people so they can become donors."

Burt looks in the mirror while straightening his tie. "Well, the fact that I was invited changes that, doesn't it?"

"Maybe."

Jolene comes into view. He smiles at her reflection as she smiles a wide smile back. He stops tying his tie and lets his hands drop to his sides. Caught in a trance, he stares at his wife's reflection. She breaks the stare and moves to his side.

"What are you thinking?" she asks.

He slides his arms around her waist and pulls her in. "I'm a little nervous, to be honest."

"Why?" She melts into him.

"It's not every day you get to go to a charity dinner and rub elbows with rich people and politicians."

"How many of them are rich in the Spirit?"

"There will be other pastors there. At least, that's what I heard. Reverend Pollard from the AME church down the street will be there. That's about all I know of at the moment."

"Just be yourself. You'll be fine. After all, it's a charity dinner about rebuilding Philly. Who talks about that more than you?"

He smiles. "Yeah."

She finishes tying his tie for him and smooths out his suit over his shoulders. He looks at her as she does it, smiling. Every so often, she glances at him, locking eyes, but looks away as if shy.

"I love you," he says.

She smiles and gives him a kiss. "I love you, too." She pats him on the arm. "Now, you better get moving. We don't make enough money for you to be fashionably late."

He looks at his watch. "I'll call you when I get a chance? I don't plan on being there too long, but I was swinging by the church on the way back."

"No break, huh?" A shadow settles over her countenance.

"Not tonight, at least."

He watches her as she quickly processes and a smile forms on her face again.

"Sure. Give me a call."

He kisses her on the cheek and heads out the bedroom. Before he completely leaves, he turns around and asks, "Where's Seth?"

"Where do you think?"

There's only one place he can think of, and that's out in the tree house with Bree. He walks to the kitchen and peeks out the window. Lo and behold, there Seth is sitting in the tree house, laughing and talking with Bree. He worries that he spends so much time with this girl, but even he must admit, there's something about them together. Even as kids, it seems like they are simply meant to be. He decides he won't disturb them and heads out the door.

He wanted to say one last thing to Jolene. He wanted to give her another kiss, but most of all, . . .

He wanted her to stop him from going.

"So, Mr. Brommels, what do you think of the events thus far?"

"This is nice," Burt says. "Thank you for the invitation."

He walks side by side with a woman who is slightly taller than he is, but he isn't at all intimidated. In fact, he is drawn to her in ways he would not like to admit. She has tremendous muscle tone and clearly isn't afraid to show it in a tie-top jumpsuit. He notices her complexion and likens it to the sweetest chocolate. He shakes his head to move away the impure thoughts.

"Are you alright?" Her voice sounds light and playful.

"I am. Well, I guess I'm a little confused." He tries to remember her name, but is drawing a blank. "When you first showed up at my church telling me I'm going to do something great for our community someday, I really had no clue what you were talking about. Then you invite me to this"—he puts a hand up—"and it confuses me even more. What is this about?"

She stops walking and turns to face him. "Your voice. It's strong. What you say. It's important. People come to you for hope."

"Well, I must be doing something wrong, because I preach about people looking to God for hope."

She smiles. "But there is a growing number of people rallying behind you when it comes to the state of this community. Weren't you the one who preached about community and keeping ours strong?"

"Yeah, sure." He doesn't want to tell her his heart isn't into preaching about community, but he keeps silent.

"Well, stuff like that needs money."

"Of which I have none."

"I know that. We don't need your money." She smiles again. "We need your voice. Your charisma. We need you." She flashes him a look that he could only describe as scandalous. "Not someone like you. The man himself."

"Who is 'We'?"

She smiles again. "More on that later. Let me introduce you to a few people." She paces forward to a couple laughing and mingling. "Roberto. Debbie. I would like for you to meet someone."

"Ah, Gretchen," the man says. "How are you?"

Gretchen. Gotta remember her name. Gretchen.

"All is well." She walks over to give Debbie a hug. "You keeping this guy in check?"

"As always, Hon," Debbie says. "How's Dale?"

"Dale is Dale. I wanted him to come but, you know . . . at work again."

For the first time that night, Burt notices Gretchen wears a wedding ring. He doesn't remember her wearing one when she showed up at the church.

"You have got to get him to slow down. He'll work himself to death," Debbie says.

"Oh, Deb, he's a man. Men work. Let him be. Hi," Roberto sticks his hand out to Burt. "Roberto Morales."

"Burt Brommels."

"Pastor Burt Brommels," Gretchen cuts in.

Roberto smiles. "Nice to meet you, Pastor."

"Please, call me Burt."

"I would never disrespect a man of the cloth in such a way."

Debbie places her hand out. "Pastor."

"Nice to meet you."

"So, you are interested in the restoration of Philadelphia, are you?"

"Restoration?"

"We're growing, sure, but there are cracks and fissures. Education is the pits. Crime is creeping up. It's starting not to look the same." Debbie flashes him a smile. "I mean, isn't that why you are here?"

Burt looks at Gretchen. "I suppose it is."

"We better be on our way," Gretchen says, cutting through the awkward silence that ensued. "It's always good seeing you two."

"Likewise, Gretchen," Roberto says. "Nice meeting you, Pastor."

Burt nods and before long, he and Gretchen are off mingling again.

"And that's Raul Valencia. He's a smooth talker, that one," she says. "He runs his own financial consulting firm in D.C."

"So why is he here?"

"He has a vested interest in the goings-on up here. I'll leave it at that. Oh, and there's Theresa Ratliff."

"She's a politician."

"Yup."

It all clicks for Burt now, and he is disappointed at how easily a pretty face could lead him into politics, which he hates.

"This isn't a gathering for just any ol' charity. This is a political fundraiser."

"Not at all. This is an event to build a new art museum on the outskirts of Philly."

"And that is part of the restoration of Philly?"

"It's part of a three-phase plan, but yes."

"Why am I here, really?" He's asking himself more than he is asking her.

She smirks. "I want you to meet one more person first." She looks to his side and waves someone on. "Pastor, I would like you to meet Congressman Burris."

Burt turns to his side to see a man who epitomizes the political look. He wears the plain-looking suit, though it is clearly tailored; the patent-leather shoes. When he puts his hand out to shake, a waft of cologne attacks his nostrils.

"Theo Burris."

Burt shakes his hand. "Burt Brommels."

"You seem insistent on shucking the 'Pastor' moniker," Gretchen says. "Sir, this is Pastor Burt Brommels."

"A pleasure, Pastor. Shall we talk?" The man's voice comes out deep and gravelly, as if he were a preacher himself.

Burt looks confused. "About what?"

"About why Gretchen invited you here, of course." He turns to Gretchen. "Could you give us a few minutes?"

"Yes, sir."

When Gretchen is out of earshot, Burris says, "Thank you for coming down here. I hope Gretchen has been treating you well."

"She has. Thank you."

"Indeed. She's my campaign fundraiser manager."

"I thought this event was for a new art museum."

"It is. It's a passion project of hers that I fully support. Come, sit." He motions toward a set of seats and a table in the far corner of the ballroom. Once they are seated, a few men dressed in black inconspicuously move closer to them.

"My security," Burris says. "I hope they aren't too much of a bother to you."

"No. It's fine."

"So, let's cut to the chase: Why are you here? First, I respect you. I respect what you have done for the community. I respect what you get up every Sunday and put out into the air."

Burt listens and doesn't respond.

"But I'm going to be blunt here; I, as a congressman, don't have such a good relationship with the religious community."

"Maybe that's because you once made claims that God can't help our children. That religious folk are purposefully covering their eyes with a —What did you call it?—veil of religiosity, so that they don't have to deal with the real issues in front of them."

Burris smiles. "Ah, so you've read the article, too. My comments were taken out of context. At the end of the day, I care for our children, and I know that many people of the faith do as well."

"So this is mostly a PR thing. You invite different church leaders to a charity event that's said to be for rebuilding Philly . . . but really, you just want to be seen . . . snap a few pictures with the same folk you isolated."

"Is that your assessment?"

Burt nods but doesn't say much more.

"Listen, this is not a PR stunt. Sure, I'm up for reelection, but all signs point to me retaining my seat. I don't need PR. I have a well-known record of implementing legislation, instituting programs that help educate and promote our youth. That's all people need to know. But this, this is about *you,* Burt." He looks to the side. "Dell, could you grab me a glass of water."

One of the men dressed in black leaves the area and comes back with a glass of water, which Burris gulps down.

"Coming out of college, how hard was it to find a church?"

"Excuse me?"

"How many churches did you interview with?"

Burt eyes him curiously. "Four."

"The last one being where you are."

"Yes."

"And why didn't it work out with the other three?"

"Because they were looking for someone different."

"Meaning?"

"They didn't want a prophetic voice. They didn't want someone with compassion, or with real vision. They wanted a placeholder. They wanted an employee, not a leader."

"I see. And the church where you are now . . . they see the visionary?"

Burt looks down, hesitant to answer. "Yeah."

"Pastor, it is unbecoming of you to lie."

"What do you want me to say?"

"Nothing. I already know the answer, and I already know what you did. You dimmed your own light and conformed, because you were afraid you weren't going to get into any church. All while your best friend moves on to a mega-church, an arrangement someone set up for him before he even graduated."

"How do you know that?"

"I know a lot. Burt . . . Pastor . . . if you had your choice . . . would you be there preaching on a part-time basis, assisting another Pastor with whom you categorically disagree?"

"You know the answer to that."

"And if an offer was presented to you for you to be more, to do more, and to do it your way, would you take it?"

"Maybe. A promise can only be fulfilled based on the ability of the promiser to fulfill it."

Burris smiles. "Smart man. Listen, I must take my leave." He stands and puts his hand out for Burt to shake. "I truly appreciate your speaking with me, Pastor."

Burt hesitates again, but eventually shakes Congressman Burris's hand. "Thank you for having me."

"Thank Gretchen for that. Speaking of which, here she comes now. Gretchen dear, I must go. Give Dale my best."

Burris gives Gretchen a wave and disappears through the front of the hotel, his guards all around him. Burt looks to Gretchen, feeling like he's been duped, even though he's agreed to nothing.

"I take it the talk went well?"

"It depends on what you mean by well. I feel tricked."

"Oh, no." She places a hand on his shoulder, making that whole area feel electrically charged. "Pastor, you are special. It will be a good day when you come to the same determination."

21.

Bree – Now

Bree has been driving for the last few hours, needing to get away, although she doesn't know what from. At one point in the drive, she felt she needed to get away from Seth, but she is just a phone call away. Not too long after that, she felt she just needed to get away from the city, away from the state. Some country air would do her some good, she thought, so she packed enough things for a day and made her way to her parents' house in Virginia.

She pulls up into a driveway and parks her car behind a shiny Lexus SUV. She takes a few moments to stretch and get the blood flowing through her body again, taking in deep breaths of the air that smells like nature. It's like aromatherapy to her, because being in the city allows for a breath of fresh smog to fill your lungs. She grabs her bag and slams the car door shut. She can't help but stare at the luxury vehicle she parked behind as she passes it on the way to the front door. Such a vehicle seems to be common for pastors now, almost par for the course, but still, her father was never one to follow the bunch. She decides to ask him about that later.

Once at the door, she hesitates for a moment before ringing the doorbell. Once she does, she waits nervously. The door swings open and a tall older man with a head full of white hair stands in the doorway, behind the screen door. A large smile pulls across his face, as if he were trying to conceal his excitement for some reason. Bree returns his smile with a bigger one of her own.

"Hi, Daddy."

He pushes open the screen door and pulls Bree in for a hug. He kisses the top of her head. "How are you?"

"I'm good. How are things at this old house?"

"Same. Nothing's changed." He grabs her bag for her and ushers her inside. "Bev didn't tell me you were stopping by. I would have planned something for us to do."

"Mom didn't know. I just dropped by . . . to see how y'all were doing."

"Oh." He adjusts his wire-rimmed glasses with his free hand. "Bev," he yells toward the kitchen, "Guess who's here."

"The fire department if you scare me like that again while I'm cooking."

Bree's father smiles and walks with Bree toward the kitchen. Once at the kitchen doorway, Bree smiles but doesn't say anything. She takes a moment to observe her mother. Beverly Connelly is a graceful woman, a woman many aspire to be; a Lord-fearing and pleasant woman who still has her good looks at her age. She has always had what many call a "glow" about her. Though to Bree, that glow is quite dull.

"Hi, Mommy."

Bev turns around and smiles. For Bree, it's like looking into a mirror. Her mother has the same heart-shaped face, and the same vivid blue eyes. She also has the same curly blond hair, just with a few gray streaks.

She wipes her hands on a cloth and walks over to Bree to give her a warm hug.

"It's good to see you, Sweetheart."

There's one thing that Bree always loved about her mother. Her voice. It's light but confident, and with a southern drawl that would warm anyone's heart. But Bree is wiser than to fall for her southern charm.

"Let me help you with dinner," Bree says. "What are we having?"

Bev smiles. "Oven-fried chicken, succotash salad, and cornbread."

Bree frowns. "That's different."

"Trying something new. Eating a bit healthier these days." She winks. "A little bit."

Bree walks to the pantry to grab a hanging apron and throws it on, securing it around her waist.

"So what do we really owe this visit to?"

Bree doesn't look at her mother but starts working with the chicken. "Why does there have to be a specific reason I'm here?"

"There doesn't. I just know that concerned look on your face."

"I just wanted to see how y'all were doing. I had off from work, so I figured it would be a good day to go out of state. Didn't want to stay in the apartment all day."

"Is that right?"

"Yes, Mother, it is."

"Well, then—"

"I see you have a new car. Pretty expensive one at that." Bree says, simply trying to change the subject.

"It was a gift," Bev says.

"Who gives those out as gifts? And where can I get one?"

Bev smiles. "The church wanted to surprise your father. It was a thank-you for his service . . . for all those years he dedicated to them." She turns on the faucet and rinses her hands off. "It's good to know you are appreciated for the hard work you do, ya know?"

"Yeah." She avoids all eye contact. "Where did Daddy dip off to?"

"I think he went in the den to watch some TV."

"I'll go see." Bree takes off the apron and hangs it on the hook on the door and heads toward the den. When she gets there, she finds her father sitting on the sofa, reading a book. She sits next to him and lays her head on his shoulder.

He gives her a pat on the leg. "What's on your mind, Sweetheart?"

"Nothing. Nothing really."

"You sure?"

"Not really. I just . . . I just need a break. I need to breathe, you know?"

"And I take it your mother wasn't letting that happen?"

"No, it's not that. I just don't have the brainpower to contend with her right now. Not at all in the mood for passive aggression."

"I see."

She sits up. "So, how have you two been?"

"Good. We've been good."

Bree gives him a look.

"Better. Maybe better is the right word."

She nods.

"Seth good?" he asks.

She wrinkles her forehead. "Yeah. Why?"

"Burt told me about Gretchen."

"Oh, yeah. He's pissed. But for more than just that." She turns to face him. "I'm kinda worried about him."

He smiles. "You've always been."

Bree pops up, unable to contain her smile. "What do you mean?"

"C'mon, Baby. It's always been obvious to me that you have some strong inclination toward Seth. But it's okay. Seth is a good kid . . . er . . . young man."

"Daddy, it isn't like that. He's my best friend."

"I understand." He chuckles. "I understand."

"Plus, you know more than I do that Mom would never go for that." She looks at the carpeted floor.

"Would never go for what?"

Both Bree and her father look up to see Bev staring at them expectantly.

"Well?"

Bree's father gets up from his seat and walks over to Bev to give her a kiss on the cheek. "Brianna was joking about moving across the US."

Bree follows suit. "Seattle." *Just like old times*, she thinks.

"Still can't stay in one place, huh? What's in Seattle?"

"What do you mean, I still can't stay in one place? And there's nothing in Seattle. It was a joke."

"An odd joke to make, I'd say."

Bree just nods, knowing if she said any more, if she tried to dig any more, it would end in an argument. She glances at her father, who has an unreadable face.

"So, are you staying the night?" Bev asks.

"Ummm. Probably not. I should get back. Got some pictures to sift through."

"It looks like you brought a lot for just a quick visit for dinner."

"Yeah."

"That means you'll be on the road late at night. Just rest up here tonight and go at it in the morning," her father says.

She makes another attempt to read his face before relenting. "Okay."

"Good. Because I already set your bag in the guest room." He smiles. "I hope you don't mind."

"Of course not." Bree returns his smile, all the while trying to figure out what made her mother appear in the first place. Before she could ask, her father grabs Bev's hand and walks with her back to the kitchen.

****

Later in the night, Bree tosses and turns in the bed, unable to get any real sleep. She figures she would have done better just hitting the road and getting back to her apartment. She flips the blanket off and steps down from the bed onto the soft carpeted floor. She stares at the glowing orange dot of her cell phone as it charges, wondering if Seth is still awake. She looks at the time to see that it's close to midnight, and hopes that he is still up on a Saturday night. She grabs her phone and dials Seth's number. It takes a few rings, but eventually, her call goes to voicemail. She listens to his greeting, almost embarrassed that his voice makes her giddy, and soon after leaves a message. When finished, she sets the phone down and heads downstairs for a sip of water.

She notices the light to the study on and makes a detour in that direction. She finds her father sitting at a small desk, the room illuminated only by the little desk lamp. He turns around and looks in her direction, giving her a warm smile. She pulls up a chair.

"You should be sleeping," she says.

"So should you."

"I don't have anywhere important to go like you do."

"So, you're not coming with us to church?"

She pauses.

"I know, I know. You're still finding your way," he says. He pats her on the lap. "You are always welcome to stop by. You know that."

"I know." She looks away. "It's not because of you, you know . . . why I don't go."

"Why don't you go? Your mother?"

"No. Not because of her. Because of what she represents. She represents what Christianity is to me now. Weak . . . fake . . . hypocritical . . . hopeless."

"Those are strong words, Dear."

"I know. And I mean them." She still doesn't make eye contact.

"Well, what leads you to that conclusion, that Christianity is weak, fake, hypocritical, and . . . hopeless? You said hopeless, right?"

She nods.

"What leads you to believe those things? What leads you to believe your mother represents them?"

"I never told anyone this . . . except Seth."

He looks at her expectantly.

"Seth's mom."

"Come again?"

"Growing up, where was I more often than not?"

"The Brommels' residence."

"And as I spent more time over there, I grew to love that family. I loved Seth's mom like she was *my* Mom. When you think of 'Christian woman,' you think of her. Her poise. Her strength. Her elegance." She plays with her hands. "I overheard Mom talking about her one day. She said some nasty things."

"Things like what?"

"What do you think?" She snaps her head up and bores a hole into her father with her eyes. "You've always known."

He holds her stare for a few moments before looking away. He turns around to look at the book he was reading. "That's not who your mother is. You know that."

"I don't. I really don't. Why would she say those things? If that wasn't who she is, why would she say those things?"

"Because your mother was jealous. She was jealous of the relationship you, her own daughter, had with another mother not named Bev." He picks up a pen to write.

"I thought that, too. I thought she was jealous and that's all it was, but I noticed a trend all the way until she dropped the word of words. Daddy, she only disparaged black people. She only talked about black people."

She hears the pen drop from his hand and to the table loudly.

"And the next day, she would smile in the same faces she just talked about the day before. She would look Seth's Mom in the eyes and tell her she was always welcome, without ever welcoming her anywhere." She stands. "Sure, maybe she was jealous, but Beverly Connelly did nothing as a mother but pop me out and parade me around."

"That's enough, Bree."

"Mrs. Brommels taught me about poise. She was the one who taught me about being a strong Christian woman. And she's gone now. And Beverly didn't bat an eye. When it comes to Christianity now, Bev is it."

"Brianna."

She presses her lips together. Her father turns back around.

"Sit. Please."

"Am I wrong?" she asks as she takes her seat again.

"Of course you are . . . but of course you are not." He runs his hand through his white hair. "Your mother . . . she . . ."

"She's racist."

"She has her struggles."

"Why are you making excuses for her?"

He sighs. "I'm not. I'm just trying to get you to understand that she, like all of us, is a work in progress. Your idea of Christianity shouldn't hinge upon the attitudes of one person."

"Maybe. But isn't it odd?"

"What?"

"That there still is such thing as the black church and the white church. Isn't it odd that there's Gospel music, and then there's Black Gospel music? Isn't it odd that the church can still seem to get away with segregation?"

"That's not a fair statement."

"How isn't it? Your church . . . how many black members?"

"Brianna."

"Just answer the question. How many?"

"None."

She stares for a few moments before saying, "I rest my case."

"I see where you are coming from, but I still believe you are wrong, or at the very least slightly misguided."

"Maybe." She stares into her father's eyes.

He smiles. "Do you always have to be so stubborn?"

"Stubborn? Hmmm. I wonder where I got that from." She smiles.

He chuckles. "Hey, have you taken any good pictures lately?"

"Just did a wedding not too long ago. Seth and I—"

"You did a wedding with Seth?" He winks.

"Stop, Daddy. It's not like that. We're just friends."

"Uh-huh. So, tell me about this wedding . . ."

22.

Tally – Now

She stands in front of a building with a sizable lot and a giant sign that says "Wild Dreams." She stares at the sign, noting is hasn't changed in years. The lot is empty, but that's to be expected for midafternoon. She strides into the building, looking for familiar faces, but in particular, one. She gets through the lobby and to the main area and looks in the direction of the bar. No one there. She looks on the stage to see an unfamiliar person dancing. A few men sit at one of the tables below, staring as she moves in a somewhat jerky fashion.

"Well, look at who it is. If it isn't 'The Desire' herself."

Tally turns around to see Jordan Strickland, a tall, dark-skinned man who dresses professionally. Suit and sharp shoes has always been his staple. He has a few more gray hairs than she last remembered, but everything else is exactly the same.

"Jordan."

"What brings you by my humble establishment?" He smirks.

Tally admits he's an attractive man, but having worked for him nearly destroyed any amount of respect she had for him.

"I was wondering—" She stops to think if she wants to go down this road again.

"Go on."

"I was wondering if there's still room for me here."

"Maybe. You know you left on some pretty harsh terms." He smooths out his hair on the top of his head, then rubs his fingers together to get rid of the oil that isn't there. "You left me in a pretty tough spot. All for ol' boy over there. What was his name? Paul. Yeah. Paul."

"I'm surprised you remember his name."

"I'd never forget a punk like that ... especially after he stole my crown jewel."

"I'm not your property."

"Sure, not now. But then." He shrugs. "I can make an argument from my stance."

She looks past him toward the entrance as a few men in suits come in. Jordan greets them and allows them to find a table. He looks back at Tally.

"A lot of corporate folk come here now. They bring wonderful business." He nods in her direction. "You want to take a walk? I need another girl out there."

She folds her arms and sighs. "Fine."

Jordan walks past her and to the left, to a door that leads to the back rooms behind the stage. "So what brings you back?"

"You know what it is. Money."

"Oh. Because I thought it was the fact that your boy toy was arrested in Atlanta."

"What?"

He stops just short of the dressing room. "I take it you didn't know?" The way he asks the question makes her want to punch him in the jaw.

"No idea. He just left. So, I did, too."

Jordan laughs. "He thought he was something. He's a Philly boy. He doesn't have the chops to be a national mover. He couldn't even get to be an East Coast mover. He should have stuck to Philly."

"How do you know this?"

"You think I didn't keep track of the chump who stole my headliner away?" He enters the dressing room. "Misty. Yelena. I need you out there. Corporate folk," he yells.

A few moments later, two girls come out, one Caucasian, the other of Hispanic descent. They both stop and stare at Tally as if she shouldn't be breathing the same air as they are.

"I would like you to meet Tally," Jordan says. "Me and her go back."

They both reluctantly greet Tally and leave for the main floor.

"Any of the old crew here?" she asks.

"Just Kierra and Dee. Oh, and Jack is still here."

Tally smiles a bit. The two she trusted the most during her first stint as an exotic dancer were Kierra and Dee. Kierra is Tally's age, and they instantly hit it off when Tally first stumbled into the then-beat-up building. Dee is the mother of the group. She's the oldest and most experienced, always willing to help any of the girls out. Jack is the main bouncer. She's always had a little crush on him, but he never said more to her than "'Sup."

"Back here. I got a new office," Jordan says.

"Someone made a come up."

"You joke. But, I'm one step closer to making this into a real thing here. You were here when this joint was just a hole in the wall. Now, it's slightly less so, but we are able to be more selective on the girls we bring in. We upgraded our clientele, too." They get to a door in the back of the dressing rooms that leads to a short but well-lit hallway. "Mostly corporate folk. We still get the so called"—he makes air quotes—"sleaze-bags, but only rarely. We've done a good job spreading the word about what we offer."

Tally listens to Jordan as he goes on about turning the place into what he calls a real establishment. By the time they make it to "his" office, she almost starts to turn around and leave for fear of him giving her another history lesson. He opens the door to a nicely decorated and spacious room. Maroons, browns, and tans fill and accent every corner of the room. A simple wooden desk sits in the middle. Jordan pulls to the side one of the cushioned chairs that sits in front of it. Tally takes a seat, and instead of taking a seat behind the desk, Jordan sits in the chair next to her.

"Who's 'we'?" Tally asks.

"We? Ah." He rubs his goatee for a few strokes before answering. "I have a business partner. Vice President of Talent Relations."

"Talent relations?"

"Yeah. She is pivotal in bringing in new talent . . . in managing our current roster. She's the reason we're moving somewhere here. And since you brought her up—" He gets up from his seat and steps to the phone on his desk. He presses a button and says, "Uhhh, excuse me, VP of Talent Relations, you are needed in the CEO's office. We have a new prospect wanting to join our wonderful staff."

"Be there in a second."

Tally tunes her face at the sound of Jordan trying to sound professional. The voice over the intercom she recognizes. Before long, the door opens and an older woman enters wearing an incredible button-up silk blouse that's tucked into a pair of slim-fitting slacks. She wears a big-buckle belt that also draws Tally's attention. Normally, she would look and think to herself, "Oh, she knows how to dress," but she has always known this about the woman who stands before her. She jumps up and dives right into a warm embrace.

"Dee!"

"Oh, my God, Tally? Tally?" She wraps her arms around her.

"Deanna has done a tremendous job of getting us the right staff and taking this club to a new—"

"Oh, stop it, Jordan. Tally isn't falling for your fake professional speak. You don't even do it well." She steps back from Tally. "Let me look at you, Girl. It's been a long time."

"Five years," Tally says.

Dee's expression changes for a quick moment, Tally notices. She can't get a good read on what that was because Dee shifts her expression right back to one of excitement.

"So, what brings you around these parts?"

She takes in a deep breath. "Well. I need some money. Fast. And this is the only place I know in which I can get to that money fast."

"And what I was explaining to her was that this isn't the same establishment. We have a strict vetting process and—"

"Oh shut up, Jordan. Don't be stupid. She wants back, she's back."

"Hey, I'm dotting my i's and crossing my t's. You taught me that. We have no idea why she needs back in. Things change in five years, Dee. And what? We're starting her with the day shift until she can earn the prime spots?" He laughs. "I doubt that. So, we're going to have to front the dollars until she starts bringing in again. Again, we have no idea why she is back."

"It's not for me," Tally says. "Well, it is . . . but not just for me."

"You looking to bail your boy toy out of jail?" Jordan asks.

"No. It's not that. I didn't even know he was in jail. It's . . ."

Dee places a soft hand on Tally's shoulder. "Don't worry about it. Listen, I'll take you to my office and get you set up. Gives us time to catch up."

"And if I don't agree with her coming back?" Jordan asks.

"Tough. But you will." Dee smiles. "The Desire is back. Flyers should be going out. Take your ego out of this. Gentlemen still ask about her as they talk about those days fondly. And plus"—she walks over to him, her high heels making deep imprints on the carpeted floor —"what better way to catapult Wild Dreams to being a true gentlemen's club?"

Jordan stares at the ground for a few moments before looking at Tally. He pulls his gaze from her just before it gets uncomfortable and stares at Dee. "I hope you're right. Throughout my entire life, a pretty face out of nowhere asking me for something usually means I'm about to get robbed."

"Oh, stop it, Jordan. You run a strip club. Pretty faces ask you for something all the time. Plus, I haven't robbed you . . . yet." Dee smiles a wide smile.

"Stop playing games, Dee. You know what I mean."

"It'll be fine. Do you trust me?"

"I'm just saying—"

"Do you trust me?"

Jordan sighs. "Yeah, Dee, I do."

"Then let me do my thing."

He stares at Tally again, this time making sure it's as uncomfortable of a stare as possible. She doesn't look away. She doesn't move, not even a flinch. He nods, and like that, Dee whisks her away to her office, which is right next to Jordan's.

As soon as they step in, Dee shuts the door. She grabs Tally by the shoulders, but this time not in happiness.

"What are you doing back here?" Dee's tone is more angry than anything else.

"I need the money."

"Are you on drugs?"

"No."

"Are you in some kind of trouble?"

"No."

She stares Tally in the eyes for a few long moments. "Sit," she says and sits down at her desk. She crosses her legs and rests her folded hands upon them. "Tally. Be straight with me."

"I am." She looks to the side. "She's going to lose the school."

"Who?"

"Ms. Xing. She's going to lose the school, and she shouldn't."

"I don't think I follow."

"My harp teacher. She's a great woman. Known her all my life, and no matter how much I've done . . . no matter how terrible of a person I've become." She looks at Dee with imploring eyes. "She's never left my side. I owe her the same."

Dee looks at her, seemingly mulling something over in her head. "Why did you leave?"

"Because I fell in love. At least I thought it was love. I know it wasn't, really . . . I just needed to get away."

"I thought I asked you to be straight with me. You weren't in love really. Were you?"

She has a stare off with Dee before looking down. "No."

"He was just a quicker ride, you thought."

"I was tired of dancing. I wasn't getting to where I wanted to be fast enough."

"But you gave up your independence. Don't you see that? Here, you had a job, and you earned more money than most."

"I know. But like I said . . . I was tired."

"I understand. Jordan wasn't the best then, either."

"He was scum."

"And that's putting it lightly." She smirks. "But he's different now. He's—"

"In love with you."

Dee looks like she's been slapped. "What? What do you mean?"

"You see it, too. Don't lie."

She sits there, quiet and nodding. "But I don't mix business with pleasure. It's all business between us. That's all it should be."

"So, you're using him, too?"

"No. No, I'm not."

"Then that means . . . ewww, Dee. Ewww. You're feeling him, too."

"Shut up. And you say nothing of this to anyone."

"Fine. Am I back in?"

Dee sighs. "Yeah, Girl. Welcome back."

23.

BURT – NOW

Burt steps out of a black luxury car and straightens out his suit coat. He pats the shoulder of the driver, who holds the door open for him, thanking him, and walks into a restaurant.

"May I help you, sir?" the hostess says.

Burt doesn't expect anyone to know who he is around this part of the country. He doesn't make too many trips to Virginia, but when he does, he makes sure to have lunch with whom he considers a good friend. He thinks that actual good friends are in short supply once you reach a certain status in life. It makes him appreciate his sole friend even more.

"Yes, I'm here meeting with someone."

"Pastor Connelly?"

"Yes." He's taken by surprise for a moment before reminding himself that this is his friend's turf. Everyone ought to know who he is.

The hostess grabs a menu and says, "Right this way, sir."

She leads him to a private booth at the end of the restaurant, where he sees Jared Connelly and his signature bright-white hair.

"Jared, my man," Burt says.

Jared smiles a bright smile and stands to his feet. "Burt, Buddy, I'm glad you made it."

The two shake hands. "Why are you holed up in the corner of the restaurant? It's gorgeous outside."

"Would you rather be seated outside?" the hostess asks.

"Yes, Cora, that would be great," Jared says.

The hostess leads both men to the outside sitting area, which is considerably vacant for the time being. Burt waits for her to place the menus on the table before turning his attention to Jared.

"How have you been?" he asks.

"Well, old friend, it seems not as good as you. Is that your Bentley over there?"

Burt chuckles. "It's not mine, exactly. It belongs to the church. We typically use it for out-of-state events. Lately, I've been in it a lot. Tons of travel."

"I've heard. Trying to become the next Jakes?"

"Ha," Burt laughs a hearty laugh. "Wouldn't dare. That's too much exposure. Too much . . ."

"Fluff? Hollywood?"

"Nail on the head, Friend. Nail on the head." He unbuttons his suit coat. "So, how's the family?"

"Good, good."

"Anything new?"

"Actually, no. Nothing new at all." He smiles. "Is it bad that I count that as a blessing?"

"Not at all, Friend. I understand. Life gets hectic at times, no?"

Jared chuckles. "Yeah. How's Gretchen?"

"Getting more and more pregnant by the day."

"Hey, I know I said this before, but congrats."

"Thanks. I appreciate it, I really do."

"Has Seth come around yet?"

"Unfortunately, he has not." Burt sighs. "I'm not sure what to do with the boy."

"What can you do? He's a man now. And you know he's still hurting over his mother."

A waiter comes up to their table and takes their orders and disappears into the restaurant when done.

"It seems like Bree is still hurting over her as well."

"Bree? Really? I didn't know she cared so much."

"She was always over at your house." He leans back in his chair. "You know, I think she has fallen head over heels for Seth."

"I knew that when she decided not to move down here with you and Bev."

"I guess it was pretty apparent." He leans back in and lowers his voice a little. "You think you would have a problem with her and Seth?"

"No. Not at all. Why would I?" He adjusts in his seat. "The real question is would Bev?"

Jared looks down in shame. It takes him a few minutes of thinking before he says anything. "I honestly don't know." He looks around as more people start to fill in outside. "Bree seems to think her mother would be completely against it."

The waiter comes out with their food. They bless the food and begin eating.

"So you've talked to Bree about the idea?" Burt asks.

"Yeah. I wanted to see where her head was at. Nothing major. Just a little snooping." He smiles. "She came down last week." He digs in his jacket pocket and pulls out his wallet. From it he pulls a picture and hands it to Burt. "Forced her to stay another day, and we finally took some recent family pictures."

Burt stares at the picture while chewing down his food. "She looks just like her mama."

"Don't I know it." He pulls out another picture, this one of just Bree. "She hated doing this, so I definitely owe her one."

"You don't have a cell phone?"

"I do. Why?"

"Then why didn't you just take a few pics with your cell?"

"Are you trying to tell me I'm old?"

Burt chuckles. "No, Friend." He looks at the second picture. "She turned out to be a beautiful young lady." He takes a long and hard stare at the picture. "That necklace. It looks familiar."

"I knew you would notice it." Jared takes another bite of his food and wipes his mouth with a napkin. "It was Jolene's."

Burt squints and nods. "How did she get it?"

Jared shrugs. "No idea. She must have given it to her . . . or maybe Seth did. I'm not sure. I didn't have much time after the picture taking to go into detail. Bev asked her about it because she thought it was beautiful, and Bree was all too happy to tell her who the previous owner was."

"I see." Burt looks for a few more seconds, remembering when he gave his ex-wife that necklace. It was for their anniversary his first year out of college. He hands the pictures back to Jared.

"You good?" Jared asks.

"Yeah. I'm good." He plasters on a fake smile to cover up the rigorous workings of his mind. "Excuse me for a second." He gets up and heads back into the restaurant. Once at an area where he could talk, he pulls out his cell phone and dials.

"Hey," he says. "There's a place we didn't check for the files."

Burt – Then

"So what is it? What is it you want? Your vision?"

"I want to preach the word of God."

"Is that what you really want? Because you can do that now."

Burt sits at a small café along the boardwalk of Rehoboth Beach. He wears a hat and comfortable beach clothing. The air is warm and salty. He simply feels great. "It is. And I can. But all people want to hear about is how we are going to be better, about how we're going to get more stuff, find more success, and respect, and a better life."

"What's so wrong about that?"

"It's a lie. A lie our people keep telling themselves . . . that someday we are going to be economic equals with our melanin-challenged counterparts . . . that all of us, we all have this idea just waiting to be birthed so we can earn millions. It's a materialistic fallacy."

"So, what's the truth? What's your vision for preaching?"

"Truth is"—he takes a bite of food—"we are all wretched and less than the dirt we step on. But we are made whole and presentable to

God, by God. The truth is this Christian life comes with more hardships than blessings. More persecution than promotion. Man, on his own, is selfish, and sinful, and violent, and lost."

"Well, let me tell you, I don't know if I would show up to church every Sunday just to hear that."

"Few would."

"So you preach money and cars."

"So I preach money and cars and numerous blessings."

"And you're growing."

"The membership of that church is growing . . . I, on the other hand, am not."

"And what does your wife say?"

Burt looks down, thinking about Jolene. He knows it isn't a good look for him to be out here on the beach having lunch with some other woman, a woman that he continues to notice looks incredible in a bathing suit. "She's neither here nor there with it. She supports me, but not in a way that helps me decide the right path." He leans up in his seat. "It's one of those 'whatever you say, Dear' kind of things."

"I see."

"Can I ask you a question?"

"Sure. Ask away."

"What are we doing here? We are both married, and here we are on a beach we believe is far enough away that we won't be recognized, but not too far we can't get back in time, just in case we need to cover our tracks."

She smiles. "This is a business meeting. Nothing more. Nothing less."

"Gretchen."

"What?" She smiles even harder. "That's what this is. Isn't it? That's what Dale knows. I'm on a business lunch. Isn't that what you told Jolene?"

Burt becomes uncomfortable at Gretchen mentioning her name.

"Look, Burt,"—she reaches across the table and grabs his hand—"if this is all too uncomfortable to you, I understand. Being completely honest, I like spending time with you. But there is some business at hand."

"What exactly is this business?"

"Congressman Burris has sent me to offer you an opportunity."

Burt narrows his eyes and cocks his head to the side a bit. "Opportunity?" He slides his hand away from hers.

"He was and has been impressed by you, Burt, and he wants to place out there an opportunity for you to grow even more. It's a chance to do more."

"What are you saying, exactly?"

"Congressman Burris would like to fund your next church."

"Fund? I'm not looking for a new church."

"He says maybe you should."

"Why would he want to do that? And what's the catch?"

"There are a few things that come with this," she says, "but we can discuss that later."

"Later when?"

"Later after we make love." She stands up from the table. "Care to take a walk on the beach?"

24.

SETH – NOW

"You gonna help me with this or what?"

"Sorry. Just a little distracted." Seth briskly walks to Bree to help her with a few of the camera bags.

"I've noticed. Everything good?"

"Yeah, everything is good. A lot on my mind lately, you know?"

"Of course I do. Want to talk about it?"

"Not really."

Bree looks at him, getting set to complain.

"Look, I'm okay. Trust me. I just have a bunch of things in my head I need to sort out."

Bree seems to accept the fact and opens the door to her apartment. "You can set those things there." She points.

Seth parks the equipment where Bree says and walks to her to help her with the other bags. He takes a bag from her and accidentally grabs her hand. Bree snaps her hand away as if Seth shocked her, dropping the bag.

Seth watches Bree as she hurriedly tries to pick up the bag. "I got it. No worries, Bree."

Bree continues to attempt to lift the bag.

"Bree." Seth grabs her hand.

She freezes.

"I got it." He removes his hand from hers.

Bree simply nods and walks to the pile of bags and sets down the other one she was carrying. She takes a deep breath and exhales slowly. "So, did you figure out what you're going to do for tonight?"

Seth notices as he moves closer to the bags, closer to her, that she moves further away from him. "I was thinking I'd just go on home. I know it's late, but I'll be okay."

She nods.

Seth takes a few steps back. "So I better just . . . make my"—he trips over the strap to one of the bags and hits the floor with a thud.

"Seth?"

"Owww."

Seth feels sharp pains on his side and his leg, but still manages to let out a chuckle as he sits up. He looks at Bree and notices she's trying to hold in her laugh.

"You think that was funny?"

Bree straightens herself out. "No. Not funny. Not at all."

They stare at each other for a few moments before busting out laughing. They both laugh so hard there are tears in their eyes. Seth tries to think back to when he and Bree laughed so hard together and came up with back in the day in the tree house. He finds himself missing those times.

Seth finally picks himself up off the floor. "Well, let me try this again. I will see you later."

"Seth, your arm."

Seth looks at his arm, in particular the area where pain seems to radiate, and finds a bleeding cut.

"You got a Band-Aid or something?"

"Get over here, Clumsy. Sit." She pulls out a stool from under the island and pats the top. Seth walks over, being mindful of the bags that seemed to grab him and trip him, and sits on the stool. Bree disappears in the back and comes out with a first-aid kit.

"I got to clean it first."

"That's fine."

"And I got to put on the stuff that stings."

"I'm a big boy. I can handle it."

"Okay, I'm just letting you know. Big boys know not to walk backward into a pile of camera equipment." She snickers.

"Look, you gonna patch me up or what?"

"I got you." Bree smiles. "Don't want you bleeding out on the bus or anything."

"Really? More jokes?"

"I'm sorry. I'll hush up." She cleans Seth's arm and puts a Band-Aid on it, the entire time not saying another word.

Seth watches her tend to his cut. Once again he notices there is something innately beautiful about her. He continues to stare at her, though it seems like she is purposely avoiding eye contact.

"I thought you were squeamish around blood."

"What gave you that idea?"

"Well, for starters, every time you see blood, you start shivering like you have the chills."

"That's not true."

"It is. At least it has been for as long as I've known you." He evaluates the handiwork of Bree and nods his approval. "Thanks, anyway."

"Anytime."

They finally catch each other's eyes. They stare at each other for moments too long, but neither looks away. Seth continues to stare even though it feels like an electric current is charging through his eyeballs. Maybe it's because of the current-like feeling he continues to stare, but either way, Seth doesn't avoid eye contact. Bree is the first to look away and cleans up the items from the first-aid kit. Seth finds it harder to breathe, like his chest is being compressed. He watches Bree move, still as graceful as ever. Before she could disappear into the back again, Seth grabs a fistful of the bottom of Bree's shirt, stopping her dead in her tracks. She looks at his hand and slowly follows his arm up to his face.

"Seth?"

He doesn't say anything, but sits there still grabbing the bottom of her shirt. He flexes his jaw muscles and looks at the floor as if deep in thought.

"Seth?"

He slowly eyes Bree, starting at the floor and scrolling up her legs, but stopping at where he grabs her shirt. He grips her shirt tighter and pulls her in closer. He knows what he is saying in his mind, to let her go and stop making a fool of himself, but his body is doing the complete opposite. He finally is able to look her in the eyes, but regrets doing so. Her eyes are telling him a story, one he desperately wants to hear. His heart thumps heavily in his chest.

"Seth. Please let go of my shirt."

Seth thinks for a moment more before releasing his grip. He tries to figure out exactly what he thought he was doing. "I'm sorry. I . . . I have no idea what that was. I'm really sorry."

Bree simply nods, collects the items from her first-aid kit, and disappears into the back. Seth curses himself in his head and gets up to leave. "Bree, I'm headed out."

Bree stomps from the back to stand directly in front of him. "What the hell was that?"

Seth is shocked to silence.

"We go back and forth, back and forth. Then, when you finally tell me how you feel, that you don't want to be with me, that our friendship is too important, then . . ." She pushes him. "What the hell, Seth."

Seth seems to absorb Bree's push, not moving much at all, and stares at her. Her face is flush.

"You know we can't just act like we didn't have that talk. We can't act *normal.*"

"Why not?" Seth raises his voice a bit.

"Because every"—she pushes him again—"little thing you do"—and again—"sets me"—and again—"on freaking fire."

Seth stares, thinking about what Bree is saying. "I grabbed the bottom of your shirt, Bree. That's all."

"Oh, yeah?" She stands in front of him with her arms folded, feet shoulder-width apart, expression defiant. "What was going through your mind when you had ahold of me?"

"I don't know. Nothing. It was a . . . I wasn't thinking. I'm sorry."

"You're a liar."

"Bree, please calm down."

"No. Tell me the truth. I want the truth."

Seth starts, but pauses. He looks at her as she stares him down. His focus shifts to her rising and falling chest. So much adrenaline pumps through his veins he thinks he is going to be sick as he lets his gaze fall to the floor. She goes in to push him again, but before she could, he grabs both her wrists.

"Let go of me, Seth."

"No." He is trying to tell himself to stop, but too much is going on too fast. His body is a wreck, and all he can think of is how much it needs her body. He tries to stop, but the closer he is to her, the less he thinks . . . the more his body moves.

He has a firm grip on her wrists, and he pulls her closer. She rigidly moves closer to him. He pulls her in slowly, looking her in the eyes. When their bodies touch, he moves her arms to rest on his shoulders and lowers his hands to grip the sides of her thighs. There's something passing between him and her through their eyes, he believes. He wouldn't know how to explain it verbally, but he gets the feeling Bree understands perfectly. He leans in and lightly kisses her lips. He then allows just enough space between their faces so they can adjust to what just happened . . . to what is about to happen. He feels her begin to shiver.

"Seth."

He doesn't let her say any more and kisses her again, with more heat. It takes only a few moments before Bree kisses him back with just as much, if not more intensity. He moves one hand from her thigh and puts his fingers in her hair. Gently tugging on a handful of her hair, he leans her head to the side and nibbles on her neck. She lets escape a soft moan. He then goes back to her mouth, exploring, tasting. She tries to push away, but he swings her around so she is pressed flat against her front door and uses his body as leverage. He grabs both her wrists again but presses them above her head, flat on the door, and continues his exploration. When he knows she isn't resisting anymore, he releases one of her wrists and takes his free hand to go up under her shirt. Her skin is soft and warm. A little damp. He runs his hand up her side and to the band of her bra. He releases her other wrist and uses that free hand to aid his first in unclasping her bra. She leans her pelvis into his and presses the top part of her back to the door. In one swift movement, he has her bra undone and keeps one hand on her back and uses the other to feel around. He lifts her shirt up, exposing her to him, and starts kissing and licking wherever there is exposed skin. He kneels in front of her.

"Oh, God," she whispers. "Seth, we can't do this."

Seth doesn't hear her and lays light kisses around her navel. He starts toying with the button of her jeans.

"Seth." She places her hands on his shoulders. "Please." She bites her bottom lip. She gives one good push, but Seth doesn't move. He gets her jeans undone. "Seth, I don't want to do this."

Seth pauses and looks up at her because her voice sounded . . . different. She has her head turned to the side, but he can tell she's crying. In an instant, he realizes what a mistake he was about to make . . . what a mistake he has already made. He stands to his feet to look her in the face. She sniffs a few times as she still bites her bottom lip. Tears stream down her face.

"Why are you crying?"

It seems that just Seth's asking that question forces Bree to cry more. "Because, Seth." She still doesn't look his way. "I want you." She takes a deep breath to calm the oncoming tremors of her sobs. "I want you so bad. But I know you don't want me. Not in the way I want you. And I want you to want me. All of me." She wipes her nose with the sleeve of her shirt. "You wouldn't be able to live with yourself. And I couldn't live with myself, knowing how messed up that would make you."

Seth gently grabs her chin to make her look him in the eyes, but she snaps her face away. Abruptly, she moves from between the door and Seth. "You have to leave." She walks to her bedroom, holding her mouth as if to stop anymore sobs. She slams the door shut.

For a moment, he stands there, trying to understand what just happened. "Bree." He walks to her bedroom door and knocks. "Bree."

Silence.

Seth stares at the door. "Look, I'm sorry." Seth goes to say something else, but stops. He listens for her but hears nothing. He slowly turns away from the bedroom door and leaves her apartment. Halfway down the hall, he hears her deadbolt locking.

25.

TALLY – NOW

It's been a couple weeks at her new/old job, and Tally is exhausted.

She was immediately put on the night shift, being fronted the money by Dee and Jordan for the wardrobe she'd need to dance again. She was able to pay them back and start making real money within the first two nights. Her first night felt too familiar, as she wasn't nervous, but ready to work a crowd of once-sleazy, now corporate men who want to blow off some steam. By the time she was on her fourth night, private dances picked up for her, and there is where she made the most money. Consequently, Dee and Jordan made the most money when she did private dances as well. One of the nights, she's had the chance to catch up with Kierra as they stayed up early in the morning after the night shift to find something to eat at a 24-hour diner. They laughed and joked and reminisced, but that came to an end when the subject of Tana came up.

Tally still refuses to talk about her.

She rolls around on the futon she's been sleeping on, finally stirring awake at two o'clock in the afternoon. She sits up to see Ms. Xing pouring a cup of tea at the stove in the kitchenette area.

"Late night?" Ms. Xing asks.

Tally stretches and rolls out of the futon. "Something like that." She walks over to her and gives her a hug. "Could you pour me a cup, too?"

Ms. Xing nods. "What have you been up to?"

"What do you mean?"

"No lessons lately. Always sleep. Depressed?"

"No. I'm fine." She hesitates on telling her any more. "I got a job . . . an overnight one."

"Not anything illegal, I hope."

"Nothing illegal. It's all on the up-and-up. In fact—"—she walks barefoot to her duffel bag and pulls out a small leather pouch—"I wanted to give you this."

She hands Ms. Xing the pouch. The woman eyes the black leather pouch curiously before setting the teapot down and cautiously unzipping it.

When she opens the pouch, Tally says, "Five thousand, three hundred seventy-two dollars. To help with the bills."

Ms. Xing stares at the money and then closes her eyes. "Why?" she asks. "I cannot accept this."

"I'm living here rent free. I owe you something."

"You owe me nothing. Nothing at all."

"Look," Tally says, trying to avoid any confrontation, "I saw the bills. The overdue bills."

Ms. Xing opens her eyes again and looks at Tally with a fire she has never seen from her before. "How did you get this?"

"I . . . I strip."

"You're an exotic dancer?"

"Yes, ma'am."

The older woman shakes her head as her eyes become glassy. "Why do you keep taking this path?"

"Path of what? I ought to be paying rent or something, and there are bills stacking up."

"The path of self-destruction. Is that why you decided to do it? To pay off a few bills?"

"There weren't small amounts on those bills. I know I needed money in abundance and fast. Stripping was the only way I knew how to do it. It was the only legal option I had."

"There are plenty of other legal actions, Tally."

"Not ones I know I would be successful at."

She sighs. "I can't take this."

"Then you insult me. And make my sacrifice worthless."

"You don't understand. Enrollment is up," she smiles. "But it still isn't enough. This"—she shakes the leather pouch full of money—"isn't enough."

"Well, how much do you need?"

"Did you add up all those numbers on the bills you snooped and found? It totaled twenty-two thousand and then some."

Tally gasps at the number.

"Landlord is nice. But he isn't that nice. I owe him a lot of money. And creditors. Owe them a lot, too."

"What about your private lessons?"

"Went up as well. But that pays for me to live in the small box across the street." She sits on a stool. "It's time I gave the school up." She hands the pouch back to Tally. "Use this to get a place for yourself. Get a regular job, and make a good living. Live a good life."

"But this school is your everything."

"No. You are my everything. And you are giving a piece of yourself away up on that stage . . . it's not okay with me."

Tally holds the pouch in her hand, feeling dejected. She doesn't want for Ms. Xing to give up the school for reasons that go beyond it being her dream. For the longest time, when Tally had no real home, the music school was her home.

"I understand. But you know I'm not the nine-to-five type. Never was."

"You're a smart girl. That will get you further than your looks ever could."

"Maybe." She holds tight to the pouch. "I'm sorry."

"It's fine, really. Good run . . . with the school." She stands. "So, no lessons, but have you practiced?"

"No, ma'am."

"Sit."

Tally sits. "I'm starving. Could we grab a bite to eat first?"

"I'll order from the café down the street. You play."

"Play what?"

"Your song. Before these doors close, I want your song perfected."

Later in the night, Tally works the crowd of fantasy-desperate men, starting on stage, moving to the floor, and eventually to the private rooms.

"He's a writer and producer," Kierra says as she passes by Tally as she is on the way to her first private dance of the night. "Get that money."

Tally prances her way into the room, and with one last glance at Kierra (who winks at her), she gently shuts the door.

"So, you, sir, must be someone important," Tally says. "I got word from Jordan that you requested me specifically?" She kneels on the couch and sits next to him.

"Yeah. Jordan knows me from when I was just a young scrap." He smiles. "So, you have no idea who I am?"

"I'm sorry, I don't. All I know is that you paid for a two-hour private."

He chuckles. "That's refreshing."

"How so?"

"It's good that there's someone who has no idea who I am. Less likely for them to try to take advantage of me."

"No worries there. So, why me? There are plenty of pretty girls here."

"None like you. And I'm writing a new song. I need a muse."

"Oh? So, what do you need me to do?" She knows she's laying it on thick by asking him, but that's part of selling the fantasy.

He reaches into his pocket and pulls out a block of cash. He sets it on the couch by her knee. "That's twenty-five hundred. It's yours."

"Okay . . ."

"I want you to be real with me. Don't sell me the fantasy. You already have my money. Be a work of art."

"I'm confused. Do you want me to dance?"

"Eventually, yes."

"What do you mean by 'be a work of art'?"

"Let's just talk for a few. Talk about stuff like how you ended up in here. Who came up with your stage name? Even stuff like your innermost desires."

"Such an odd request."

"Again, I'm writing another hit."

"What is this song going to be about?"

"Beauty . . . and pain. Specifically, your beauty and my pain."

"Sounds interesting." She looks down for a second. "But I don't know about a tell-all. I don't know you."

"That's fair." He shrugs. "Maybe we should just start with a dance."

"Are you disappointed?"

"No, not at all. I still get a dance from one of the most beautiful women I've ever seen."

Tally gets up from the couch and walks over to the private sound system. She puts on a song she's been dancing to lately, one she's become fond of.

"That's my song," he says.

"You really like this one? It's great to dance to." She slinks over to his lap and begins to dance.

"No, I meant this literally is my song. I wrote it and put it together in the studio."

Tally pauses for a moment. "Oh. Okay Mr. Songwriter-Producer, what is this one about?"

"Loss."

Tally stops dancing. "How? It talks about being the best in the world."

He laughs what seems to be a genuine laugh. "All of the songs I put out have a dual quality to them. There's the message I want to get out, and it's couched in a message people want to hear. Put on a fresh beat and boom. Number-one hit."

She starts dancing again. "So, this song you are working on; the message is about your pain, but it's couched in a message of my beauty."

"Seems like you get it."

"And you needed my history for that?"

"Not quite. I just wanted to get to know you more. Maybe find your pain. Adds flavor to the experience, adds flavor to the song."

"Spoken like a true artist." She turns around and continues her dance. She looks back at him. "My pain is too much for one song."

"So is mine. That's why I put it in multiple songs."

Tally continues to dance, thinking that this unnamed music guy is pleasant. The two hours will pass quite quickly, and she has twenty-five hundred to boot.

"Do you dance like this for everyone?"

"Like what?"

"Like you're making love to them. Do you look at them the same way you're looking at me?"

"You don't want the fantasy, right? You want real?"

"Be straight up."

"I do."

He nods. "I appreciate your honesty."

She doesn't know why, but she grabs his hand and places it on her hip and continues to dance. She looks at the camera in the corner of the room (which is in the corner of all the private rooms) and motions with her hand that everything is fine.

"Ain't no one gonna come and throw me out, are they?"

"No." She intensifies her movements. "Hey, you worry about your song. I'm the beauty, remember?"

He laughs. "I dig."

The rest of the two hours pass and just before Tally leaves, he takes her hand.

"What are you doing after your shift?"

Tally pulls her hand away, but gently. "What do you mean?"

"I mean, there was something good going on in there." He hangs up on his words. "I . . . I never had a conversation like that with a female before . . . and I for sure haven't had one with a stripper. But I get the feeling that you're different. I mean, not anything against strippers in general, but I've never run into a smart one. One that was real with me. And I would like to see who is behind that mask."

Tally smiles. "Sorry, but that sounds a lot like you're trying to get me into bed."

"I'm not. I swear on my life, I'm not. I'll tell you what. There's a cafe at the bottom of the hotel I'm at. Let's go there."

"I can't just leave my job. I still have an hour left."

"I can talk to Jordan. I'll drop another twenty-five hundred if I have to. Let's just continue this."

"I don't know. I mean, I don't even know your name."

"I'm Eddie. Well . . . you can call me Eddie . . . everyone else calls me Big Ease."

"Big Ease?" Tally smiles.

"Still can't believe you don't know me." He laughs.

Tally thinks for a few moments, not wanting the night with Eddie to end, and definitely not wanting to finish out her night grinding on now-sweaty, drunk men.

"Fine. See what Jordan says." She can't stop smiling. "Either way, it was nice meeting you, Eddie."

Seth – Now

Seth, Bree, Cam, and Tony all move around their largest wedding to date: a lavish event in the ballroom of a five-star hotel. Each has their separate job, all orchestrated by Bree, and Seth is making sure he gets his shots. The thing is, he knows Bree has been avoiding him all night, not saying more than a few commands.

"Bree." He catches up to her at the reception when he feels he has a window of opportunity. "Hey. How are you?"

She has a pained expression. "I'm fine, Seth."

He looks at her, trying to understand why she is acting in such a way. "Is everything okay? I mean, between us."

"Yeah. It's all good."

"Then why are you acting—"

"Not here, Seth. I'm not doing this right now."

"Doing what? I'm so confused."

"Yeah, well, so am I." She turns to walk away, but he grabs her arm before she can go. "Get off of me." She yanks her arm away.

"Bree."

"No. Stop it right now. You still have a set of pics to take. Get to them." She walks away.

Seth watches her stride away toward the bride and groom, smiling.

"She's not so graceful anymore."

Seth looks to his side to see Cam with a confused expression, shaking his head.

"Yeah. Guess not. I think I really messed things up though, Man."

"What did you do?"

"I let go. I stopped thinking and . . . yeah."

A few moments later, Bree comes back to Seth, with Cam standing next to him.

"Cam," she says. "I'm headed out early. Let Tony know, and we should be good."

"But the fun is just getting started," Cam says.

Seth stands there looking incredulous. "Bree, are you serious right now?"

"Goodnight, Seth." She glances at Cam. "Have fun."

She walks off, and Seth is about to follow, but Cam grabs his arm.

"Leave her be, Bro."

He turns back to look at Cam, not understanding what is going on with Bree.

The rest of the reception goes off without a hitch, but the only thing clouding Seth's mind is the look of disgust Bree gave him. They all start to pack their things when a partially drunken groom comes up to the three of them.

"Gentlemen, thank you so much for doing this."

"It's our pleasure," Tony says, being ever the professional. "We wish you many years of marital bliss."

Cam smiles.

"Well, listen, we have to be out of this ballroom in a little bit, but we were going to continue the party out in the café. You guys are more than welcome to grab a few drinks and party a little."

"Thanks, but we really should go," Tony says.

"Actually, I think me and Seth will take you up on that," Cam says.

Seth looks at Cam, shocked.

"Good deal. See you guys in a few."

The groom almost stumbles away.

"Cam, what are you doing?"

"Being a friend. You don't have to drink. But, for goodness sake, blow off some steam once in a while. Plus, these people are kinda fun."

He considers what his friend is saying. "Fine. Let's do it. Tony?"

"That's a no-go for me. I'm taking the Bree route and getting my behind home. It's one in the morning."

"Old man," Cam says.

"Yeah, yeah. Have fun, Gentlemen." Tony finishes packing and leaves the hotel.

"What a treat for you," Cam says to Seth. "You get to party with the life of every party."

"Self-proclaimed."

"Nope. These are facts based on hard evidence."

"No comment." He zips up his camera bag. "I'm not drinking. You know that."

"You don't have to. There are other vices to partake in."

"C'mon, Cam."

"I'm kidding. Just talk to people. Have fun. Forget about Bree. Maybe grab yourself a bridesmaid."

"Goodness, Cam, stop talking about it like it's a market."

"That's what weddings are. But I'm not going to disgust you with the details. I might not get invited to do another." He laughs.

Before long, both are in the café on the main floor of the hotel, talking, laughing. Seth is trying his best to avoid thinking of Bree. At the moment, he is leaning over the main counter, talking to one of the bridesmaids. He knows she's dropping a lot of hints of her desire to go upstairs with him, but he obviously is avoiding that. He looks past her to see Cam talking to two women, one of them older. He chuckles. He excuses himself from his current conversation and makes his way over to Cam. He stops in his tracks when he sees a familiar face. She sees him, too, because for the longest time, they lock eyes. Something about her look freezes him in place. It's plain, but it's like she sees right through him. She sees all his mistakes. She sees all his hopes. She sees him for the wonderful and wretched person he is. He can't move. And it's clear she's making no attempt to look away. He notices she's with someone, and he tries to pull his eyes away. He can't, at least not in time, and who she's with looks back at him. Seth recognizes him, but he isn't sure where he's seen the guy before.

She gets up quickly and says something to the guy. Moments later, she's weaving through the crowded café to get to the exit. He follows her. On his way out the café, Cam taps him on the shoulder to introduce him to the women he was talking to, but Seth ignores him and continues to pursue the girl with the pretty eyes. She makes it out into the hotel lobby as Seth just makes it out the café.

"Tally," he says.

She stops in her tracks but doesn't turn around. He jogs to catch up and slows when he's closer. He notices her hand shaking.

"Hey, Tally. That's your name, right? I almost—"

She turns around and looks at him with tears in her eyes. "Why?" she asks.

He doesn't know what's going on, nor does he understand why she looks so distraught. "Why what?"

"Why are you here? Why did you stop me? Why do you remember my name?"

"Because someone like you is hard to forget. Are you okay?"

"No. I'm not. I look at you and feel low. I feel terrible."

"That seems to be a general consensus of females lately."

"What?"

"Nothing. Listen, I can leave you alone. I didn't mean to interrupt your date. I just wanted to say hi."

"It wasn't a date. And isn't it late for you?"

"What are you, my Mom now?" He feels weird about making that joke.

Yet she smiles, and his whole world lights up. He still can't place it, but there's something about her that he is naturally drawn to. He's drawn to her in a way that isn't purely physical, and he knows he's never quite been drawn to any woman like that before.

"Why do you feel low? Why does seeing me make you feel terrible?"

"Besides the obvious?"

"I mean sure, you held me at gunpoint and robbed me." He wriggles his nose. "Yeah, maybe I shouldn't be chasing you down." He rubs the back of his head and smiles.

"You probably shouldn't." She wipes away the tears from her bloodshot eyes.

"But, here I am . . . at two o'clock in the morning. Here we are."

"Here we are. At two o'clock in the morning, again. Thank goodness it isn't raining now."

Seth smiles. "So, if that wasn't a date, what, you're just hanging out with a friend? In a five-star hotel cafe?"

"You ask a lot of questions."

"I do. Yeah. I'm sorry for prying. I was just curious. I've seen that guy before."

"He makes music."

"Oh, wait, I know who that is. Big Ease?"

"It seems everyone knows him."

"Yeah. I just know him because he's from this area. I don't care too much for the music he creates."

"Neither do I."

Seth frowns but doesn't say much more.

"Listen, I have to go."

"Yeah." Seth unintentionally was starting to linger. "It is late."

"I'll see you around, I guess."

"Wait. Listen, this is weird, but . . . do you feel that?"

"Feel what?"

"I'm about to sound really corny, I openly admit that. And a little crazy. I'm about to sound crazy."

"Okay." She looks at him weirdly.

"When we locked eyes, what did you feel?"

She squints one eye and looks away. "Why do you ask?"

"Because, I felt something. And I have no idea what the heck it was. It just felt like you knew me . . . like you know me. And we don't really know each other. There was something there, though. I couldn't look away. You wouldn't let me look away."

"I wouldn't?"

He sighs. "I sound crazy, right?"

"You do."

"Yeah, I thought so." He nods. "Lemme ask you something else."

"That's all you've been doing, is asking questions."

"You don't seem to have an issue answering them, though." He smiles.

"Last one."

"Fine." He takes a deep breath. "Why did you ask me out? The last time we saw each other, you asked me out."

"It was a lapse in judgment. That's all."

He nods. "Okay. I get it. I just . . . I just find it strange that we keep running into each other."

"Well, if you would stop stalking me," Tally says with a smile, "then we wouldn't keep running into each other like this."

He laughs. "I suppose you're right. Well, I better let you go. It was . . . it was good seeing you."

She smiles. "Yeah."

He doesn't want her to leave, and he doesn't understand why. Maybe part of him is hurting because of what is going on between him and Bree, but he believes he would feel the same way regardless. He waits for her to turn away, but she doesn't, and he doesn't move. "So one of us has to call it."

"Then turn away, Seth. Go back to your party."

"I would like to . . . but . . . I'm enjoying your company a lot more. Still, it's late, I know. Hey, but . . . maybe . . . maybe I can give you a call sometime?"

She looks down with a concerned expression. "You think that's a good idea?"

He laughs. "Nope. But I'm full of terrible ideas. You'll learn that as you get to know me."

"As I get to know you?"

"Yeah. I'm convinced we're going to keep running into each other. I don't know why, maybe some divine intervention . . . either way, we'll be talking again."

"I'm not a church girl."

"I know. Church girls don't typically find themselves on a date with a record producer who puts out club music."

"I already said it wasn't a date."

"I know." He chuckles. He looks at her, just wanting to take her in a little more before they should say goodbye.

"Okay, fine." She pulls out her phone. "Give me your number."

He tells her his phone number, and she calls him quickly so he can program hers into his phone.

"Oh, God, you're still using a flip phone?"

"Hey, times are rough." He notices Bree called him a few minutes ago.

She smiles. "Don't I know it."

"I'll call you sometime, or, you know, you can give me a call."

"Sounds good. Have a good night, Seth."

"Thanks. You, too."

She turns to walk out the hotel, with Seth watching her until she turns the corner. He starts back to the café to see Cam staring at him, shaking his head.

26.

BREE – NOW

She couldn't do it. She tried to grin and bear it, but she knows she couldn't stay at that wedding with Seth any longer. And she knew for as long as she was there, he would try to talk about what was wrong with her; about *what was wrong with her, not about what is wrong with what he did.* She's angry at him for pulling her back and forth in the way that he has. She's even angrier at herself for allowing him to jerk her around.

She gets back home and throws her keys on the table by the front door. Pulling her camera bag behind her, she stomps into her apartment, unable to stop thinking about the night. She flips the lights on in the kitchenette and props her camera bag against the island. She sighs, knowing that she is mad at Seth, but she still loves him. She is hopelessly in love, and she knows that he didn't intentionally screw her over and play with her emotions. He isn't, nor has he ever been, that type. Seth is good-natured, an outstanding and caring human being. What she can't quite understand is how things haven't worked out between them.

She begins to undress but stops. There's a feeling settling deep in her gut that has only been perfected through years of living alone.

That is, the feeling of not being alone.

She stops dead in her tracks and listens for something strange, but hears nothing. Slowly, she backpedals toward her kitchen and goes into the drawer to grab a knife. She stops still and slows her breathing to hear, but all she hears is her raging pulse throbbing in her ears. She steps to her camera bag to grab her phone while making sure she faces the darkness of the short hallway and bedroom. Bree grips her phone and keeps backing toward her front door. She looks down to dial and call the only one who she could call at a moment like this. She dials Seth's number hoping he would pick up, but it goes to voicemail. She bites her bottom lip so hard she thinks it's going to bleed. Still holding the knife, she grabs her keys from her camera bag and continues backpedaling toward the front door until her back is against the door. She unlocks and opens the door without ever looking away from the bedroom, steps out, and closes the front again. She thinks about hopping into her car and driving away, but she can't think of anywhere to go. Seth was and is her go-to. He was always there when she needed him. Always. She sits by the front door of her apartment and cries. She messed it up, she knows, even though she blames him.

But, those years ago, when he was about to make the biggest mistake of his life, according to her, in marrying Kylie, she indeed messed things up. Back then, Seth was hers, and the thought of him being someone else's husband was enough to drive her mad. It surely drove her actions that night when he helped her move. She saw her last shot, her final chance at making him hers. But, the next morning, he was gone, and for a while, he acted like it never happened. The marriage was still set to take place. They still saw each other around school and talked and hung out, but he never mentioned a word about that night.

Then suddenly, the wedding was called off. She didn't find out from him, but from her father instead. She knew for sure that was her shot, though. He had finally come to his senses and realized she was his, and he was hers. All he had to do was take that step into the new territory on the landscape of their relationship.

Where she was waiting, and hoping, and most of all, ready to fill him with love.

She wipes her tears away and reenters her apartment after determining it's her own paranoia that caused her to panic. Everything seems to be in place, the way she left it. If she were in her right mind, she would have noticed that and the fact that nothing seems to be broken or rifled through. She slaps the knife on top of the counter and walks to her bedroom, flipping the light switch on as she enters. As she ties her hair up into a bun, getting ready for a shower, she sees something on the floor at the foot of her dresser that sends a current of fear up and down her spine.

A boot print.

She turns on her heel and makes a mad dash toward the knife on the island, but is tripped up. As she tries to get to her feet, a blunt force in the small of her back forces her to the ground, knocking the wind from her. She feels a hand cover her mouth. Before the mystery hand can get a grip, she wriggles her body enough to shift the balance, then bites down hard on the hand. A man grunts as the weight that was on her is released. She gets to the island and grabs the knife and starts swinging it wildly, landing a few slashes on her assailant.

She stands somewhat hunched because her back is on fire, and she holds the knife in a defensive position in front of her. The man standing ready is in all black and wears a mask. He doesn't say anything, nor does he move to get away, even after being told multiple times to leave. She slashes the air a few times as her assailant moves with fluidity to dodge. She screams again, which causes the man in black to lunge at her. Both fall to the ground. As she falls, she's able to stick the knife in her assailant. Where, she has no idea. All she hears is the muffled scream. In an instant, the man in black wraps his arm around her neck, his bicep bulging into her throat. She reaches her hands up to get to his face, though she can't see him, and tries to dig her fingers into his eyes. He doesn't release his grip around her neck. She starts to see bright little floating dots in her vision as she continues grabbing and pulling at whatever she can get her hands on. She grabs and scratches but comes up with only the mask, a mask she now holds in her hand, and in near-perfect clarity, in the reflection of her window, she sees the man's face. The man's bicep bulges even more as her face becomes redder and redder. She feels a slight but quick tug, accompanied by a sharp pain in her neck, and finally, nothing.

27.

Burt – Now

Burt sits at his desk in his office after a counseling session with a married couple that is considering divorce. It forces him to think about his own marriage, not with Gretchen, but with Jolene. He thinks of all the things he would have done differently, and that leads him into thinking about all the life choices he's made and how most of them he would have done differently.

"Come in," he says as he hears a knock on his door.

Dell enters and gently closes the door behind him. Burt notices he walks with a noticeable limp.

"Everything okay?" Burt asks.

"No, sir. We have some . . . issues."

"With what?"

"With the files."

Burt stands and looks out the window. "What kind of issues? Were you able to confirm if she had anything?"

"She's dead."

Burt feels like the air has been let out of him, but he doesn't move more than leaning his forehead on the glass of the window. "I told you not to hurt her."

"She came back earlier than expected. She was supposed to be at a wedding. Didn't think she would be back." He grips the back of a seat. "She saw my face."

"Did you confirm if she had the files?"

"Didn't get a chance."

Burt closes his eyes as a headache is starting to form. "I can't believe you. I cannot believe you."

"Sir, I apologize."

Burt snaps around and speaks through bared teeth. "Apologies don't mean anything. How could you mess this up so badly?" He tries to keep his tone low so no one else but Dell would hear. He wants to make sure the venom he spews suffocates Dell and only Dell.

"Sir, I . . . I have already provided a way to clean it up. I just need a bit of cash."

"How much cash?"

"Twenty grand."

Burt sighs, still trying to control his anger. "Have you provided a way to confirm if the files are there?"

"Sir, the cops are going to be there soon."

"I don't care. Confirm if the files are there."

"Yes sir." He takes a step back. "And the cleanup?"

"The money will be wired to the account."

Dell is just about to turn and walk away when Burt says, "You know I've known her all her life. She was good, Dell. And now, I await a call from my best friend . . . as he tells me his daughter has been murdered." He tightens his face as his eyes get glassy. "Leave, Dell."

Dell releases his grip from the chair in front of him and skulks out Burt's office.

Burt refocuses his attention out the window. He pulls out his cell phone and wipes his face with the back of his hand. He punches in a few numbers with a shaky hand.

"So," he says. "We've got a problem . . . one that I need you to sort out before things really get out of control."

SETH – NOW

Seth stands outside the mega church where Bree's father used to preach before moving down to Virginia. He's stood in the lot for a while now thinking, not wanting to enter the church, not wanting to let go of his best friend.

After his night of partying with Cam, he got back to his apartment and slept for what seemed like forever. By the time he got back home, the sun was starting to rise. It was a good night, one that was particularly memorable because of his run-in with Tally. He finally woke in the afternoon to his phone buzzing and falling off the nightstand. Not too long after that, he heard a banging at his door.

He trudged out of bed and opened the door to see Cam.

"Dude, did you sleep?" Seth asked. "You look like trash."

"I did, Bro. It's when I woke that I realized I was in a nightmare."

"What? What's wrong?" Seth let him in and swung the door shut. "You did something with one of those bridesmaids? I told you to leave them alone." He stopped talking because Cam wasn't answering him. All he did was look Seth in the eyes in a way that scared him. He'd never seen Cam like that before. He knew something was seriously wrong.

"Bree's dead."

He snaps to, still standing in the middle of the lot as vehicles park and people flow into the church. The way the lot was filling up, you'd think it was for Sunday service. He supposes Bree had an impact on quite a few people . . . or maybe these are people here to support the family. He doesn't know, and that bothers him. He doesn't know why it bothers him so, but it does. He moves further to the back of the lot and further from the church as more vehicles fill in.

He feels he doesn't belong in there with the family and friends who cared about her. He pushed her away and pulled her back in so many times . . . and she was always there to love him. He doesn't deserve to be in there, and he doesn't deserve to feel anything other than pain during this time.

Cam sat on his couch as he stood, staring, disbelieving.

"He got in last night. Was tearing the place apart. She came in at the tail end of him cleaning the place out. They struggled. He . . ."

"He what?"

"He stabbed her to death."

"He who?"

"Police found the guy trying to get away, driving into New York." He wiped a tear from his eye. "Her blood was in the car. He admitted to everything. Apparently, this guy has a history of violent crimes."

"Why Bree? Why her place?"

"He said it looked like she came from money."

Seth walked to the dining table and gripped the edges of it. At the time, it was the only thing holding him up. "It's my fault."

"Don't do this, Seth."

"No. If I hadn't tried to . . . she wouldn't have been so upset . . . she wouldn't have left early . . ."

"Bro, don't start down this road. There's nothing but pain and suffering at the end . . . if it ever ends."

"Maybe that's what I deserve."

He leaves the parking lot and walks to a part of the campus that has a small pond and sits on the bench that overlooks it.

"You coming in?"

Seth didn't hear anyone approaching, being intensely lost in his own thoughts. He looks up to see Bree's father. For a moment, he wonders why he is out with him and not inside. He also wonders why his own father hasn't come out to check on him.

"I don't know if I can, sir."

He nods, his white hair popping up gently in the wind. "It's not your fault, Seth."

Seth flinches. "Who told you?"

"Your father."

He thinks to how his father would know, because Seth never told him he thought it was his fault. The only person who could have said anything was Cam.

"She was mad at me. She left that wedding early because of me." He's uncomfortable driving into any more detail than that.

"But no one could have known that sick man was going to be there. Don't hold yourself hostage like that." He has a bag next to him, Seth notices for the first time. He grabs the bag and hands it to Seth.

When he holds the bag, he notices it's Bree's camera bag. It's too light to have a camera in it, but he feels something in it.

"Open it."

He unzips the bag to find the jewelry box that she held so dear, the one that belonged to his mother. He runs his hand along the cherry-wood finish.

"It's a little girly, I know, but maybe you can take the inside cushion out and replace it to hold a few watches, or cufflinks."

He opens the box to see his mother's necklace.

"I thought it was only right for you to have these things." He gets up.

"Thank you, sir."

He nods. "Now, unless you want to make one of those cheesy grand entrances, you probably should head in with me."

"What do you mean?"

"You and your father . . . you're up front with Beverly and me . . . as you should be . . . you're family."

"Thank you, sir."

After the funeral, Seth gets a ride from Cam back to his apartment. Cam offered to stay with him, but Seth declined. He wants to be alone.

He holds the camera bag with a particular reverence and unzips it. He pulls out the jewelry box and carefully opens it. He remembers when he and his father gave her the box. It was around the time of his mother's funeral. He leans back in the couch, finally letting himself weep for his lost friend. He holds the box with a firm grip, playing with the cushion inside, picking at it. He thinks he will turn it into a watch case, even though he doesn't own a watch. He yanks at the cushion that was glued down, pulling it up by the centimeter. Halfway through the process, through the blur of tears, he sees a small manila envelope. He looks at it strangely, but slides it out and opens it. He pops it open and pours out the contents. A business card flops out, and a key hits the floor. He grabs the business card and reads it.

"Clarence Jergins, PI." He squints as he reaches to grab the key. He recognizes the kind of key, the kind used for P.O. boxes, because it looks like an older version of what he has. He sits thinking about why those items would be in the jewelry box. Did Bree put them there? Did his mother?

28.

JOLENE – THEN

She's insecure. She sits in an old and worn-out leather chair, in front of a desk, a private investigator's desk, awaiting his return. She scans the room, noting how plain it looks. It's three o'clock in the afternoon, and the sun shines brightly, yet each window is blocked by shut blinds. Streaks of sunlight still make it into the room, highlighting only the dust particles floating in the air. The door behind her swings open, and a large man enters the room, holding a manila envelope.

"Mrs. Brommels."

"Please, call me Jolene."

The man gives a curt nod and maneuvers himself to sit at his desk. He is too big of a man for the chair and desk, making both look like they are from grade school. He places the manila envelope on the desk in front of her and sighs. She's unable to tell if he sighs from difficulty of delivering bad news, or if he simply finds it difficult to breathe. Either way, Jolene is as nervous as a woman could get in a situation like this.

"I found something," he says.

"And?" Her heart is in her throat.

"I'm sorry," the man says. "It is what you suspected."

Jolene stares at the private investigator for a few moments, trying to keep her composure. She takes a few deep breaths and closes her eyes. "How long?"

"By my estimation, three years."

She gasps and holds her hand to her mouth. The man motions toward the manila envelope.

"All the information is there." He leans back and watches her grab the envelope and read through its contents.

Jolene reads through papers and observes pictures of her husband gallivanting around in different states . . . but with the same woman. She remembers each time he said he was going out of state. He said it was for a Pastors' conference, or he was preaching at a church event. At four different locales, she—this other woman—was there. Jolene flips through more papers that she spread out on the desk in front of her, to find the woman's name. All the while, the private investigator observes her with a cool stare.

"Gretchen Chambers," she says. She frowns. "She's married?"

The PI nods and leans forward to the set of pictures. He slides out a picture of a man. "Her husband, Dale." He allows Jolene to scan the picture. "He's been labeled as an abuser. Supposedly, he beats her at night. Forces her to do unspeakable things . . . sexually."

"It is true?"

"Not from what I can tell. Not from what people say the man's character is like."

"So this . . . Gretchen already has a cover in place."

"Albeit a flimsy one." He moves to his right and digs in a drawer. He pulls out another envelope, this one bulkier. He sets it on top of the papers and pictures. "When you're ready."

"What is it?"

"I happened upon a video recording."

Her eye twitches. "A video recording of what?"

"Them." He clears his throat. "Together."

She looks down at the bulky package. "How easy was it . . . to get all this information?"

"Not easy at all. But that's what you hired me to do, correct?"

"It is. I just didn't expect all of this." She digs in her purse and pulls out a white envelope, clearly full of cash. "Your fee . . . and a little bit more for your service."

"You are too kind." He takes the envelope from her and places it in the still-open drawer. "If I may, a word of caution."

Jolene begins gathering the found information. "I'm listening."

"I ran into trouble trying to get all of this together. He has people . . . protecting him."

She pauses. "Okay?"

"Powerful people. Law-enforcement people. Maybe government people, I don't know, but I had to call in virtually every favor I had just to get this."

She leans back in her seat. "What are you saying?"

For the first time since meeting the man, Jolene realizes he has started to fidget. "Listen, I'm ducking out of state for a while. Until things cool off a bit. But I ask that you not go crazy with all of what I presented to you today. It would be in your best interest to hide this stuff somewhere . . . or destroy it."

"Why would I do that? What aren't you telling me?"

He leans forward and folds his hands, placing them on top of the desk. "I'm saying you have in your possession comprehensive and undeniable proof that your husband, a well-known pastor of one of the fastest-growing churches in our area, is having an affair. That much you know. But what you don't know is this . . . In my search, I ran into a few guys, law-enforcement guys, who, short of threatening my life, tried to get me to back off. These guys I have known for years. I don't have all the pieces to know why these guys are protecting this man, but I know it's for a good reason. If you make too much noise . . ."

"What? They're going to take me out? Don't be silly."

"Mrs. Brommels, please."

"Jolene. I asked you to call me Jolene."

"Jolene, I'm being completely up front with you. With info like this, and not knowing how deep things run . . . just take caution."

Jolene closes her eyes and takes a deep breath. "Thanks, and I will."

"And one last thing."

Jolene slides open her eyes.

"You have never met me."

She nods, her face turning to one of steel determination.

She's made copies. There was a print shop just down the street from the PI's office. She hurried in, made copies of what she could, and left the print shop to head straight to the post office.

A couple days before that, Jolene had purchased a post office box, and paid cash for it.

She paid for the next twenty years.

She steps inside the small building, noticing it's empty, which is a usual for this time of the afternoon, but feels particularly lonely at the moment. The clerk, Jane Pearlmutter, greets her with a smile. Jolene forces a smile back.

"Jane, I need some help."

"What do you need?" Her thick glasses shake as she wriggles her nose.

"I need a box."

"Jolene, you just paid for one from now until the end of time."

"I know. But I need something safer. One that doesn't have my name on it. Do you know where I could go, if not here?"

"I . . ." She looks around. "Is everything okay?"

"Jane, please. I need to hurry."

She presses her lips together. "I may know a spot."

"Thank you. I just need a place that can't be tracked to my name."

"Are you into anything illegal, Jo?"

"No . . . I just . . . if something happens to me, I don't want the contents of these envelopes to disappear."

"Now I'm nervous. What's going on here?"

"Things are wrong, Jane. Things are wrong . . . and I want to set them right. But I need help."

Jane looks down, then sharply into her eyes. "What do you need me to do?"

"I need a safe place to put a few folders. A place no one will touch."

"I have a safe, here under the counter. Will that work?"

"It would. Are you the only one with access?"

"For as long as I run this place, I am."

Jolene sighs. "I need you to guard these folders."

"Here, I also have a little security box with a key. Put your stuff in there, and I'll put it in the safe." She jumps to grab a metal box with the key dangling from the keyhole.

"Jane. No one sees these until it's time."

"How will I know it's time?"

"I don't know. But, I trust you to know what to do."

Jane's face shifts to one of determination, showing Jolene she understands the importance of what she is being asked to do.

"Thank you so much. I'll be back soon."

29.

BURT – THEN

Burt pulls his car up to a dusty lot, where he sees Gretchen's BMW. He parks and gets out the car to see her standing between a seemingly unkempt field and an old, abandoned warehouse. He squints under the beaming afternoon sun.

"What on Earth is she doing?"

He walks out toward her. When she sees him, she smiles.

"What are you doing out here?"

"This plot of land is owned by a man named Simeon Lannister."

"It's huge. But who is Simeon Lannister?"

"He doesn't exist. But, this land, is where your new church will be built."

"Really?" He looks around. "Did they ever think of cutting the grass once in a while?"

"Ha. I wanted to tell you Congressman Burris is pleased to hear you've accepted his offer."

"He made me an offer I couldn't turn down." He looks out into the field and back at the warehouse. "The representative he's sent didn't hurt, either."

He looks at the side of her face as she smiles. He inches up to her and runs his hand under her skirt, up along the back of her thigh.

"You shouldn't do that."

"Yeah? You're not stopping me."

"It's the middle of the day. Someone could be watching."

Burt looks around. "I don't see anyone." He looks back at the cars. "But I get it. Listen, I better get back." He turns to walk back to his car.

"And you're just going to walk away?" she says.

"Yup. It's the middle of the day . . . and I've got work to do."

He hears her footsteps through the tall grass behind him. "Ugh. Get in my car."

"Excuse me?"

"Get in my car, Burt." She grabs his arm and pulls him to her car, which has tinted windows.

****

Burt gets home after a long day and sees that Jolene has dinner ready to go and is at the table. Seth sits, kicking his feet under the table.

"Stop kicking your feet, Boy," Burt says.

Seth looks at his mother first and stops when she nods. That irritates Burt, for as much as he's done, he still can't seem to gain his son's respect, even at this early age. He sits down at the table and partakes in a silent dinner. No one says a word, but he notices Jolene staring at him. He doesn't understand the look, but he knows it isn't a loving one like it once was.

It's been a long time since he's seen that look from her.

After dinner, she clears the table and sends Seth up to his room. He is about on his way to his study when she asks him to talk.

"Okay. Sure. What's on your mind?"

She sits and folds her hands—what she does when she's nervous and is trying to keep her hands from shaking.

"I want a divorce."

He jerks his head back as if he was just slapped. He examines her face to see if she's joking, but when there isn't even a hint of a smile, he knows she is not.

"What are you doing, Jolene?"

"I think you should be asking yourself the same."

Burt squints. "What do you mean?"

"Gretchen. That's what I mean."

Burt doesn't flinch. "Who is that?"

She smiles and shakes her head. She gets up from the table and walks to the dining room cabinet. She pulls out a bunch of papers and throws them onto the table. She sits back down, this time looking at him with a frown. He moves some of the papers around, seeing pictures of him and Gretchen. He also sees a few papers that concern him even more. They seem to be profiles written up about him, and Gretchen, and some other mystery person who is possibly in the political realm.

"Do you know who she is now?"

"Jolene."

"Do you?" She slams her hand on the table.

He grinds his teeth.

"What have I done? Hmmm? What have I done for you to treat me so badly?"

"I haven't treated you badly. I've provided for you. I've done everything I could to make sure you are taken care of, provided for, and happy." He frowns. "So you're telling me that's not enough?"

"Stop it. You are not going to turn this on me. You stepped out of our marriage, Burt. Do you understand what that means?"

"I haven't stepped out. These pictures prove nothing. Gretchen is a business acquaintance."

"Burt." She shakes her head again. He finds it irritating and wants to slap her. "I have a recording. So, stop trying to play me for a fool and tell me the truth."

"If you have all of this information, why do you need me to say anything?"

"Because I need to know why. I need to know what it means."

Burt looks down and doesn't say anything. He doesn't know what to do, but he feels for sure everything crumbling around him.

"What does it mean, Burt?"

He stands up from the table. "It means you aren't going anywhere." He grabs all the papers. "Where's the other stuff?"

"What?" She pops up. "It's over, Burt. It's all over."

"Shut up."

"And once I get the copies to the authorities—"

"What?" He steps to her, dropping the papers to the floor. "What did you say?"

"Yes. Copies. You think I would be dumb enough not to make them?"

"Where are the copies, Jolene?"

"They're safe where I want them to be."

He stomps over to her and grabs her by the hair, pulling her back. "Where are the copies?"

"Let go of me."

"Where are they?" He wrenches her head back to stare her in the eyes. He's never seen fear like that on anyone, let alone his own wife. "Tell me." He didn't realize how angered he's become, as he screams in her face.

She starts to cry. "No." She struggles against him. "What have you become?"

He looks into her eyes, still enraged. "What do you know?"

She continues to struggle. "I know you should lose it all. You weak and pathetic hypocrite."

He's had as much as he will take from her and her prying ways . . . her accusatory tone . . . her judgmental eyes. He feels himself slipping as he stares at the papers scattered along the floor. He knows what he has to do.

"I'm . . . I'm sorry." He pulls her to the kitchen and throws her to the floor. She hits her head on the tile and barely moves. He grabs a cloth and a plastic bag.

"Wh-What are you . . ."

He steps over to her and straddles her back. He balls the cloth up and jams it into her mouth so she doesn't make any more noise, and uses his weight to keep her from moving too much. He reaches into the under-sink cabinet and finds some duct tape. In robotic fashion, he slides the plastic bag over her head and wraps a few rounds of duct tape around her neck. He watches her as she struggles for air. With tears in his eyes, he leans over and wraps his arms around her, making sure she can't pull the bag off. As she tries to kick out of his grip, he closes his eyes and leans his chin on the back of her shoulder. He tries to block out the sound of her gagging, struggling for air, but he knows he will remember the sound for as long as he lives. After a minute or so, she stops moving, but he continues to hold her.

Eventually, he lays her gently on the kitchen floor and dials a number on the phone.

"I . . . I . . ."

"Burt?"

"She's gone. I did it. She found out."

"Wait. What are you talking about?"

"I killed her, Gretchen. I killed Jolene."

"Oh, my God, Burt. I'm sending someone. Don't go anywhere."

"My son . . . he's upstairs."

"Okay, Burt; let me make a call."

He hangs up without saying anything else and stands there, looking at Jolene's lifeless body.

30.

Mathias – Then

Mathias is learning the ropes. He and Dell have had great success recently, but the number-one thing he has learned from Dell is that the ropes are a little loose and are prone to moving. This is especially the case when working with Dell. To date, they have done everything from paying informants to letting other criminals slide in exchange for their cooperation. He finds that Dell has a completely different network of criminals which he taps to solve various other crimes. It's strangely effective, but it isn't quite his idea of justice.

"How much longer?" Mathias asks.

"Don't get too antsy. A stakeout can take days. We're gathering intel."

"We're wasting time."

"Hey Justice League, this is how we bust the bad guys."

"Or become one of them."

"There something you need to get off your chest?"

Mathias sits in a chair and stares out the window. "Nope." He looks at the sky. "It's about to rain. What do we do then?"

"Same thing we're doing now."

Mathias sighs. "You know—"

Dell's pager beeps. Mathias watches him as he pulls his pager from his hip and stares at the number on it. His face shifts slightly. He grabs his jacket.

"I got to go."

"But we're on a stakeout."

"I'll be right back." Dell pulls on his jacket and is out the door.

After an hour of looking across the street with a set of binoculars, he gives up. It's raining way too hard to notice anything anyway. The door swings open as Dell barges back in.

"We gotta go," he says, virtually out of breath.

"What's up?"

"Accident. Sarge is pulling us off to get to it."

"What? Why would he do that?"

"It's bad. Victim is stuck in the car. Doesn't look like anyone else was involved."

"Alive?"

He looks down. "Don't think so."

"Where?"

"Down the street."

Mathias squints. "I didn't hear anything."

"How could you, when it's raining this hard?" He starts for the door. "We'd better get there. Hey, Kid."

"Yeah?"

"You take lead on this one. You've worked hard enough."

Mathias nods. It would be the first incident he's taken the lead on.

"I'll be right there with you," Dell says.

Seth – Now

Seth gets to the only post office he knows of in the area and walks to the front desk. The clerk, Ms. Pearlmutter, has always been in this post office, at least as far back as he could remember. He steps to the counter and rings the bell. When she comes around the corner and sees Seth, Ms. Pearlmutter smiles.

"Ah. Seth. What can I do for you today?"

"Hey, Ms. P." He digs in his pocket. "How are you today?"

"I'm well. You?"

"Good." He places the key on the counter. "You ever seen a key like this before? It looks like a P.O. box key, like the one I have, but different."

She grabs the key and adjusts her glasses along the bridge of her nose. She flips it a few times as Seth looks on.

"Where did you find it?"

"Well … it was in my mom's jewelry box. Hidden inside an envelope."

"You don't say."

"Yeah." He looks down.

"What's wrong, Seth?"

"Just how I got this key that means something … but may mean nothing."

"Explain."

"Ma'am, my best friend just died, and she had—"

"You're not talking of that young Brianna girl that's on the news?"

"I am, ma'am."

She gasps.

"She had my mother's jewelry box . . . well, we gave it to her when she passed, my dad and I. And—" He looks up at her to see she's crying. "You knew her?"

"No." She shakes her head. "I didn't. But I know what this key is to."

"What is it to?"

She walks to the back. A few minutes later, she comes back with a metal lock box. She hands him back the key. He takes it and put the key in to open it. It slides in and turns, but before he could open it, she slams it shut.

"Hey."

"Not here."

"Huh?"

"Seth," the wrinkles on her face become pronounced as she seems to hold back tears, "Your mother gave this to me to keep safe. She said I would know when to release it. My gut is telling me it's time."

"Do you know what's in it?"

"Folders and envelopes." She takes a deep breath and sighs. "I think . . . I think she was killed. She was killed over this."

"She got into an accident."

"I don't think there was an accident." She shrugs. "Or maybe these are just random mutterings. I've just had a long time to think about this."

"Ma'am, what are you saying?"

"Soon after you mother's passing, your father came here looking to see if there were any items Jo stored in a box. I directed him to her box that had her name on it. She placed something in there, that he pulled out and took with him. But, I feel that he was really looking for this." She places a hand on his. "So be careful."

Seth stands almost in shock, nervous about the contents of the metal security box. He slides it off the counter and cradles it. It takes him just a quick bus ride to get back to his apartment, and when he does, he opens the box and examines every paper. There are some cassette tapes inside envelopes as well. Luckily, he still has an old tape player he just could not get rid of. He doesn't have much, and what he does have is old, outdated, or broken, but in this situation, especially, he is thankful for what he does have. He listens to each tape, hearing conversations between his father and Gretchen, and his father and some other guy he doesn't recognize. Much of it is in code, but he's able to surmise that his father isn't as holy as he made himself out to be. He also now understands that his father has lied to him for years. He is the reason she was in the accident. They likely were arguing about Gretchen. It all falls into place for him, so he thinks. The question remains, now that he knows this info, what is he going to do about it? Here is where he's stumped. There's just too much going on for him to process.

Normally, he would call Bree. She always helped him get his thoughts together. But she is no longer here. He leans back in his couch and cries. In the middle of his tears, he tries to ask God for guidance. He asks for understanding, but he knows he isn't much open to listening.

31.

TALLY – NOW

"I couldn't believe it," Tally says. "He was there, too. Another late night. Another time I tried to get away but couldn't. He was there."

"So what did you do?" Ms. Xing asks.

"I didn't know what to do. He made me feel special . . . and ashamed, and beautiful, and wanted, and excited. He made me feel so much all at the same time."

"Why ashamed?"

"Because he's this faithful Christian guy. I remember seeing him in church, the way he looked. It's hard to describe, but there I was, after what I had just finished doing."

"You were on a date?"

"No, ma'am." She looks down. "I just got finished with a shift."

"Still dancing?"

"Yes, ma'am, and that night, there was this guy in the music industry . . ."

"So cliché."

"Isn't it?" She laughs. "He's trying to write a new song, and I was his muse . . . or something like that. He told me he wasn't trying to get me into bed . . . but that's what guys say to get girls into bed. Still, he paid a lot of money, so the least I could offer was my time. And that's when Seth showed up."

Ms. Xing frowns. "What ever happened to bad man?"

"Oh, get this. He's in jail. Got arrested in Atlanta."

"Serves him right."

Tally smiles. "So, you really letting go of the school?"

She nods. "I have to. I'll make a living from private lessons. Just like it was when you were younger. Would like for you to come with."

"And teach?"

She nods again. "You are an adult, and you make your own decisions . . . I just wished you picked a different occupation. You should be solving world problems somewhere . . . find the cure for cancer . . . something that. Not rubbing up on nasty men, telling them their lives don't stink because you're beautiful and want them."

She laughs again. "But it's just so easy. Men are so pitiful; they drop their hard-earned money in front of an illusion. They set themselves up to be used every time."

"Tally."

"Look, I just need to get on my feet. I thought I was saving the school by dancing, and when you told me you don't need it . . . the money is coming in so fast right now."

"Do you like it?"

"A little. I like the money."

"Don't let money become the driving force for everything in your life. Don't think because it's so easy to use men, that you should." She smirks. "You think Seth would mind you being a dancer?"

Tally sighs. "That's not a fair question."

"Why isn't it? Because you already know the answer?"

Tally doesn't say anything. She just gives Ms. Xing a look.

"Fine. But, I'm serious, I want you to teach with me."

"I'll think about it. I would love nothing more than to—"

Her phone rings and when she grabs it, she freezes.

"Are you going to answer it?"

"It's Seth."

"Why are you staring at it googly eyed? Answer it."

She stares at it for so long, the phone stops ringing. She froze because she didn't expect him to call at all, and she wasn't going to call him, for no reason other than being stubborn. She quickly calls him back.

"Hi, Seth?"

"Yeah. Tally?" His voice sounds gravelly enough for her not to recognize him.

"Yeah. What's . . . up?"

"Listen, I . . . I'm sorry for bothering you."

"You're not bothering me at all. I was just hanging out."

"I . . . I really need someone to talk to right now. And . . . I just . . ." He sighs loudly over the phone.

"What's wrong?"

"I'm sorry. This was a mistake. I have to go."

"No. Wait. Are you at your apartment?"

"Yeah."

"I'm leaving now. Be there in a few."

"Tally, you don't—"

She hangs up the phone and rushes to grab her keys.

"Is he okay?" Ms. Xing asks.

"Doesn't sound like it." She grabs a jacket. "I'll be back in a little bit."

She smiles. "No, you won't."

Tally would have some other comeback, but she is already out the door.

When she pulls up to his apartment building, she sees him sitting on a bench next to the steps. The way he just sits there looking out into space unsettles her. She parks and gets out the car. He doesn't move or smile, or even look her way. She quietly makes it to the bench and sits. Still, for a while, he doesn't say anything. People walk by them, too concerned with their own lives to notice they just sit there on the bench in complete silence. A few look at her, mostly men deciding if she is with Seth or not. One man approaches Tally, and that's when Seth simply looks over. The man takes a glimpse at Seth and continues along his way. Seth then returns to his listless stare out into the streets.

She considers moving closer to him and holding him, but thinks better of it and decides to wait until he's ready.

"I people-watch every now and again," Seth says. His voice comes out small and timid almost, which is different than how it was when he called.

"There's nothing wrong with that."

"I have a friend who can figure out people by the way they move. I've tried for years to hone that skill, but not to much success."

"Oh."

He nods. She wishes he would stop looking so lost. It pains her to see him this way, and she has no idea why.

"I, um, thank you for coming," he says. "Do you pray much, Tally?"

"I honestly can't say I do."

"I get it. Have you ever?"

"No. Not really."

He nods. "Well, I do. All the time." He straightens up. "And I'm not saying that to make you feel bad or guilty or anything like that. It's just, I've been praying for you . . . ever since you robbed me, and even more after you returned my things."

That makes Tally feel nervous.

"But I'm going through a really rough time right now . . . and I don't know what all of it means. So, I prayed, and I just got this feeling in my gut. It was urging me to call you."

Tally listens to him as he explains that feeling that urges him to move, and she remembers her own similar experience in leaving Paul's apartment for the music school. She unknowingly nods as he speaks, fully understanding what he is saying.

"You watch the news?"

"No. Not really. I don't watch much TV."

"I get it. Neither do I." He takes in a deep breath. "My best friend . . . was killed."

She gasps. "I'm sorry to hear that."

He nods. "I just don't understand why." He looks down at his lap. "We grew up together. We were . . . inseparable. And she—"

"She?"

"Yeah . . . she."

"Did you have feelings for her?"

He looks up into the sky. "I did. And then I didn't. But, she was . . . special."

"I see."

"Can I be honest?"

"I don't see why not."

"We slept together."

"Oh."

"You look surprised."

"No, I just took you for the wait-for-marriage type. Isn't that what you believe?"

"Yes. It is." He chuckles for the first time since she showed up. "Wanna know how much of a scumbag I am? I slept with her, and I was engaged to someone else."

"Whoa. But I wouldn't call you a scumbag."

"Yeah, but I've done some pretty crummy things."

Tally looks at him and smiles. "We all have. Hello?"—she starts waving her hand—"Girl who robbed you at gunpoint."

Seth chuckles a bit more. "Yeah." He contorts his face into a frown. "But, I pushed her away, and pulled her back in . . . back and forth . . . I toyed with her . . . without ever thinking about it and . . ."

He looks down and places his face in his hands.

She stares at first, unsure of what to do. She simply didn't expect to see him sobbing in front of her. She didn't expect to see him so . . . vulnerable. She slowly moves over toward him and wraps an arm around him. She holds him as his body shakes in her grasp, not caring about the people walking by and the weird looks they are getting. All she cares about is comforting him, because he needs someone. She rubs his arm and whispers to him, "It's okay. Everything will be okay," repeatedly. Eventually, his sobbing subsides, and he straightens up.

"Thanks," he says.

"No need to thank me. I'm . . . I'm here for you." Looking up at the sky, she sees clouds coming in. Drops of rain speckle them and the area around them. "I guess I better get out of here."

He looks around, seemingly timid to look her in the eye. "It's been one rainy summer."

"Yeah." She gets up from the bench. "Listen, if you ever need someone to talk to, you can call me. It doesn't matter when."

He looks at the ground in front of him as the rain starts to pick up. "You want to come up?" he asks. "Unless you got somewhere to be."

She thinks for a moment, realizing she has to get ready for a shift tonight. "Ummm."

"It's cool. Don't worry about it."

"No. I would love to."

"But?"

"There's no 'but.' Lead the way."

He gets up from the bench, and they go to the front doors of the building. He opens the door and waits, holding it. She hesitates for a second because no one has opened the door for her, ever. And for him to do it, it seemed so natural. He did it without even thinking, like that type of treatment has long since been ingrained into his being.

"Thank you," she says.

He nods and then leads her to a flight of stairs. "I'm on the second floor."

"How long have you lived here?" She continues the small talk as they climb the stairs.

"Around four years. Honestly, I'm not sure how."

"Meaning?"

"I'll tell you more once we're inside." He stops on the second floor and holds the door open for her again, making her feel special in a weird way.

"Now, I have to warn you, my place is a mess."

"I don't mind."

"Okay," he says. "You've been warned."

They get to a door in the middle of a long hallway, and he pulls out his keys to unlock it. For a third time, he opens the door for her, and she enters his apartment.

"You know, no one has ever held the door for me before," she says.

"Really?" He looks like he's trying to find something to say.

"Yeah. It's different." She walks in and changes the subject. "Oh, it isn't a mess in here at all."

"You're being nice." He offers her a seat on the couch.

She takes a seat on the couch. "So, what did you mean you're not sure how you've been here for as long as you have?"

"Well, I probably shouldn't have said I don't know how. The guy who runs this building, he's real cool. I'm so far behind on rent, I should have been kicked out. But every time I go to see him and pay down on what I owe, he waves me off. Tells me it's paid for."

"That's not a normal landlord."

"Yeah. Not at all. I mean, he knows I'm as broke as broke can be." He sits down on a chair near her. "But I don't want to take advantage of that. I owe him a lot of money."

"I understand. You take pictures, right? There isn't a lot of money in that?"

"There could be if you're good and put yourself out there. And I've tried. Well, the group I'm with . . . we've tried."

She nods but thinks back to when she robbed him. She feels even guiltier for doing so, because now she knows those few dollars she took was all he had to get a good meal. She typically didn't think about her victims, but ever since him, all she could think about were the victims—the men she's made victims.

"So, listen, thanks for . . . thanks for being here . . . especially when, you know, when I'm bawling my eyes out in public."

"Sure." She looks around awkwardly, finding not much else to say.

"So, tell me about yourself, Tally."

She stiffens up. "Huh?"

"Well, besides the girl who robbed me and then stalked me to return my things . . . who are you?"

"Oh. Okay. Well, there isn't much to know about me, I guess." A blatant lie.

He smiles for the first time since meeting up. "I'm sure. How did you end up robbing me? I'm guessing I wasn't the only one, so how did you get into that? Do you still?"

"Well, I don't do it anymore."

He stares at her expectantly.

"Okay, look. There are some things you don't want to know about me. Some roads I don't want to go down."

"Maybe there are roads you don't want to go down, fine. But, I want to know all about you. So, are there roads you can go down?"

She feels a burning in her gut as she looks at the area rug on the floor. It has a blocky design, but the more she looks at it, the more it blends into itself. The blocks turn to blobs. She bites her bottom lip while thinking. "No," she finally says.

He nods. "Okay. That's fine. I just thought . . . I don't know what I thought."

"You're emotionally raw right now," she says without looking him in the eyes. "You shouldn't worry about . . . getting to know me."

For a moment, both sit in silence. Tally is afraid to look Seth's way.

"That's an odd thing to say," he says. "But very . . . emotionally aware."

"Maybe. I just know a bit about reaching out to anything . . . to anyone when emotionally torn down."

"But you're not just anyone . . . right?"

She takes a deep breath. "I don't know."

"Well, let me clear the air; you aren't just anyone. I know that much for sure. Who you are is still a mystery."

She struggles with the idea of telling him who she is, but recognizes that he is and has been completely open with her—at least that's the way it seems to her. She goes to speak when he gets up and grabs a metal security box.

"Can I show you something? I'm trying to make sense of this, but can't."

32.

Mathias – Now

Mathias sits in a parked car, his cell phone on his ear.

"He's sitting there . . . yeah . . . wait. A female just sat next to him . . . I don't know. Never seen her before. I'll keep you updated . . . yes, sir . . . yes, sir, that situation has been handled."

He hangs up and continues to stare at Seth as he sits on the bench with a mystery woman. He watches him as he puts his face into his hands and sobs. That's when it becomes too much for him to watch. He starts the car and drives off, hoping to make one more stop before finally going home.

He's made detective, one of the benefits of learning under the tutelage of Dell. Once Dell retired from the force, he was given a new partner for a small moment in time. Now, he's the go-to as Dell once was. His father and grandfather would be proud, at least, of that part of his life. Everything else around that fell apart for him. His fiancée, Wren, packed her bags and left years ago for reasons he still cannot come to terms with.

But he still sees her every now and again.

He pulls up in a residential neighborhood and parks the car across the street from a set of homes. He pulls out a snack cake and rips it from the plastic packaging and takes a large bite. He waits for some time when, from the third house down from where he was parked, a woman comes out. He stops chomping on his snack and stares at her. She wears a floral-print dress that flaps in the slight breeze. He barely sees the paint on her toes as she walks down her walkway barefooted. He smiles, thinking about how many times he's told her about that, but she's always been the free-spirit type. Shoes just became a restriction to her. Wren walks down to the mailbox and grabs the mail. Joggers run by and greet her. She smiles and waves. The good Lord knows what he would give just to wake up to that smile again. He watches her as she snaps around and a tall man walks up to her and gives her a kiss.

The snack cake sours in his stomach almost immediately.

Garrett is his name, and he's been staying over a lot more lately. He's an FBI agent, but he couldn't figure much else out about the man. Mathias watches him as he wraps his arms around Wren and gives her a kiss. His body naturally reacts as if he is in protection mode. He has to protect Wren from predators. Unfortunately, there was no one who could protect her from him. They both look back at the house. Wren skips to the front door and comes back into his vision holding a child, a little girl. Mister FBI walks to his car and gets in. He drives, with the two waving goodbye to him. It makes Mathias' blood boil. Whoever this man is, he surely doesn't deserve to be waved off by Mathias' woman . . . and daughter. He sits in his parked car long after Wren and his daughter go back into their home.

He left when the sun was setting, and by the time he gets back home, it's dark, but not pitch black. He pulls up into his driveway and shuts the car off. He pops open his car door and slides out. He should be getting some sleep, but he knows none will come. He enters his home but doesn't cut on any lights. He makes sure the curtains are closed before turning on a small table lamp. He walks back to the kitchen and to the fridge to grab a beer. He sticks his head in the fridge just far enough to get a cool blast.

"That seems to be all you have in here. And not even the good kind."

Mathias pulls his head out the fridge to look up at the kitchen table. "Are you complaining? You shouldn't even be alive right now." He sticks his head back in the fridge.

"I suppose you're right."

Mathias hears a hard gulp. He grabs a beer after indulging in the cool air and shuts the door. He flips the light switch on to see Dell sitting at his kitchen table, with a few empty bottles of beer in front of him.

"Didn't stop you from drinking half my stuff," Mathias says.

"Yeah, well . . . I needed something to take off the edge." He taps his hand on the table gently. "Tell me, Justice League, why did I do it?"

"Do what?"

"You know . . . this stuff for Burt."

"Because he called."

MATHIAS – THEN

He couldn't place his finger on it. That accident, the first incident he handled, he handled well. That is, up until he was asked by Dell to omit a few details and gloss over a few things he noticed during the investigation. Indeed, Mathias felt something was off, so he asked questions, questions that Dell swiftly avoided. Then, when Mathias was filling out the report, Dell asked him to change some details, minor ones, but ones that tell a different story. He didn't do it, but somehow they were changed anyway. He asked Dell about it, but he claimed he knew nothing about it. It seemed everyone from other officers on the force to the coroner knew something that he did not know. Still, he had no idea what. Not too long after the investigation wrapped up, Dell retired from the force, and Mathias was promoted to detective soon after that. Things moved quickly.

Things moved too quickly.

Things between him and Wren are changing. He knows he has something to do with that, as he comes home more tired than anything. He also comes home more depressed. He was never a drinker before, but slowly, alcohol crept up on him like a snake in the grass, poised to bite. So, some nights, he comes home drunk. Their wedding isn't too far away now, but from the looks of it, they might not make it.

He sits at an outside table at a café down the street from where he lives. A man in a suit approaches him and simply slides into the seat across from him, as if Mathias had been expecting him.

"Do you know who I am?" the man says.

"I do." He straightens up.

He puts his hand out. Mathias shakes it. "Pastor Burt Brommels."

"Mathias Reid."

"Mathias, I wanted to thank you for your handling of . . ." He looks down for a second. "I wanted to thank you for keeping the investigation into my wife's accident going smoothly. I know she was driving too fast in the rain. So, I understand that there wasn't any foul play here. It was just an unfortunate accident."

Mathias feels his stomach turn. He debates whether he should say anything about his concerns with the investigation.

"Dell Crawford was your partner?"

"Yes, sir."

"Well, as you know, he's retired from the force. But I wanted to let you know, he's heading up the security at my church."

"Okay. Why did you want to let me know?"

"Well, this is where the conversation gets interesting." Burt smiles. "We both know Dell has his . . . ways of doing things."

"Yeah."

"Those ways, I know, aren't always on the up-and-up. Some of his methods are rather . . . questionable."

Mathias scans Burt's face, trying to understand what angle he is taking here. "Then why hire him?"

"Well, I didn't . . . not exactly. The church did."

"But you run the church, do you not?"

"It's more of a team effort. One that I lead, sure, but the idea of adding security and adding him to the staff was thrust upon me, more or less."

"More more, or more less?"

"More more, but you don't need to worry about that. Look, Mathias, I need a guy. I need someone to have my back, because I don't know what is going to happen with this Dell character. And I would much prefer to have someone on my staff who at least believes in justice. I knew your Daddy. He was an outstanding cop. I know your Granddaddy was, too. I need to be able to count on honor and integrity like that." He looks Mathias in the eyes. "Can I count on you?"

It's a no brainer. Justice. Honor. Integrity. Burt mentioned all the key words that makes Mathias believe what he says is true. "I'm in. What do I need to do?"

Burt smiles. "Just be ready when I call." He pulls out an envelope from his suit coat pocket and slides it to him. "For your troubles."

"Sir, that's not necessary."

"It is. You are on my staff now. You're part of my secret service, so to speak." He taps the envelope that rests on the table. "Everyone could use a little extra to help them along their way."

Mathias nods. "Thank you, sir."

"Once a month, expect an envelope from me."

He nods again. Burt gets up from the table and puts his hand out to shake. Mathias shakes his hand.

"Welcome aboard, Mathias Reid."

When Burt leaves, Mathias slips open the envelope to see a check made out to him in the amount of six thousand dollars.

33.

SETH – NOW

He knows his father lied to him. That's about all he knows at the moment, as he is still trying to grasp exactly what all the information means. When he originally brought the security box home, he was only able to scan a few papers that meant nothing to him initially. When he and Tally went through everything, they scanned every paper, looked at every picture, and listened to every audio recording. The more he found out, the angrier he became. He woke up today feeling two strong and distinct emotions: anger at his father, and a longing to see his mother again.

Tally had to leave after they went through the box. He wanted her to stay, but she became mysterious about where she had to go. He wasn't going to hold her hostage or anything like that, but he sure did enjoy her company. She patted him on the shoulder when it became clear to him that his mother had been out in the rain because his father had an affair. He didn't want to confront his father about anything until he put together the last little bit of the puzzle. Among the other notes and folders was a little piece of paper in someone's handwriting he didn't recognize. In all caps, the phrase "POLITICAL TIES" was written. Neither he nor Tally understood what that meant.

He needs more answers, and who better to answer his pressing questions than the PI who presumably found the information out?

He enters the warehouse-looking building at the address printed on the business card. He gets to a second floor, which smells like dust and mold. The carpeted floors look worn, and there are doors lining up on both sides of the hall. He walks by the doors, noticing each has a number on it. He refers to the business card again and finds he should be looking for room 104. He gets to 104 and knocks. As he's waiting for an answer, he notices it is extremely quiet inside for an office building. He knocks again.

No answer.

He starts back toward the stairwell when another of the offices opens. Seth jumps as an old man pops out right next to him.

"What do you want, Kid?"

"Ummm. Hi. I'm looking for"—he looks at the business card—"a Mr. Jergins."

"Who is looking for him?"

"I just said, sir. I am looking for—"

"Don't play coy, Kid. Who the hell are you?"

"I'm Seth Brommels. My mother— "

"Brommels. Brommels."

"My mother came to you, I think."

"She insisted I call her Jolene." The old man squints. Seth can't tell if the man's hand was always shaking, or if it just started. "Get out of here, Kid."

"Excuse me?"

"Get out of here. Leave the past alone." The old man goes back into the office he came from and slams the door.

Seth, feeling dejected and shocked, leaves the office building. He came a far way to get to the rundown building and had expected to obtain some real answers. He walks to the bus stop that's at the end of the street but has a feeling someone is following him. He looks all around but finds no one. He sees a car with tinted windows pulling up to the stop. The passenger window rolls down just as he sits on the bench.

"Hey, Kid."

Seth looks up to see Dell and some unknown in the driver's seat. "What do you want?"

"We need to talk."

"What do I have to say to you?"

"Probably a few choice words. But this is more about what I need to tell you."

"Yeah, right."

"I know you're looking for the truth. I know the truth."

"The truth about what?"

"About your mother."

Seth freezes. "Who says I'm looking for anything?"

Dell nods. "Okay. So, what if I told you there are still yet-to-be-uncovered details to Brianna Connelly's death?"

"What? What do you mean?"

"We can't talk out here, Kid. It's not safe."

"What do you need to talk to me for?"

"Because we think you have something that could . . . that could help in what we are trying to do."

Seth snaps his head up. "What are you trying to do?"

"Serve justice."

He looks to the side, not believing he's even considering what Dell is saying. "Say I do know, or have an idea on what you are talking about . . . so what?"

"C'mon, Kid. There's a part of you that always wanted the truth. You seek it out every chance you get. I'm offering a chance to uncover the truth and do something about it."

He looks down. "Mom didn't die in an accident, did she?"

"No, Kid."

"And Bree wasn't murdered by some psycho who thought she had money."

"Sorry, Kid. No."

Seth nods and gets up from the bench. He hears the car doors unlocking, and he opens the rear door and hops in.

"Who's your friend?" Seth asks.

"Mathias Reid, aka Justice League."

The man keeps a straight face while driving away.

"That name sounds familiar."

"He's the one who was in the papers about your mother's case."

Seth catches eyes with him in the rearview mirror. "Hey."

The man gives a curt nod and refocuses his attention on the road.

MATHIAS – NOW

"Yes, sir. He's headed into the building now . . . I'm not sure. It looks like an old office building. One of the ones where small-business owners rent out the space . . . Don't know. I'll keep tabs . . . Another update soon." Mathias hangs up his cell and places it on the dash of his car.

"So, what's the situation?" Dell asks.

"He thinks the kid has the files." He massages his forearm. "Says it's a hunch."

"So he's having you follow him? Don't you have a job, Detective Reid?"

Mathias looks over at Dell and scoffs. Dell looks at him like he deserves an answer to his question. Mathias provides none. He looks at the building.

"You think the kid is going to come with?" Mathias asks.

"He will. He won't want to, but he will."

"What makes you so sure?"

"He knows he's onto something. And if he does have those files . . . look, there he is."

Mathias watches Seth as he walks from the office building to the bus stop. "Looks like no dice."

"Looks like. Pull up to him."

Mathias pulls the car up to the bus stop as Dell rolls his window down to talk to him. It takes some convincing, but Seth hops in the backseat of his car. He turns the car around and heads back to his house, where they can fill him in on the truth and details of their next plan of action.

BURT – NOW

He sits at his desk before afternoon Bible study after getting off the phone with Mathias. He sighs, thinking to himself that it is difficult to find loyalty these days. Throughout all his years, his gut hasn't led him astray. At times, it came down to life or death. His gut forced him to open his eyes before a man stabbed him to death during prayer. His gut moved him toward preaching the word of God. But lately, his gut has been off. It rumbled in his belly, the notion that somehow Bree had the files, evidence of his crooked dealings. He was wrong, though maybe he wasn't. Maybe Jared Connelly has the files now and is just waiting to take him down. He shakes his head. He's becoming too paranoid, and that's when people make mistakes. Still, a little paranoia is good. Keeps everyone else on guard, and it easily roots out deception. But his gut . . . his gut tells him that Seth knows more than he lets on. His gut tells him that Mathias has betrayed him.

He grabs a cell phone from his desk drawer, a burner, and texts to a number he has memorized, "report." He places the phone back in the drawer and waits. For a second, he thinks to call Gretchen, to let her know of the issues at hand, but he thinks better of it. To date, she knows nothing of his newest attempt at finding the files. She's always believed they didn't exist. Burt knows better. If Jolene said there were copies, then there were copies. The phone buzzes in his drawer, startling him. He grabs it quickly and answers.

"What do you have?"

"Quite a bit, sir," a voice other than Mathias' says. "Looks like you are right about Matty."

"Explain."

"Seth comes out the building, which I found out what was there."

"Just stick with Mathias right now."

"Yes, sir. Seth comes out and Matty pulls up to him. At first I thought he was talking to him, but there was someone in the passenger seat."

"Dell?" Burt feels his blood turn to acid.

"You got it. And some words were exchanged. Couldn't make out what was being said. Seems like Matty has a jammer. Anyway, Seth gets into the car with them and they drive off."

"Where to?"

"Don't know. I stayed behind and searched the building."

"Good call. What did you find?" He stands up from his desk and walks to the window.

"Clarence Jergins, private investigator. An old man now."

"So, Seth is getting a private investigator?"

"No, sir. Your late wife did."

Burt feels another headache coming on and tries to breathe it out. "He's who she went to those years ago?"

"Yes, sir. And he had quite a bit to tell me. He found out about you, the current Mrs. Brommels, and Congressman Burris. He told me he gave her detailed files and audio recordings on everything. Stuff everyone could go to jail for."

"How did you find this out?"

Long pause. "You don't want to know."

"And what of him?"

"He had an accident."

Burt nods. "Your prognosis?"

"I can't tell you if Seth has the files or not . . . but I know him meeting with Matty and Dell is bad. If he doesn't know what happened . . . he soon will know the truth."

Burt unknowingly has been grinding his teeth.

"Sir? What would you like me to do?"

Things are moving too fast for him, so he takes in a few deep breaths.

"Sir?"

"Track them. Find out where they are . . . but don't approach. Call me as soon as you find them, and I'll give direction from there."

"Yes, sir."

He hangs up the phone and yanks open the drawer. He throws the phone in, then slams the drawer shut. He punches a button on his desk phone. "Tina, please get Assistant Pastor Fredricks to conduct Bible study today. I'm feeling a little ill."

"Yes, Pastor."

He flops into his chair and folds his hands, waiting.

34.

SETH – NOW

They took him to his place so he could grab the security box, and before long, they were on the road again, going somewhere. He had no idea.

It's nighttime, and they pull up into a driveway to a nice-sized home. Mathias puts the car in park, but keeps his stony demeanor. Dell looks out the passenger window as if searching for something.

"Hey, Justice League, you feel that?"

"Yeah."

Seth watches as both men pull out guns.

"Let's go, Kid," Mathias says.

Seth is almost frozen in place, but he forces himself to move. All three briskly walk into the home with Dell giving a last look outside before shutting the door. Mathias grabs Seth's arm and pulls him away from the windows.

"Basement," Dell says.

All three go to the basement to a card table.

"How much you want to bet he's sent someone else?" Dell asks.

"Wouldn't doubt it," Mathias says. "We better move fast here."

"Agreed." Dell grabs a chair and sits at the card table. "Let's see the box, Kid."

Seth tries to slow things down. "No. Not until you tell me the truth."

"C'mon, Kid, we don't have time."

"The truth."

Mathias paces back and forth. "What do you want to know?"

"Everything. Start with my mother."

Dell shifts in his seat. "Fine." He looks down as if suddenly scared. "You sure you want to know these things?"

"Yes. There's no turning back now, is there?"

Dell shakes his head. "Your mother. She wasn't killed in a car accident. She died well before that."

"How?"

"Your father."

He feels like he just has been punched in the gut. He feels it so viscerally, he hunches over. "What did he do?"

"He suffocated her."

"And you helped cover it up?" He looks to Mathias.

"No, Kid," Dell says. "Mathias knew nothing about it. He did everything he was supposed to do. I was just behind him changing things . . . messing with the investigation."

"Why?" His voice cracks. "Why would you do such a thing?"

"Because, Kid, we all made a deal with the devil."

"My father?"

"No. Congressman Burris."

"What?" He frowns, but mostly because he is trying to stop from crying. The last thing he wants to do is cry in front of two men.

"Burt, your father, owes a lot of his"—he makes air quotes—"success to the congressman. He bought the church, had it built. Gave Burt free reign over staff and the like. He made Burt a pastor of a mega church."

"Why?"

"Money and influence. Plain and simple. Burris gets a payment every month as a return on his investment, and Burt preaches about having a strong leader for a few sermons, leading people to vote for him as needed."

"Where does the money come from?"

"Where do you think?"

Seth shakes his head.

"Religious folk pay a lot of money if they think there's a blessing somewhere for them involved." Dell leans his elbows on the table. "Then Burris takes the money and uses it to fund campaigns . . . or for more influence in other areas. And that is just one of his illegal income streams. He takes charitable donations from everywhere and funnels them into personal funds. His team of accountants . . . scary good."

"But what did my father . . ." It disgusts him to call that man father. "What did Burt get out of it?"

"What do you mean? He's one of the most well-known pastors in the world. People just drop money at his feet. For all intents and purposes, he's running a multimillion-dollar corporation. And that lady of his sweetened the deal even more."

"Gretchen?"

"Yeah, Kid. She put it on him so good, he had to say yes." He looks up at Mathias, who remains with a stern face. "Sorry. Yeah . . . Gretchen's sole purpose was to convince Burt of making the deal."

"So these files," He didn't realize he was clutching the security box to his chest. He sets them on the table. "They prove what? Corruption?"

"We hope."

"And what do you have to do with all of this?" He looks to Mathias.

Mathias seems to think for a few moments before answering. "I was just supposed to be a second set of eyes for Burt . . . and if there ever came a time when Dell needed to be . . . handled, I was supposed to be there."

"So you're a criminal, too?"

"That's harsh, Kid," Dell says.

"But it's accurate," Mathias says. "I took money from your father to act as his insurance against Dell . . . against—"

"Being found out," Seth says. He puts his head down, not knowing how much more he can take. "And my mother found all this out, and she was killed for it." A realization smacks him in the head and makes him feel even lower. "And so was Bree."

"Brianna didn't know anything," Dell looks down. "But she was killed for it."

"Who?"

"Listen, we need to get to those files, Seth," Mathias says.

Seth looks at Mathias, then back at Dell, who doesn't look him in the eyes. "You did it, didn't you?"

"I'm sorry, Seth."

He looks down, trying to compute everything he's been told, but finds his mind is simply burned out. He slides the metal box to the middle of the table and slouches in his seat. "There are the files."

It takes a few moments before Dell pops open the box and scans the papers, with Mathias looking on.

"Has anyone else seen these?" Mathias asks.

"Just one other person. Her name is Tally."

"The girl you were sitting with outside your apartment?"

He nods.

"Call her. She might be in danger."

MATHIAS – NOW

It broke his heart. The look on Seth's face as he and Dell revealed to him the answers he needed. He was losing a grip and fast, Mathias could tell. But they had to keep moving forward. They knew they were running out of time. Dell sat for a while, staring at his hands. Mathias thinks all of his dirty deeds have finally caught up with him, because before him sat a kid who is completely blameless, yet his life has been ruined. While Seth called Tally, Mathias looked through the files. Once done, he looked at Dell and nodded.

"This does it," Mathias said.

"And the confession?" Dell asked.

"It's enough."

"Well, we better get it in the right hands." He got up.

Mathias looked over to see Seth staring at his cell phone. He couldn't get in contact with Tally, and he looked more lost than ever.

"Seth, it's time to go," Mathias said.

Seth looked up with an expression that nearly destroyed him. He asked, "Where?"

Mathias gave him a rundown of the plan.

It's only now that Mathias knows what Seth meant. His life is in shambles, and he has no idea where to go from here. He hears Seth's cell phone ring and a crushed Seth talking to her in low tones. He looks to the side to see Dell staring out the window. He hasn't said much since revealing to Seth everything he did. Mathias knows that Dell's actions are weighing him down. After years of cover ups, illegal deals, and the like, it seems that Dell is reaching the end of his rope. Mathias glances at Dell again, knowing the parts he didn't reveal to Seth are eating him up inside. The things he had to do to cover up his part in the death of Brianna Connelly won't leave his mind easily.

Mathias pulls up into the driveway of a home he's never actually been this close to. He grabs the security box and hops out the car, striding to the front door. He knows it's late, but he forgets about it when he rings the doorbell. It takes a few moments for someone to come to the door.

"Garrett," Mathias says. He holds out his hand to shake.

"Do I know you?"

"No. I'm Detective—"

"Mathias?"

Mathias looks past Garrett to see Wren standing at the steps in a bathrobe.

"What are you doing here?"

"It's important that I speak to Garrett."

"It's eleven o'clock in the evening, Mathias."

He always loved the way she said his name. And she always said his full name, no nickname that has been given to him over the years.

"I know. But it's a matter of life and death." He refocuses his attention on Garrett. "You're an FBI agent, correct?"

Garrett takes a step back.

"You have nothing to worry about," Mathias says. "I wouldn't dare try to harm you with Wren around."

"Wren," Garrett says, "Who is this?"

"He's my ex . . . my ex fiancé."

Garrett looks plain. If that tidbit of news surprised him, he sure didn't let on.

"Okay. So, what is your ex fiancé doing at our front door?"

"Again, it's a matter of life or death. Very serious stuff. Please."

Garrett eyes the security box he holds in his hands. "What's in there?"

"Evidence. Enough to get you started."

"On what?"

"Congressman Burris' federal corruption case."

"Come again?"

He shoves the box into Garrett's chest. "It's there. Conspiracy, corruption, misappropriation of funds, murder. Congressman Burris is dirty. Pastor Burt Brommels is right there with him. Files, audio recordings, a confession. How much more do I need to say before you take this?"

Garrett grabs the box. "Nothing. Let me look through it. I'll call you if I need anything else."

"You won't need anything else." He takes a few steps back. "I got to go. I don't want anyone to see me here."

"What do you mean? Are we in danger?"

"No, but I am." He turns to head back to the car. "You take care of them. Don't toy with her. If you're serious about her, then let her know. But don't you mess with them." He jumps into the car, not giving Garrett a chance to respond. A few seconds later, he's speeding off down the street.

"Where are we headed?" Mathias asks Seth.

"Not too far from here. She said she would meet us at the music school."

35.

TALLY – NOW

She didn't know what to make of it, either. When Seth pulled out the metal security box, she didn't know what to expect. He went on to explain a lot of stuff about his mother, who she learned died in a car accident, and a lot about his father, who based on the files and pictures, looked mighty suspect. He told her he even had audio recordings, but didn't go as far as playing them for her. She wasn't sure why he showed her that stuff, though she felt she gave him good advice. She told him to go see the private investigator who was on the business card, assuming he was the one who got his mother the information in the first place. That's about all she had.

Tally is working another shift at the club, and simply put, she is exhausted. She does a couple songs on stage before taking a break. She goes back to the dressing room and plops into a chair.

"What's wrong, Sweetie?"

Tally cocks her head to the side to see Dee out of her periphery. "Tired."

"You've been going at it pretty hard. Why don't you take a day or two off?"

"'Cause I don't get money those days."

Dee sits next to her. "Everything okay?"

"Is it ever?"

"You want to talk about it?"

"Nope."

"That's fine." She stands. "You know, that record producer came back looking for you."

Tally laughs. "I bet. Typical. I know what he came back for." She shakes her head. "So easy."

"You're not running away with him, are you?"

"No, Dee."

"Tally, I really think you should take a break."

"I will when I've made enough. And"—she grabs her cell phone, seeing that she has three missed calls from Seth. "What?"

"What's wrong?"

"Ummm. Nothing." She puts the phone up to her ear and listens to the voicemail Seth left for her. The more she hears, the more her face contorts. "I think . . . I think I may take that break. Just for a day."

"Tally."

"Dee, I gotta go." She jumps up and starts changing into her street clothes. "A couple days?"

"Sure. What's going on?"

"I don't know yet. I just need to get home."

"Okay. Sure. Just let me know if you need anything."

And like that, Tally leaves the strip club with her suitcase rolling behind her. She throws it all in her car and calls Seth back.

After getting to the school and taking a quick shower to clean off the glitter and rose-scented oil from her body, she stands at the bottom of the stairwell looking out the window for a car. The streets are mostly empty this time of night on a weekday, so she would be able to notice any changes. Seth's call has her on edge, and she wonders if he took her advice and went to the PI. She wonders what he found out, and most importantly, she wonders why she is all of a sudden in danger. When a car pulls up and the back door opens, she briskly walks to it and gets in. She sees Seth and smiles, but the weak smile he gives back puts fear in her heart.

"What's going on?" she asks.

Seth looks at his hands while talking. "Tally, this is Detective Mathias . . . retired Detective Dell."

She tenses, thinking he sold her out. Maybe this has to do with Paul? Why doesn't he look her in the eyes?

"Listen, I'm sorry for dragging you into this. I should have never showed you those files."

"That's what this is about?"

"The kid put you in danger, Darlin'," Dell says. "Because there's someone who will stop at nothing to make sure those files don't reach the light of day."

"My dad . . . my dad, Tally. He's as shady as they come. And those files . . ."

Tally grabs his hand and kisses the top of it. "It's okay. It'll be okay." She looks around the car, eventually locking her eyes on Mathias, who doesn't say anything.

"So, what are we doing? Where are we going?" she asks, noticing she grips Seth's hand, finding the warmth comforting.

"We are getting you to safety," Mathias says. "And we are—"
CRASH!

She doesn't know what just happened. She hears voices, but she can't see anything. It takes great strength to simply open her eyes, and when she does, everything is a blur. She's still in the car, that much she knows for sure, but it feels like up is down, and down is up. Her head feels like it's being split right down the middle. As she continues to fight to regain her senses, she realizes gravity is forcing her hands above her head. She sees the two detectives in front of her. Things fade to black again as she fights. She slowly turns toward where Seth is, to find an empty spot. The car door is wide open.

More voices, closer this time.

She struggles, trying to unbuckle herself, as she finds she has little to no strength. Her vision goes black again as she hears one voice clearly.

"Hurry up. Grab her, and let's get out of here before it blows."

She thinks she's making progress on that seat belt, but she's barely moved a finger. Her car door creaks open. The next thing she knows, she's being dragged from the car, her heels scraping against the pavement. She's hoisted up in the air and thrown down hard on a semi-solid surface. Everything shuts down. Against her will, she succumbs to the darkness. She hates herself because she's done that once before.

Something cold and hard hits her face, forcing her to come to. The front of her shirt is wet, so she realizes water was just thrown on her. She blinks away the water from her eyes and looks around. She observes she's in a small, dusty room, her hands tied behind her as she sits in a chair.

"Alright, Sweetheart," a man says. "Make this easy for me, okay? Now, where are the files?"

She says nothing.

"C'mon now. I don't want to hurt you, but goodness, I will if you don't tell me what I need to know."

"I don't know what you're talking about."

The man steps up to her and slaps her across the face with the back of his hand. "Again, where are the files?"

She smiles.

"Is there something funny?"

"Yeah." She licks the open cut on the inside of her mouth. "After everything I've been through, you're gonna have to do better than that."

SETH – NOW

Seth opens his eyes with great struggle. He blinks a few times and tries to lift his head.

Another great struggle.

He remembers riding along in the car, then a loud noise, but nothing else. He knows he's been in an accident. He takes a deep breath and realizes it hurts, and he groans in pain. The shooting pain in his leg forces him to be aware rather quickly. Almost immediately after lifting his head, he sees he's at his father's church, in his office. His father sits directly in front of him, staring.

Seth tries to move his arms, but finds them bound behind him. He stops the struggle and stares his father in the eyes. Burt gives him a look of disgust.

"Where are the files?" Burt asks.

"What files?"

Burt unbuttons the cuff on each sleeve and rolls them up. "One more time. Last chance, Son."

"What are you going to do?"

"I'm sorry about this. I really am." Burt punches Seth square on the jaw. "Where are the files?"

Seth coughs. "You're not sorry. You're scared."

Burt punches him again. "Where are the files?"

It takes a little more time for Seth to come to. "And you're too dumb to know it's over. I know what you've done. Others know what you've done."

"Where are the files?" A little spittle flies from his mouth. "Tell me where the files"—he punches him—"are." And again.

"With the FBI," he spits out. "They're with the FBI."

Burt pauses. He idles over to the desk and leans over it. He grabs the cell phone sitting on the desk and dials. Seth doesn't hear much.

All he wants is rest.

Mathias – Now

The smell of smoke and antifreeze wakes Mathias as he hangs upside down in the driver's seat of his car. He feels around for his seat belt and unbuckles himself, falling to the roof of the car. He groans before looking to the side to see Dell. The sound of a spark concerns Mathias and tells him they must get out before it's too late.

"Dell, wake up, Man."

He pulls on Dell's arm, but he doesn't move. A fire breaks out above him as he takes a glance to see both rear doors open and the back empty.

"Dell, they got them. We gotta go."

Still Dell doesn't move.

Mathias feels around Dell's neck for a pulse. There is none. Smoke starts to fill the car and escape out the back doors. He crawls backward out the car and stumbles away and into an alley behind a dumpster. The car explodes, the sound of it alone enough to cripple a man. He takes a few moments to breathe before getting to his feet and going to where he knows the two were taken.

36.

Tally – Now

Tally sits in the chair with her head leaned to the side. Her kidnapper stares at her, though he stops asking if she knows where the files are. He got a call on his cell phone and ever since then, he's just sat, holding a gun in his hand. She knows he's just waiting for the cell to ring again, and he is going to shoot her.

"Hey," she says. "Can you loosen these?"

He ignores her.

"My wrists really hurt. I'm not asking for you to let me go." She looks at him with an expression that gets her paid each night. "I can make it worth your while."

He stares at her for a few more seconds before looking down and away. She knows he's considering.

"You know we're in a church," he says.

"So?" She tries to remain as playful as possible, but still, that statement gives her pause.

The man smirks but doesn't move.

"Tell you what. Let my hands free, and I'll give you a show."

"Yeah, right."

"I'm serious. You have the gun, so it isn't like I'm going to try anything." She pauses. "It is, after all, what I do."

"What do you mean?"

"I work at Wild Dreams."

The man grunts. "Okay, fine. Show me what you got." He gets up and walks toward her, with a predatory look in his eyes.

She knows she has him. She keeps a straight face as he moves closer to her, but when he reaches behind her and cuts her loose, she smirks. She feels around her wrist, massaging the area, then stands up.

"Wish I had some music," she says.

"Dance." He points the gun at her while backing away and sitting back on his chair. "Make it good."

She hears a song in her head, and she starts dancing, trying to be as seductive as possible. Ironically, she hears one of Big Ease's songs in her head, and begins to do her routine as if she were on the stage. She knows, though, that she has to get closer. She gets her shirt off and continues her routine.

"You know you want more than this," she says.

"What are you thinking?"

"Right now, it's like I'm on stage." She peeks back over her shoulder. "I give private dances, too."

"Yeah?"

She slides her yoga pants down. "Yeah."

His phone rings while she dances. "So, what do you say?"

He doesn't respond to her but answers the phone. A few grunts later, he hangs up.

"Alright. I'm good with a more up-close-and-personal dance."

She walks up to him with as much hip swaying as she can muster, knowing she's getting very close to the time she must act. He starts groping her all over her body with one hand while still pointing the gun at her.

"Turn around," he says.

She doesn't want to, for she knows he's going to shoot her in the back while she's dancing.

"Not yet," she says. "You know this is turning me on?"

He doesn't say anything as he seems to be intensely focused on her chest. She then unclasps and slips out of her bra. She knows she has to increase intensity to get him to let his guard down. She stuffs her emotions and the disgusting feeling in a little box inside herself. She grabs his hand and places it on her crotch. He seems to be delighted about that, as a smirk is plastered on his face.

"It's warm just for you." It's harder and harder to stuff the disgusted feeling away.

"You don't do this at the club, do you?"

"Not at all. Not allowed. This is what happens when I can do what I want."

"But you don't really want this. It's not real."

"How do you know?" She smiles. "And does it matter?"

"I guess not."

"I don't think it does." She places a hand on his crotch and moves it away.

His jaw starts flexing. "Turn around."

"Awww. Come on. I'm not done yet." She moves closer to him and puts her bare chest in his face. She looks down at him, waiting for the right moment, which is soon, she figures. He can no longer aim the gun at her. She takes his free hand again and makes sure it's firmly between her legs.

"Get me started," she whispers in his ear.

He grunts and starts massaging around her crotch, and she knows she has him. She keeps dancing. With a swiftness that he isn't able to keep up with, she knees him in the crotch from an angle, coming forward and down. At the same time, she's able to knock the gun away from his hand. The gun skids across the floor as he screams in pain.

She jumps from him and dives for the gun. Before she can get to it, he grabs her ankle and yanks her back.

Tally kicks him in the face, hard, busting his nose open.

She crawls to the gun and finally gets it in hand. She stands to her feet and points it at him. He gets to his feet and stares at her, then at the gun. She notices the safety is on, and turns it off.

He makes a dash for her, but she is able to fire off a few shots as he lands awkwardly on top of her.

She moves from under him, realizing she's covered in blood. She dashes around and finds takes an old cloth on a shelf. She snatches it and wipes herself off, then gets dressed. She stuffs the gun in her waistband and leaves the room.

She looks down a long stone hallway, confused. She thought the man said they were in a church. She takes off running down the long hall and gets to a set of stone stairs, which she climbs with ease. She gets to a door and bursts through . . . to end up in a closet. She has to get to Seth. That's all she thinks about. She has to get to Seth. She steps out of the closet and looks around a semi-dark room. She finds copiers and computers all around: the church's print shop. She finds an exit and gets to the main lobby, where it seems a crowd of women gather. Passing through the women in hats, she overhears they all meet up for the women's ministry night prayer. If she could freeze-frame some of the looks she's getting, she would. She moves through the crowd and notices movement out the corner of her eye. She turns to see Mathias making his way through the crowd as well. He notices her and nods toward an empty spot in the lobby.

"You okay?" he asks, looking at the bruise under her eye.

"I'm fine. Where's Seth?"

"Dell told me about this place under the church where I think he may be."

"He's not there. That's where I came from . . ." She looks down at her feet. "There's a dead body there."

Mathias looks stern. "I have to get to Seth. You hide somewhere safe."

"What? No. Aren't you going to call for backup?"

"I will. You need to find a safe spot until this is all settled."

"What are you going to do?"

"Get Seth, make sure he's safe, and continue with the plan."

"What plan?"

"Too many questions." He starts on his way. "Somewhere safe. Now."

She nods and walks down a hallway, trying any of the doors to see which one opens. When she finally opens one, she steps in the room. She sees Mathias standing in the middle of the crowd of women. She keeps her head poked out to hear him say, "Ladies, I am Detective

Mathias Reid." He holds out his badge. "I am very sorry, but I will need all of you to exit the building. Please, for your safety."

Tally notices they don't move at first, but when he pulls out his gun they make haste out the front doors. She looks back into the room, finding it to be a janitor's closet. She steps in and closes the door. Her heart races as she pulls out the gun from her waistband. She holds it in the ready position and waits. There's only one thing she can do at a moment like this, and it surprises her that it's a thought. Maybe it's because she's in a church, but the one thing she thinks of doing is praying. So, that's what she does. She prays for Seth because that's all she cares about right now. She earnestly hopes this time of prayer in a closet turns out better than her last.

BURT – NOW

Burt leans over his desk, having difficulty breathing. He sucks in air quickly, trying to keep the room from spinning. He thought he was prepared. He turns around to see what he's done to his son and realizes he wasn't prepared at all. There might be a way he can still spin this, he thinks. But again, he must act fast. He picks up his cell phone and calls his new right-hand man, who is keeping watch over the girl.

"Kill her," he says. "I have the information I need."

He responds with nothing more than a grunt.

"Then head on up to regroup. We'll deal with the cleanup later."

Another grunt.

Burt hangs up, being annoyed, and makes another phone call, this one to Gretchen.

"Babe, we have a problem."

"What do you mean?"

"We . . . I need to get in contact with Burris. We need to batten down the hatches. A big storm is on the way."

"Burt, what's wrong?"

"Look, Babe, remember our plan? The contingency? We need to start moving in that direction. I need you to get out before the FBI starts knocking on our door."

"No. Burt, no." He hears her crying over the phone. "Not now."

"Yes, now. I . . . I need you to start moving, okay? You get moving, and I'll meet up with you soon."

"Okay. Okay." He hears rustling over the phone. "Moving now."

"That's my girl."

"Burt."

"Yes, Dear."

"I love you."

"I love you, too." He hangs up.

"Did you ever love Mom like that?"

Burt turns toward Seth to see him awake and aware again. His face is severely swollen.

"I think you already know the answer to that."

He watches his son as he struggles to speak.

"You're a sellout, you know that? And a hypocrite."

"You have no idea about my struggles, about what I had to go through just to get to a point where people listen to what I have to say."

"And there within . . . is your problem. It's all about you. Your messages reek . . . of arrogance." He takes a deep breath. "There's a special place in hell for you."

"You're in no position to judge me."

"But I know who is . . . and who will." He coughs. "And He will deal harshly with you, I'm sure."

Burt turns his back and dials on his phone.

"Sure. Turn your back on me like you always do . . . like you have always done. For what, Dad? Why? You can't be a man and look me in the eyes."

"Shut up." The phone rings.

"What did I ever do to deserve you treating me so badly? Was it because I didn't want to preach? Because I wanted to do photography? Because I broke it off with Kylie?"

Someone picks up the call, but says nothing.

"It's me. The FBI will be paying you a visit sooner rather than later. Better get your affairs in order."

"Noted." The phone clicks.

He sets the phone on the desk. "It's because you are just like her. Stubborn and, for the most part, right in your thinking. But you're a dreamer . . . and reality is often harsh . . . and unforgiving."

"I . . . call . . . bull."

Burt turns around to see Seth, his chin to his chest. It looks unnatural to him, so he walks up to his son. Stopping him in his tracks is the pool of blood under his left leg. Just at the moment he reaches for him, he hears a gunshot outside the door. He sighs and stands tall. He walks to his window and sees the flashing of blue and red lights. He knows that it's all over. Looks like he won't be meeting up with Gretchen after all.

The door busts open, but he doesn't flinch at all. He merely glances at the door and refocuses on the increasing number of police cars in the lot. "Mathias."

"Burt Brommels, you are under arrest."

"No, I'm not."

"Get down on your knees, facing the window, and place your hands on top of your head."

"No."

"If you do not comply, I will have to use force."

"So formal. And it's Pastor Burt Brommels to you."

"I repeat, I will have to use force."

Burt turns around and in a fury screams, "Then force me. Force me to my knees, Mathias. 'Cause life tried to do the same, and it failed. You don't have the power, that's for damn sure."

Mathias fires off a shot into his leg. He's never felt such pain before, and he leans on the desk in front of the drawers. A searing hot fire rages up and down his leg. He leans heavily over the desk on one arm and with the other makes it seem like he's holding his leg, but he's fumbling with the drawer.

The one that holds his gun.

"You know," he says through clenched teeth, "you're just as dirty as I am."

That seems to give Mathias pause.

"No one is clean in this one. And you're going to go down just as hard. But it doesn't have to be that way, Mathias. It doesn't have to be. We can help each other."

"No. Down on your knees. Hands behind your head." He takes a couple steps in his direction.

Burt gets his hand on the gun grip and cocks it. He knows it's all over. A thought creeps up in his mind to get on his knees and ask for forgiveness, but he frowns at the idea. God wouldn't hear him anyway, he thinks. In a fury of motion, Burt feigns falling to the floor while pulling out the gun and firing a shot at Mathias.

But Mathias is faster, and by the time he fires his one shot, Mathias fires three.

And all of them land.

Burt falls to the ground, the still-smoking gun he fired falling from his hands. He can't move, and the burning is now in his chest. It hurts so bad, but then it feels cool.

Then numb.

He turns his head to the side to see Mathias stepping toward him. He moves in slow motion. Burt blinks his eyes as tears fall from his face. He looks at his son, who hasn't moved from his previous position and mouths out, "I'm sorr—"

His mouth hangs open, his eyes wide, as the rest of his life leaves him.

37.

Tally – Now

Tally sits in a chair next to Seth's hospital bed. His leg is suspended and in a cast. She's been staring at him for the past few hours, waiting for him to wake.

Back in the church, in the janitor's closet, she heard footsteps moving quickly in one direction. She went to the door to see it was the police, so she took the gun and hid it in a bunch of cloths. She stepped out the closet and was escorted out the building. On the way out, she saw the detective and screamed out for him. He jogged over to her and nodded at the officer who was escorting her out.

"Did you find him?" she asked. "Is he okay?"

He wouldn't look her in the eyes. "He's okay."

"Listen, I . . . I hid in the janitor's closet."

He squinted.

"There was nothing but dirty cloths on the shelf."

He seemed like he understood.

"No worries," he said. "I'll find some new ones."

"Call me and let me know what's going on." She saw a stretcher being rushed by her. "You understand? Call me as soon as you know."

"I will."

Someone knocks on the door to his room and enters. Tally sees a taller Hispanic man, presumably Seth's friend, as she has seen him with Seth before. He looks startled at her existence.

"Hello," is all he says. No introduction at all.

"Hi."

He looks hesitant to say anything. "I'm just here to check on my homeboy." He walks up to Seth and sighs. She sees a tear trace down his face, one he tries to wipe away as quickly as possible. "'Sup, Bro." He places a hand on Seth's chest. "I need you to heal up fast, Man. We've got"—he chokes up—"we've got some more weddings to raid." He smiles and gently pats him on the chest. He turns around to head out. She can tell he is not at all used to seeing anyone in the condition Seth is in. Right at the door, he stops.

"I'm Cam," he says, his back facing her.

"Tally."

"You're the mami who robbed him. Yes?"

She feels awkward answering. "Yes."

"I told him to stay away from you. You have too much baggage. Don't ask me how I know. I just do." He leans his head on the door. "But you're here. And he has no one. So, if you are going to be here "— he turns around to look her in the eyes—"you better be here. You understand what I am saying?"

She hears him loud and clear and nods her understanding. He leaves the hospital room leaving her and Seth alone again. She looks down, knowing what she wants to do.

She wants to open up to him.

"Seth, you want to know me. How I ended up robbing people . . . how I ended up robbing you." She takes a deep breath. "Well, here it is. It was all about survival . . . and an advantage I've found many ways to exploit. And a plan gone wrong. The short is this . . . I use people, men in particular, because it's how I made it. It's how I'm alive. Throughout my entire life . . . I used men for survival. I used my looks . . . I used sex . . . because men are so easily manipulated when it comes to that. It's how I survived being kidnapped. It's how I got through life . . ."

Tally tells a sleeping Seth everything: from what she witnessed her brother doing to the kidnapping and surviving the shack. She tells him about being an exotic dancer and meeting up with Paul, thinking he was an easier ride, but being wrong. She even opens up about her mother . . .

"After we lost everything because, well, Daddy wasn't there to bring in any more money, Mom got strung out on drugs and . . . it was just a really bad time. I finished school, though, and for the whole time I had this question to ask her that pressed itself out more and more. Finally, I just asked her. I asked her if she was at that shack, if she knew I was there, if she was part of putting me there. She denied everything . . . and I believe her . . . but I have my suspicions. But at the end of the day, she is wherever she is . . . and I'm here."

And she opens up about Tana, though it is with great struggle.

"She's the one who introduced me to the dancing world. She was my best friend, and after all the mess with my family, her family decided to move out of the area. And by some stroke of luck, we ran into each other. And I lived with her for a while . . . but her life was . . . destructive. And that's the Cliff's notes version."

She slides into the hospital bed next to him and whispers in his ear.

"So, that's how I ended up robbing you. And let me tell you, there's not one day I don't regret doing that to you. But, somehow it brought us into each other's realm. And I'm thankful for that. But Seth, I am scared. I am scared because this is all new for me. These feelings are all new. I've never felt this way about someone before. I can't use you. I don't want to. I mean, I freaking went to church for you." She smiles. "Someday, I hope to tell you all this when you can hear me . . . when you're awake. I promise it will be soon." She falls asleep lying next to Seth.

When she opens her eyes, she sees Seth wide awake, staring at her, smiling. She pops up.

"Hey," she says.

"Hey." His voice is hoarse. His eyes, weak.

"How long have you been awake?"

"Long enough for the nurse to come in and check on me. I asked her not to wake you." He smiles again. "You know you snore?"

She slides out the bed and sits back in the chair next to him. She smooths her hair out. "I do not."

"You do. It was cute, though."

"How do you feel?" she asks, changing the subject.

"Groggy and light. Can't feel that thing that's hanging there at the moment."

"You mean your leg?"

He smirks. "Yeah. It doesn't even feel a part of my body." His smile fades. "So, what happened?"

She feared the dreaded question, but knew he would ask. "Do you want to watch the news?"

"I don't know. Do I?"

"I couldn't explain it properly."

He nods and she grabs the little control that's connected to his bed. She presses the button and flips to CNN. It only takes a few minutes for the breaking news headline to appear and a complete rundown of the "church scandal of the century." She watches with Seth as the news report runs down most of what Seth was told, his father's part, and the connection to congressman Burris. It's a pretty extensive report, explaining there's a confession recording from Dell Crawford to the murder of Bree and the cover up of his mother's murder some odd years ago. Other details were reported on, such as Gretchen Brommels' getting stopped and arrested at an airport as she was on her way out of the country. The report digs into how most of the members of the large church stand in shock at Pastor Burt Brommels' deceit and death.

Seth leans back in the bed, stone faced, and she turns the TV off.

"There's more, but . . . I figured you heard enough. On a positive side, there's a big effort going on out there to . . . help you out . . . medically."

"Yeah." He stares at the ceiling, looking like he isn't quite paying attention to what she is saying.

She watches him as tears fall down the sides of his face. A nurturing side she never knew she had kicks in, and she crawls back into the bed next to him. She wipes his tears from the sides of his face.

"Thank you for being here with me," he says.

She leans in and kisses him on the forehead. "It will all be okay. I'm here for you."

"Tally."

"Yes, Seth."

"Who are you?"

Her breath catches. "I'm a pretty terrible person."

"I still don't believe that."

She looks at him with kind eyes. "Heal up first. I promise I will tell you. Maybe over dinner?"

He closes his eyes, on his way to another rest. "I'd like that."

MATHIAS – NOW

He had to turn in his gun and badge, and he made no qualms about it. He took the money Burt was offering . . . money that was dirty. It doesn't matter that he used that money so Seth could live rent-free where he is. It doesn't matter that Mathias never actually spent the money on himself.

It just matters that he took it.

He was suspended from the force, though getting the information to the FBI and attempting to arrest Burt has earned him some goodwill in the impending investigation and hearing. He had to shoot one of the church security members before getting to Burt, but he made sure he didn't shoot to kill. He covered for the girl after finding the gun she used to shoot the man in the basement of the church. He wiped it clean of her prints, and made sure he returned the gun to the basement.

Not too long after he turned his badge and gun in, he was called to come down to the station, where they placed him under arrest.

So far, he's spent a night and part of the day in jail, thinking, counting the number of bad decisions he's made in recent memory. Still, after thinking about all the wrong ones, he can only think of one he would actually change.

He would have fought harder to make things work with Wren.

His life quickly cascaded down into a deep and dark pit after they split, and he would give anything to have a do-over. He wouldn't be a detective, but he would have her and his daughter.

He realizes now that is the life he's always wanted.

A guard appears at the front of his cell and unlocks and opens the door.

"What are you doing?" Mathias asks.

"Someone is here for you, Mr. Reid."

Mathias frowns. He gets up from the cot he's been lying on for most of the day. The young-looking guard moves out of Mathias' way as he walks out of the cell. He sees a man whom he has never seen before.

"Mathias Reid." the man says.

Mathias doesn't say anything.

The man holds his hand out to shake. "Logan Simms."

Mathias doesn't shake his hand.

"Come with me."

"I'm sorry. Where do I know you from?" Mathias asks.

"Let's get you processed and out of here first."

Mathias gets processed, and he walks out of the building with this Logan Simms at his side.

"Looks like they didn't impound your car. How nice of them," Simms says mockingly. "I'm a former detective, D.C. area."

"What do you want?"

"Do you like being a detective?"

"Yeah."

"Well, let me be honest: you aren't going to be one for much longer. You may skirt away from jail time . . . but you aren't getting your badge back."

"Your point?" He moves toward his car.

"Wait, Mathias. I want to help. I know you believe in justice. So do I." He pulls out a card and hands it to him. "And so does my employer. There's a way you can still help. You can still be a man of justice. Just . . . consider my words." Simms looks around. "My employer wanted to actually see you in person."

"Your employer: He's the one who posted my bail?"

"Correct. And here he is pulling up."

Mathias looks out into the street to see a limousine pull up. As soon as it rolls to the curb, Simms heads straight for it. Mathias, on the other hand, remains cautious.

Simms stops and opens one of the doors. "Please."

Mathias reluctantly walks to the vehicle and gets in. He sits across from an older man who is sharply dressed in a suit. His face has hard features, and there's something about the man's eyes that leads Mathias to believe he's under a microscope.

The man holds his hand out. "Ramses."

Mathias slowly shakes his hand. "Is that a first name or last?"

"With as much power as he has, he doesn't need another name," Simms chides.

Ramses looks over and smirks. "So, I know you're wondering what this is about."

"A little."

"Well, let me start by saying this: you're going to need some help."

"What do you mean?"

"You have a federal prosecutor who is sniffing on your trail, looking to make an example of you. Police corruption is high right now. It's not a good look for you to appear corrupt at a time like this. Even worse, you worked with one of the most corrupt individuals on the force."

"Dell." Mathias looks down. "I was told I've earned some goodwill."

"That only means ten years in prison instead of twenty." He sighs. "I'm being facetious, but the point remains the same. There's only one way you get out of this without going to jail."

"And that is?"

"That is if you hire me."

"I have no money for that."

"I'm offering my services pro bono."

Mathias pauses.

"I'm sure my associate here has informed you of your murky future. It is likely you will never hold that badge again. But, you can still be someone. It's in your blood, after all."

"How do you know so much about me?"

"I've done some vetting. Which is to be expected, based on what we're offering."

"And what exactly are you offering? Because let me be honest, I'm done accepting shady deals. They don't work out so well for me."

"Understandable. But there's no shade in this deal. I'm offering you a chance to be a hero."

Mathias sits back as both men stare at him. "I'm hoping you don't need an answer right at this moment."

"No. Not at all." Ramses smiles. "Take some time to think. You have Simms' card. Call when you've decided. But, I would like to at least offer you my services, no matter what you decide regarding our secondary offer."

"You'll still represent me if I decide to . . . not be a hero?"

"He won't only represent you, he will clear you of everything," Simms says.

"I will represent you no matter what you decide. Take your time, Mathias," Ramses says. "We'll be here. Just call whenever you're ready."

Mathias nods and leaves the limousine. He gets into his car and stares at the card with a simple phone number printed on it. He doesn't trash it, but he flips it into his glove box and starts the car to drive home.

38.

SETH AND TALLY – LATER

It took some time, but Seth healed up from his wounds and breaks as if nothing happened at all. What still takes some time is to heal up the wounds on the inside. Seth and Tally stayed friends for some time as Tally opened up more and more to Seth. Seth, at the very same time, opened up to her, and they both formed a trust that neither would even think about betraying. Just recently, they started dating, though it didn't feel any different than when they were just hanging out.

"Tally, you ready?" Seth calls out from the living room of Tally's apartment. "You know we can't be late."

"Keep your pants on, Old Man," she says as she makes her way from her bedroom to her front door. "How do I look?"

Seth takes a moment to slow things down. "You look exquisite."

"You're so dramatic."

"I mean it. You look great."

"Do I look ready?"

"Of course you do. You're not getting nervous, are you?"

"Well, yeah. This is my first wedding, after all."

"Oh, you'll be fine. You teach this stuff. You play at the hospitals. You play in front of thousands at church. This is nothing."

"But they're paying me a lot of money to do this. What if I mess up my notes?"

"They're paying me a lot of money to take some pictures. What if I miss an important moment?"

"You don't, though."

"And you won't, either. Trust me. You are supremely gifted. Now, let's rock. 'Cause neither of us will get paid if we don't show up."

"Is Cameron assisting?"

"Oh, my goodness, will you stop calling him by his full name? You know he hates that."

"That's why I do it. Plus, that's his name."

Seth smiles. "Yeah. He'll be there."

"You think he'll ever settle down?"

"Now, you're stalling. Let's go." He turns on his heels and walks toward the front door.

"Seth, wait." She skips up to him, and just as he turns back around, she kisses him, deeply, on the lips. "Thank you."

"Okay. I'll bite. For what?"

"You know what you did."

He winks. "I've done nothing. God has done it all."

She nods. She thanks God every night for this happiness she feels; that has become a part of her. She smiles, remembering when that was such a foreign thing to her: God moving in her life. She thinks about Seth, the man whose life she pretty much stormed into, and the extra bit of happiness she feels whenever she's around him. "Seth, I think I love you."

"Well, dang. It took you long enough."

"What?" She frowns.

"I loved you from the moment you put that gun to my head." He laughs. "Let me rephrase that. I've loved you for a very long time, and I knew . . . I know there's something special about you . . . that God placed something in you that when taken care of will grow and blossom into something . . . beautiful." He grabs her hand and kisses the back of it. "So, I know I love you, and someday it will be an honor to be your husband . . . someday." Seth feels a tad bit vulnerable, but he's always found that Tally is the only person he can be vulnerable with.

"I'm not gonna lie," she says, her smile reaching from ear to ear, "that was real smooth."

Seth bursts out into laughter. "You ready to go?"

"I am."

Thank you for Reading this J. Evan Johnson Book

Sign up for his FREE newsletter and be first to get updates on new releases, sneak peeks of future stories, completely free books and short stories, bonus content,
AND MORE!

Visit him online to sign up at
www.thejejstory.com